T0116814

THE WORDS OF MY ROARING

THE
WORDS

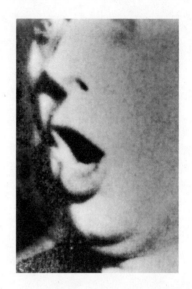

OF MY
ROARING

ROBERT KROETSCH

 The University of Alberta Press

This edition published by
The University of Alberta Press
Ring House 2
Edmonton, Alberta T6G 2E2

Printed in Canada 5 4 3 2 1
Text copyright © Robert Kroetsch 1966
Introduction copyright © Thomas Wharton 2000
A volume in (cuRRents), an interdisciplinary series. Jonathan Hart, series editor.

CANADIAN CATALOGUING IN PUBLICATION DATA

Kroetsch, Robert, 1927–
    The words of my roaring

    ISBN 0–88864–349–7

    I. Title.
PS8521.R7W6 2000   C813'.54   C00–910501–8
PR9199.3.K7W6 2000

Printed and bound in Canada by Friesens, Altona, Manitoba.
∞ Printed on acid-free paper.
Interior photo courtesy of National Archives of Canada.

The University of Alberta Press gratefully acknowledges the support received for its
program from the Canada Council for the Arts. The Press also acknowledges the
financial support of the Government of Canada through the Book Publishing Industry
Development Program for its publishing activities.

"My dear friends, rain..."

In *The Words of My Roaring,* Robert Kroetsch's second novel, the telling of the story becomes the story. The narrator of *Words,* the voice we hear speaking to us, is everything. John Judas Backstrom of Notikeewin, Alberta, undertaker and candidate for public office, is many things, most of them unredeeming, but he is first and foremost a voice. And this voice, with its unflagging energy and verbal inventiveness, is directed primarily toward the task of embodying itself. Incessantly, compulsively, Backstrom talks about Backstrom. Or rather, Backstrom talks Backstrom, into being. Like so many of the great voices in the western tradition, he is a kind of monster of self-creation, a figment of his own gift for words.

The novel's historical setting, Alberta on the eve of the Social Credit landslide of 1935, makes Backstrom an ironic version of the Depression-era dream of the "self-made" man. Throughout the novel he reminds us of his size ("six-four in my stocking feet, or nearly so"); his remarkable set of teeth; the sandy colour of his hair. He forgets he's already told us umpteen times about his success with women (always bemoaning the "curse" of his attractiveness), about his long-gone glory days as a baseball wunderkind, about his gargantuan capacity for alcohol and food and whatever else he can get his hands on. Lusting after Helen, the daughter of his political rival and surrogate father Doc Murdoch, Backstrom tells us he's always been a sucker for "women who see through me." The point being, of course, that he himself, rather than the woman, is the worthy object of scrutiny (although here too is one of many hints that there is nothing to see; that the voice is everything). Even when lying naked in a garden with the pale, beautiful Helen Persephone, a ghostly figure in her own right, Backstrom marvels not so much at her as at what her love has made of him.

For all his bluster about actions speaking louder than words, Backstrom's convictions rarely outlast the cloudbursts of (usually borrowed) rhetoric with which he proclaims them. In that regard, he serves as a fairly realistic portrait of a political opportunist, riding a wave of public anger and desperation into power. Backstrom's fitful, halfhearted quest to get elected—and his wild campaign promise of rain by election day—appears to be motivated only by the thought of riding out the tough times in the comfy shelter of the Legislature. To get there, though, he has his work cut out for him. Somehow, in the next thirteen days, he has to entice a weary and suspicious electorate away from the much-loved old Doc. And so off he roars in his wonderful campaign vehicle, a battered old hearse, up and down the dusty roads of south-central Alberta, and into Kroetsch country.

Backstrom's restless lunge from auction to beer parlour to stampede (much of which involves activities unbecoming a candidate for public office) allows Kroetsch to widen the novel's scope beyond the narrator's narcissistic monologue. Out of his manic peregrinations comes a kind of *Johnny Chinook* collection of colourful characters, anecdotes and turns of phrase, much of it very funny. In Kroetsch's Alberta, however, the "bull" of a good yarn is an animal of the unpredictable, bucking kind. As we laugh, Kroetsch reminds us that the source of "prairie humour" lies in the things that can't be changed, in adversity and loss.

The west's specialty, the tall tale, makes its appearance, of course. We hear the one about the dust being so thick that gophers climb right up out of their holes and into the air. When the wind carries off the topsoil and turns green farmland into wasteland, when drought and grasshoppers and remote market forces all strike at once, there are, the novel suggests, two creative responses: prophesy the end of the world or turn it all into a joke. In either case, the only way to change a brutal reality that can't be changed is with words.

But the novel doesn't only contain tall tales; it is one. In Kroetsch country, prairie politics, like so much else, takes on mythic dimensions. And so, while grim dustbowl reality intrudes for a while, we keep returning to the not-so-reliable source. Everything we see in this novel, we see through its larger-than-life narrator. And in fact sight is the wrong metaphor. This is not a primarily visual novel. Kroetsch is not a primarily visual writer, and that turning away from the painterly codes of realism, the effort to make one's words fit a predetermined concept of what reality *looks like*, is one of Kroetsch's important contributions to the Canadian novel. As faithful as Kroetsch's Alberta settings are in many ways, grounded in geography and climate and culture, they are also emphatically worlds constructed of words. The journey down the Red Deer River in Kroetsch's later novel *Badlands*, for all its marvelous specificity and evocation of place, is more a journey through the dense, jumbled strata of the English language. Kroetsch reminds us, as no other western Canadian writer does, that we ourselves have created the prairies, the parklands, this perennial borderland, through the stories we tell and retell about ourselves—through our endless talk, our long poem, as Kroetsch himself calls it. In *The Words of My Roaring* (as the title suggests), we don't really see Backstrom's world. Instead, we hear it.

That "roaring" (the title is a line from the twenty-second Psalm) is a reminder not only of the desperation of the era but also implies that the protagonist's voice is too loud for anyone else to get a hearing. And as we read, we notice just how many of the conversations in the novel are one-sided, how much of what we hear either comes from, or is directed to, persons unseen. Backstrom's wife Elaine calls to him up the stairs. As a prelude to his actual disappearance, Jonah Bledd's voice is heard worrying over his bleak job opportunities from inside a rail car. Backstrom hammers on Doc Murdoch's door, begging forgiveness, and gets no answer. One of the most important characters in the book actually never appears in person. John George Applecart (a paper-thin disguise for "Bible Bill" Aberhart) makes his prophecies, and his pitch for votes, through the "complex machinery" of the almighty radio. Here is the other response to calamity, and one which can also be quite profitable: foretell the end of the world and the beginning of a new one.

> Follow me, is all that voice would say. That hollow voice. Send in your contributions. "Send us your nickels," Applecart said, "your dimes, your precious dollars, my dear friends." He paused, and I heard the gurgle of water. "For remember," Applecart said. "Remember that promise. Do as I ask you. And there shall be no more death, neither sorrow, nor crying, neither shall there be any more pain—"
> "A pig's arse!" I shouted.

Fittingly, what follows is Backstrom's most sincere and impassioned speech—to someone who can't hear him. During his campaign, Backstrom makes a few Applecart-style speeches of his own, but here he rejects this apocalyptic, Utopia-around-the-corner rhetoric. His own authentic words are never alpha and omega. Backstrom turns off Applecart's voice, but we don't turn off his because this is a voice that is constantly shifting, changing, recreating itself. Like water, the element Backstrom promises the drought-stricken farmers of Coulee Hill, he himself is unstable, mercurial, liquid. His self-glorifying bombast always paddles against a strong undercurrent of self-doubt. His restlessness seems the result of a nameless urgency or even fear. And his fixation on his own physicality suggests someone who is terrified that he may at any moment simply wink out of existence, and who must therefore recreate himself again and again, word by word. Italo Calvino has defined humour as comedy that has lost its bodily weight, usually under the impact of suffering. In that notion there may be a way to link some of the novel's seemingly incongruous elements: the realistic Depression setting, the "tall tale" voice, and Backstrom's obsessive self-reference. (In Kroetsch's later novels, as well, a remarkable number of bodies lose their earthly weight in "humourous" circumstances.) The dreadful possibility that he is only a voice, or that he is nothing at all, sounds beneath every word Backstrom roars:

I was born out here in a farmhouse, remember. The first
thing you hear is the wind. And going upstairs, at the turn of
the stairs in that first house; a window looked west; and westward in the summer you could see the green of a windbreak,
elm and maple and Russian poplar and caragana.... And then in
the fall you could see through the bare branches out across a
mile of wheat stubble; a gradual rise to the horizon, a clump of
poplars, a line of telephone poles along a road a mile away....

Backstrom starts to tell us about his childhood, but an odd thing
happens in this lovely passage: he disappears, in the space between
"that first house" and "a window" that does the looking for him. The
ubiquitous "I" vanishes, his place taken by a nameless "you," by an
empty house, by the landscape. Like Jonah Bledd, who vanishes
beneath the waves of Wildfire Lake, Backstrom is never really
"there," at least to himself. His self-creation, like that of a novel, is a
creation *ex nihilo*. *Words* is words is *Words*.

Myth-minded literary critics have had a field day with the arche-
types in Kroetsch's fiction. His work has been characterized as
postmodernist, in the sense that his use of myth is not straightfor-
ward but proliferative, prodigal, ironic (piling up the mythic parallels
supposedly undercuts them). Like the parodic questers of Kroetsch's
later novels, Backstrom has been seen as a fool-king pieced together
from shreds and patches of various mythologies. He is Orpheus,
Hades, Frazier's scapegoat god. He is Coyote, the fool-hero of Native
tradition, covered in scars but still loping determinedly along through
an indifferent cosmos, in search of sex, a good feed, more life. In this
context, the long-awaited rain that Backstrom promises by election
day takes on all sorts of mythical meanings. But since voice is everything in this novel, it's inviting to read the rain another way.

In the opening scene, Backstrom, desperately trying to top Doc
Murdoch's campaign goodies, offers the cynical voters not money or
even Utopia, but a small miracle, a sign from above that things might
just get better rather than worse. Through most of the novel we (like
the voters, like Backstrom himself) are waiting for this promised
deluge, imagining it, wondering if it will arrive in the nick of time.
The truth is that the rain has been there all along. The rain that
Backstrom really foretells, and delivers on, is the novel's rain of

language. The flood of words and wordplay that Kroetsch's later poetry and essays and fiction so brilliantly embark upon, and that this early novel heralds. The life-giving rain of *Words* becomes the fire and ice of *The Studhorse Man,* the tricky currents of *Badlands,* the bee-swarm and blizzard of *What the Crow Said.* John Judas Backstrom, not John George Applecart, is the true prophet of another world: Kroetsch country, where the rain always arrives, again and again. *The Words of My Roaring* fittingly ends with an invitation to go out into that downpour with our eyes and ears open and our cupped hands outstretched: "My dear friends, rain...."

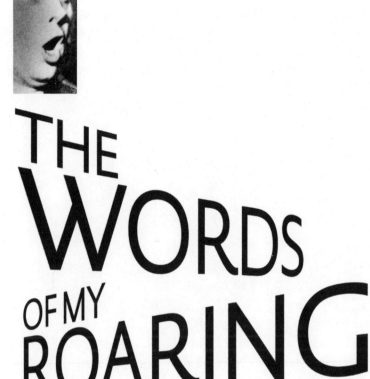

THE WORDS OF MY ROARING

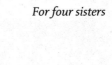
For four sisters

Why art thou so far from helping me,
and from the words of my roaring?
PSALM 22

SATURDAY

OLD MURDOCH was up on the fancy platform with all the flags and the bankers, promising relief and better prices. Promising new markets. Up there looking like a million dollars, showing his gold teeth and nodding his flat pink face as if drought and hard times and mortgages were just something those three hundred people had dreamt about last night. Promising we could all be as rosy and rich as he was, if we'd just smile when he smiled—and make our X's on the appropriate line.

Old Murdoch up there on the stage, he saw me sneak in and he bowed and said, "My worthy opponent."

That brought the place down. By God, the Union Jacks stood straight out in the gales of laughter. That old community hall just wheezed. The windows rattled their putty loose. The streamers overhead, red, white and blue, curled and uncurled in the raucous air.

Old Murdoch had packed them in and he was laying them out. "My worthy opponent," he said, "has come to bury us not to praise us."

I could find absolutely no place to sit down. What empty seats there were were smack up front. I didn't simply stand at the back of that hall, I loomed. My name, let me say once and for all, is Johnnie Backstrom, and I am six-four in my stocking feet, or nearly so, a man consumed by high ambitions, pretty well hung, and famed as a heller with women. Or at least I was, until the eldest unmarried daughter of the Burkhardt clan proved marvelously fertile on the strength of an awkward and hurried trial.

"Only," old Murdoch was saying. "Only let me say this."

I had, unfortunately, worn my black suit; it looks good with my huge craggy head and my fair hair. Except that it made me stand out like a preacher in hell.

People were holding their sides so they could listen. "Let me say," the Doc said, "that whereas my worthy opponent has come in here this Saturday night, perhaps from the beer parlor down the street—whereas my opponent has wormed his way in here uninvited, fragrant with stale beer—" The Doc couldn't contain himself. He had to break out in a golden smile. "Whereas he has crept and crawled in here to make us cough at the reek of his grouching and complaining—" I hadn't spoken a word. "Whereas he comes to bury our province in further debt and grief and misery—he himself, thirteen days hence; he himself shall be buried—in a landslide of votes."

Applause. Applause. Wild applause. Three hundred people knocking their calluses together, crying their joy. Cracking the rafters with their ignorant scorn. What could I possibly say? I who could not so much as find a place to sit down. Not a corner to hide in, not a hole to swallow me up. Sweat was beginning to pour down my neck. It is part of my profession to wear a black suitcoat; my armpits were awash.

"Let me say," the Doc said, "that the situation is a serious one." And suddenly he stopped smiling. He dabbed the sweat out of his eyes with a clean white handkerchief. "So serious that only maturity can serve our needs. Only experience, only a close familiarity with the long and painful past, can guide our decisions." His square pink face became serious; he hulked forward over that decorated kitchen table and its pitcher of water like a bear scenting honey. "For six long years the whole province of Alberta has rocked in the throes of a terrible calamity. For six terrible years, since that October day when grown men leapt in despair from skyscraper windows; when money turned to wind and hope turned to despair."

That whole hall full of people became serious. Old Doc was not a tall man, but he was big; he had a presence that nearly crowded his banker friends off the stage. His heavy body strained at a leash, his thick white hair fell over his forehead, his pink face took the light like a slab of gouged and polished granite. He was an old white bear ready to do battle. He squared his shoulders, his jacket off; he had stripped it off, something I could not do with mine because of the holes in my shirt sleeves. He cleared his throat. The plutocrat bank managers or whatever they were in a row on kitchen chairs behind him, they crossed and uncrossed their spindleshanks and nodded their five bald heads in unison; and the girl sitting on his right poured him a glass of water. But the old Doc was warmed up and looking for action. Sniffing the breeze for action.

"My worthy opponent," he said, "is a dear friend of mine. Johnnie Backstrom was the first child I brought into this world. I remember with great affection that day, that blustering windy day a mere thirty-three years ago when I rode a horse toward his mother's travail. I remember picking up little Johnnie Backstrom by the heels and slapping his purple hind end."

I'll be damned if that didn't bring the place down once again. There I was, embarrassed and looming at the back of the hall, nearly six-four in my stocking feet. Hundreds of faces came twisting and craning around to take one more look in utter disbelief. In grinning hick astonishment.

"Little Johnnie Backstrom," the Doc said, "grew up in sunny Alberta. He was here, worrying his mother half to death and messing his pants, while we turned the Indian trails into highways. He was here. Hunting crows' eggs and making mud pies and drowning out gophers, like any normal child. We tore down the sod shacks and the tarpaper shacks and worked hard for real homes and real stores and real farms. He was here, hiding in the wheat stooks and playing tag in the school basement, carefree and innocent." The old Doc raised his arms as if to hug his many children to his happy square body. You could practically smell the warm fur. "And now little Johnnie Backstrom wants to sit for us in Parliament. With all his fine background, with his three years of experience as an undertaker, he wants to go up to Edmonton and run our government."

I wanted simply to disappear. I slouched into myself, trying to conceal my huge frame. I couldn't even spare the three-fifty to rent the hall in that one-horse town. I had to go worming in and do my scrapping from the back row, hoping to hurl a few wicked barbs free of charge.

There I was, the best undertaker in the whole constituency—the only one, except for a deaf hardware dealer who couldn't endure the sight of an empty crate. There I stood, humiliated; a man who cannot abide humiliation.

And I knew all the time that a single funeral, the cheapest kind of funeral, could save me. Just a few dollars in the old tin cash box and I'd campaign Murdoch right off the dirt roads. Out of the farmer towns and the skating arenas and the country schoolhouses. Just one hundred dollars cash from one man who was rich enough to die; I'd be a Member of the Legislative Assembly come September. You bet your sweet life. Let the snow fly and I'd be sitting up there in the Parliament buildings, gawking out a window at the streetcars crossing the High Level Bridge. The micks and bohunks be damned; let the krauts and the crazy Swedes bury their own dead. Tough titty, boys. No more digging the grave myself to make the extra two bucks. Not for John B., M.L.A. Indemnity, they call it; nothing so crass as salary. Compensation for money that was never yours to lose. Five solid years of good green indemnification.

The Doc was ranting on, making his alibi sound like manna. Talking like Santa Claus while three hundred people bowed before him, the men in overalls with patches on the patches, the women in bloomers made of flour sacks.

He must have been listing his virtues. Because all of a sudden, after a very short statement, he stopped; and some joker with his arse beginning to ache from sitting too long on a nail keg had to clear his throat and chip in, "Backstrom, what you got to offer that can top that?"

I hadn't heard what the that was. Mostly I heard only the creaking of benches and planks as people turned once again to face the back door. Let me say flatly that when I walked into the doctor's rented hall there in that water stop called Coulee Hill I did not intend to promise anything. But we are so often mistaken; we confuse beginnings, endings. They are so alike so often. Especially when it comes to politics. Politics, or, I might add, love. They had me cornered all right, the bastards. And then the answer came without my thinking—I had been drinking a little; I looked at the speaker and saw he was a farmer and I said: "Mister, how would you like some rain?"

More laughter.

"Right after the election," the farmer said, "if we vote for Johnnie Backstrom."

"No, sir," I said. "That's not what I said."

Murdoch started to pour some water from the sweating pitcher and found his glass was already full. I would have given him two of my remaining thirteen dollars for one sip; my throat was drier than the ditches I'd noticed on the drive out from my happy home in Notikeewin. "It's easy," he said over the raised glass, his white hair sticking to his forehead, his face pink and flat above all the sun-tanned faces that were turned to the back door and me. "It's pretty easy to say it's going to rain in the next thirteen days."

"It hasn't rained in the last twenty-four," I said. "Or haven't you noticed, Doc?"

Followed by a new ripple of laughter. Only it was different kind; fidgety, embarrassed. I'd like to say—well, embarrassed was the right word.

I've always been polite, basically. Maybe that's why I'm a married man. I looked up, almost sorry I'd pinned the Doc down; and that pretty girl on the platform on Doc's right was watching me. Watching me closely. Hardly listening to the Doc. It was enough to make a man fell a little horny. She was pretty; she was more than that, with her dark eyes and that new white dress that looked just a little too cool around the neck for Coulee Hill, even in the middle of a hot spell. She was so beautiful she struck me into wonder.

"So you're going to bring us some rain," the Doc said.

He set down the empty glass on the red white and blue crepe paper that covered someone's table. "Well, come to think of it— settling the dust is your specialty."

That shabby old community hall just about exploded. People laughed so hard they slapped a couple of whirlwinds out of their dusty clothes. A stout lady in front of me was shaking so hard she split the back out of her gunnysack dress. The Doc was a real crowd-pleaser. I grinned a little myself, trying to look mysterious and calm; I have this amazing set of perfect teeth.

"As I was explaining," Doc Murdoch said, reaching back to one of his starched and ironed cronies to take up a sheaf of statistics. "I can deliver you." He gave us a glimpse of the gold in his mouth. "I can deliver you out of this predicament—and it won't be done in the manner of my worthy opponent."

I didn't wait for the guffaws.

Don't tell me I should have waited. Why embrace the boot that kicks and stomps and tramples you? I simply fled. I confess—I turned at that moment and I bolted. Why turn the other cheek when you can turn both? I took to my waiting heels. I nearly wore the door frame as a collar when I crashed into the open air. I burst out of that prison like a startled Hungarian partridge. I flung myself like so much dishwater into the darkening street.

I was perfectly justified: it was hopeless. It was worse than hopeless, I saw it all clear as day. I could no more beat old Murdoch in the forthcoming election than hope for a sudden plague. Why argue with the hobnails of fate? The game was over, the jig was up. I should have openly wept. I should have sat right down on the sidewalk and dumped a handful of ashes onto my sorrowing head.

B U T I galloped straight back to the beer parlor from which I had crept and crawled. A red brick institution located, as Murdoch had explained to his mob of raving teetotalers, down the street. I slammed in through the screen door, my fists clenched until the knuckles shone white, and I ordered a round for the house.

The Coulee Hill beer parlor was host to exactly four customers. The four men who had ridden out with me in my hearse from Notikeewin and who hoped, upon the conclusion of my political activities, to return the seventy-two miles in my hearse to Notikeewin. The Wild Rose City.

"Are we ready to go?" one of the four men asked, sweeping his change off his table.

"I am drought-stricken and parched," I said. "We are ready to drink."

So as I say, I ordered a round for the house. I bought and paid for that round and not long after I ordered another, I had to, the pain still knocking in my breast, and by that time there were nine people present. Not exactly a tumult of votes. But Jonah Bledd advised against even that act of generosity.

"You're a damned fool," he said.

Jonah is my best friend. Or was my best friend. He was my best friend but could not bring himself to enter an undertaker's place of occupation. He simply would not enter. Wild horses could not drag him into my residence, even when I had no customers. Thus my wife treated him alternately as an agent of perfidy and a figment of my imagination. But he was nothing if not a good man. He counseled against the third, the fourth, the fifth and subsequent rounds which I purchased for the house, each consecutive round proving somewhat dearer than its predecessor.

"You are a damned fool when it comes to money, women, alcohol, or politics," Jonah said, his hair as usual standing straight on end; his astonishment perpetual. "You are," he went on, "a meathead, a fathead, and a shithead."

But I was electioneering. By God, Murdoch or no Murdoch, I was back in the game. People were listening. People were looking my way. I felt I could lick my weight in bobcats. I searched through the pockets of my old black suitcoat, cautiously, trying to count the change without jingling the coins. "Duncan L. Murdoch," I said, for all to hear, "is tighter than a hen's ass on a frosty morning." The two remaining one-dollar bills were folded into a pocket of my shirt. "Duncan Murdoch, M.D.," I said, "would not be man enough to walk into a beer parlor and buy *himself* a glass of beer."

And I searched through the pockets of my pants. I had forty cents somewhere. Two dollars and forty cents. Twenty-four beers. I looked around once more, counting. Half the tables were empty on a Saturday night. By the sweating balls of Abraham, that's hard times for you.

I raised my left hand; I'm left-handed. I started to draw a circle around the table. Then I stopped; I made sure the slinger was watching; I made sure a number of people were taking note. And I drew a circle around the room. The old magic circle with my old magic arm.

I have this powerful left arm; I pitched for three years for the Notikeewin baseball team. I didn't ask, I was sent for. Try that young Backstrom kid, he is the only hope; they phoned my mother. Notikeewin was away from home at a sports day and they got into the final game and found their pitcher had given out. They sent a big car to get me. My first game; I fanned twenty-seven men in a row— my enemies hated me. People still talk about it. You could walk into any beer parlor in this constituency and mention that game and have a good fight on your hands inside of twenty minutes.

The screen door banged shut and I looked around. Four more men had just come in. I looked away; but the slinger caught my eye, waiting for instructions. The son of a B. There were twenty-four people in that room. I'd counted twice. Only now there were twenty-four plus four.

So for some damned fool reason I nodded. Just like that, I ducked my head down and up, and before I could give it a quick shake the slinger had turned away.

I had at least forty cents in change. The quarter and nickel were safe in my right hand in a pocket of my coat. And somewhere—I fingered the string, the clots of fuzz, a broken shoelace, the peppermints, a half stick of Juicy Fruit, two buttons that fooled me for a second—I found it; a dime.

So all I needed was forty cents more. I dug thoroughly into my pants pockets, my coat pockets, my shirt pockets. I pretended I was getting too warm, thus all the activity. I complained about the heat, kicking up both legs as I did so, squirming in my chair. I fingered the bottom fringe of my coat; sometimes a coin becomes lodged in the lining. The four men pulled up chairs at the table behind me. I started to empty my glass and found it already empty, the foam drying inside the rim. I glanced around again, as if looking for someone—and this time I recognized one of the men as the farmer I'd spoken to at Murdoch's rally. He had one eye that looked off to the side. His right eye. I should have told you that. He was walleyed. It made me uneasy.

I just for good measure reached into the pockets of my coat one more time and once again I encountered the peppermints, the string, the half stick of Juicy Fruit I was saving for later. I had chewed the missing half before going home the previous night. The slinger was delivering a tray of beer around the room, swaying recklessly from table to table, banging the glasses down as if they were only half-full, now and then dumping an ashtray into a larger ashtray he carried on his beer tray, now and then mopping beer circles off a table. I felt in the cuffs of my pants, pretending I had dropped something, very nearly plunging my hand into a full spittoon; sometimes a coin gets lodged in the cuffs of my pants. Jonah had left his change on the table; seventy-five cents. I forgot to mention: he did buy a round. He was the only one of the lot who did; the others were free loaders to a man. I had no choice. I slapped down my change with his and covered it all with two one-dollar bills.

"We caught a frog beside the railway track the other day," Jonah was saying. "We threw it into a pail of water and it drowned—didn't remember how to swim."

The men at the table behind me must only have smiled; I didn't hear any laughter. Then a finger tapped my shoulder. I nearly had heart failure. I ignored the intruding finger and it tapped again, with a kind of slow steadiness that seemed to imply it could go on tapping all night. Forever, if necessary.

Against my better judgment but for some reason I put my left hand on the edge of the table, pushed back thirty degrees so my chair was balanced on one leg, and I swung in what was a perfect semicircle. Then I let the creaking old armchair come to rest again.

I expected an accusing finger to point to the pile of coins.

"You say you're going to make it rain, Backstrom."

Not a question. A blunt simple statement. The walleyed farmer addressed me distinctly as if to teach me a very difficult equation or to ask me a very tricky riddle. His peculiar eye distracted me.

The slinger was at that same moment banging down four beers on the farmer's table; gratitude is a rare commodity. So for a moment I was irritated. I was joking when I said that, about the rain. I had to give old Murdoch a smart answer. Why in hell couldn't people forget something?

"You can't spend rain," I said.

Another smart answer that fizzled out. The farmer guzzled the free beer. "I'd have something to eat," he said, "by the old Harry. And if it doesn't rain, better prices aren't going to do me any good." He raised his voice to the watching men, a kind of croaking voice, and he cast that strange eye around the room. People really sat up and listened.

"Backstrom here was at Murdoch's spiel tonight. He says it's going to rain before the election."

This time I could feel little fragments of laughter pricking my skin. Sheer humiliation; from the very people who were pouring my last cent down their gullets. Splinters of laughter pierced my soul.

The slinger was standing at my elbow, waiting for the money.

"You going to *make* it rain?" someone asked. I swear, voices just seemed to speak at me out of the walls. I was confused. Jonah's three friends there at my table were silent and fidgety, the three of them alike were wearing old blue suitcoats and red ties over their work clothes. They were so uneasy they didn't even snatch up the fresh beer as they were wont to do.

"I just said it would rain." I pointed to the pile of bills and coins. The slinger picked up two dollars and eighty cents.

"Have one yourself," I said.

It's a general custom. He took one more dime, leaving two dimes and a nickel.

"You say you're going to make it rain, Backstrom?" someone was calling from across the room, his voice hollow and echoing out of a fresh glass of beer.

"I just said it'll rain before the election."

"Oh I see." The walleyed farmer let out a guffaw, his voice croaking again. "You're backing down."

"The hell I am. Hell no." I raised my new glass and emptied it with one long hard swallow—I could feel my throat working, partly out of thirst, partly to control my temper. I have a fairly quick temper, my wife tells me. And she is quite a specialist on the subject herself. Jesus H., they knew nobody makes it rain, even if in the morning they'd all parade into church, headaches and sore peckers and all, to pray for a cloudburst. But if they wanted to believe—holy baldheaded Moses, it was bound to rain in thirteen days. That was a blue-eyed grizzly cinch. "Sure," I said. I damned near put that empty glass through the table top. "Hell, yes. Sure I said it'll rain. I promise you that, you clod-hoppers. You prairie chickens. And when it's so goddamned wet you can't drive to the polling booths, I hope you'll be men enough to walk, wade or swim so you can make a cross for John Backstrom."

I thought that was a good touch, reminding them of my name. Someone gave a cheer. A kind of wild whoop. The man next to him said, "You better lay off drinking, boy. You'll soon be as goofy as Backstrom himself."

That was too much for me to bear cheerfully, good-natured though I may be. Too much. I said, "Look, mister." I said, "When I say it's going to rain it's going to pour. And I say it's going to pour. So if I was in your boots I'd start shopping for a boat. You lazy pack of stubble-jumpers. I'd start building an ark."

Well sir—everybody must have heard. Maybe I raised my voice a little. Anyway, I'm a little vague on exactly what happened next. Things seemed to bust loose. Bedlam. Men who were supposed to be hard up started buying drinks for me and my table. That walleyed farmer pulled out a dime you could just about see through and he said, "This is my last goddamned dime and I'm using it to buy you a goddamned drink, Backstrom." What could I say? That man was a real sport. Even the owner of the place bought a round. People started talking to each other. Of a bumper harvest and where could they get extra help in a hurry. Of shopping trips to the city and winter clothes for the wife and kids. Of paying off the interest on the mortgage for another year. Of the money barons in the East who were getting rich on the sweat of our honest brows; the coupon clippers who were bleeding us white. We all talked at once. Men were buying whole trays of beer, standing us beers all over the place, so I did my duty. I was touched. The floor was sticky with spilled beer. Beer flowed. I was a candidate for public office; I had to demonstrate my worth.

I was demonstrating so hard that when the slinger flicked the lights and said it was closing time, I offered to keep the place open of my own accord. I offered to close the owner's eyes. I said that when I got to Parliament I'd change the closing hours, so he had nothing to worry about. I said a number of other things, and I rose from my chair and picked up same to give added emphasis to some of my stronger assertions.

But Jonah Bledd persuaded me to leave without rearranging the furniture. He offered to buy a case of beer. Then he tried to persuade me to let him drive, but I said no man drives my hearse but me.

And so we drove, with big John B. at the steering wheel.

We drove through the cooling night, and we felt pretty good, I can tell you. The crows had stopped knocking around in the sky. All day they were boss, but now it was ours; the sky, the horizon, the fields of wheat. The moonlit night was ours. A dozen bottles of beer were ours. It was all listed under our names, we were certain, and we drove and stopped and we drove and we had to stop again.

Man, it felt good, just to be half-loaded and the pressure easing up in your bladder and the old tool held firmly in the right hand. For that one beautiful moment you feel you've spent a lifetime looking for a place to pee, and here you've found it. We watered the parched earth. You could hear water running, and that was a mighty pleasant change. Oh show me the way to go home. That clear sky above all rashed over with millions of stars and the baked earth letting out the breath it had held all day; the cowshit and buckbrush and a drying slough hole scenting the air; a little rank yet fertile with hope. It felt good. Giving yourself a flick or two. Three is playing, somebody said—one of Jonah's triplet friends, in an old blue suitcoat and a worn red tie. And wild roses in the glare of the headlights, a little dusty, but full of color because no rain had washed the petals white. The telephone line; the poles all throbbing, setting up a hum that lulled the sleeping grasshoppers.

"Let's go," I said. "Let's travel. It's traveling time."

We all piled into the hearse once more. The three in the back were singing: Oh show me the way to go home, I'm tired and I want to go to bed. We hit the gravel, all of us singing. The hearse swayed onto the road, the flight of stones knocking the still air. I was feeling pretty fine. The three men behind me were trying to harmonize: wherever I may roam. Old friends, you might say; they were friends of Jonah and therefore friends of mine. I was gone for so long, I'd just been back three years. We all sang.

But Jonah was getting sour-faced. His voice told me that. Jonah who was always steady as a rock; not much given to laughter, but steady, reliable, levelheaded. A man people leaned on; I was always leaning on Jonah. We were singing maybe for the tenth time, O'er land or sea or foam. Nobody can get that part wrong. But he was doing it. He was starting to worry.

"I didn't tell you," he said, right in the middle of the song. I stopped singing myself. I was almost hoarse. For another thing, I can't sing a solo. "How do you mean, Jonah?" I said.

"Today at noon," he said. "I got laid off."

I was frantic for a moment. I should have kept on singing, giving myself time to think. One of my biggest weaknesses is not giving myself time to think. I groped for something to say; my mind raced in circles, dodging a wild impulse to tell him to go consult my wife. She thinks I don't know she smokes. My dear wife who is full of useless and cryptic advice. Who also sprung a surprise remark on me, while I was driving her back from a church bingo at which she had won a set of matching pillowcases: HIS, HERS. "I have news for you," she said.

As I say, I *was* a heller with women.

"Today at noon," Jonah repeated.

I was speechless, you understand.

Women sort of go for undertakers; a phenomenon I have never quite penetrated to its root.

"I got my walking papers," Jonah was saying. "What should I do?"

He worked for the railway. He used to.

"Can you be a Rawleigh man?" I burst out at him.

"A what?" he said.

For some crazy reason that came into my head. My wife owed our Rawleigh man nearly two dollars. He drives around uninvited in a car that should be junked and heaps useless items on kitchen tables before hundreds of gullible women. "Sell door to door," I said. "You have that sheepish grin that will disarm people. I wish I had that grin of yours instead of my own damned lecherous face." I saw I was getting off the topic. "A Rawleigh man, they have an excellent line," I said. "Especially their ointments and salves. Also their spices. My wife swears by them. Their salves and ointments, she claims—"

"I'd end up giving things away." He took a bottle that someone handed forward from the dark behind us.

"But you'd learn," I said.

"I'd need a car," he said.

"Can you cut hair?" I said. I was still frantic. His hair, I could see in the dim light from the dashboard, was standing straight on end.

"Johnnie, can I cut hair?"

"You're asking me?" I said. "There's a barber shop for sale in the Royal Hotel. Clippers and everything, dirt cheap, I heard. I thought about it myself. Even if you had to hire a barber—"

"I couldn't trim a horse's mane." Jonah said. "And I'm broke."

"My wife," I said—I was being irrational—"buys all our pepper, red black and white, from the Rawleigh man, and from the Rawleigh man only. Also our cloves, for baking and for toothaches. Also paprika." I couldn't stop myself; I recognized that. I was turpentined and running. "Also bay leaf, also cinnamon, nutmeg, sage, dill." I could have gone on forever. I desperately wanted to go on, never stopping. "Also mustard, very good for a chest cold. Also rosemary—"

"No," he said. "I'm serious, Johnnie. I should have gone East when you did. It's too late."

"Never," I said. I took a pull from the bottle and handed it back. "Never, Jonah."

We were driving due west at the time. The road from Coulee Hill into Notikeewin runs due west, parallel to a branch line of the railway which begins in Notikeewin and ends in Coulee Hill. If you follow me. Seventy-two and a half miles. Jonah and I applied for the same job when we finished high school. We were close friends, but given to competition. The life force of the nation, competition. But for some reason, maybe pull, he got the job.

"You did all right staying here," I said. "With the railway. You've got a fine wife and five strapping kids."

"And no way to support them."

"Business will pick up the minute harvest begins."

Jonah actually laughed. His scalp always seemed too tight; it pulled at his eyes in a funny way. The three men in the back of the hearse were singing at the top of their lungs: I had a little drink about an hour ago. "Harvest," Jonah said. "What the hell are you talking about, Johnnie?"

"I'm talking about trainloads of wheat and new machinery; loads of gas and oil; bindertwine; lumber for new granaries."

"One sack of twine will take care of the whole bloody crop. We could haul it to town in our pockets."

"There'll be wheat trains again," I said, "so long you won't be able to see from one end to the other."

"Sure," Jonah said. "Tomorrow."

"Really," I said. "They'll have to hire extra crews just to ride in the middle and relay the signals. You'll be getting bushels of overtime. Fat bonuses—"

"Tomorrow is Sunday," Jonah said.

"The day after—" But I stopped talking.

I wheeled hard for the next town. Five towns in a row break the monotony between Coulee Hill and Notikeewin. We were past Roundhead and St. Leo. We were passing Burkhardt; the village of Burkhardt, founded by my wife's forebears, who made a little money by charging too much for machinery and then got snooty and moved to Notikeewin. My wife's illustrious forebears whose departures, terrestrial or eternal, did not hurt the beer-parlor trade, but who in the last twenty years had never, the multiplying hundreds of them, cast one vote for any candidate but Duncan L. Murdoch, M.D.

Jonah was sort of hurting my feelings. I had to exaggerate a little, both my talking and my driving. I'm that way sometimes. He didn't believe in my rain, Jonah Bledd of all people. My closest friend. Jonah, who was basically what I would call a good man. We were hitting sixty-one on that gravel road in a hearse that was built to do around twelve miles an hour.

"Look at the country out there," I said. The land is nearly flat and out ahead we could see the lights of two towns and then of Notikeewin; three clusters of lights, like fallen stars on the dark earth. A total distance of thirty-some miles. "She'll look like one big garden," I said.

"Another dead soldier," Jonah said. I saw that he swung his arm and I knew an empty bottle was spinning away behind us, spinning off into the night. It was our last one, we had passed it around. He wiped at his mouth with the back of his hand. I strained hard, trying to get a glimpse of his face.

There's a little curve in the road just there by the Esso station. Outside of that it's as straight as a die for twenty miles. I was thinking hard by this time, remembering how a souser of a rain can alter the whole picture. I was born here. I know what a bumper crop looks like—how a good soaker at the right time can do the trick. I knew that right along that highway the scrutineers would count the winning votes. The constituency is framed by the railway track on the north, with a loop of river hanging below. The towns are strung out along the railway. The whole thing is shaped vaguely like a collection plate, if you've ever been inside a church, and an undertaker, let me assure you, has. I positively hate going to church.

To tell you the truth, I forgot about the curve. I'm sure I forgot. Maybe I couldn't see it, the lights weren't very good on my hearse. I was somewhat irritated. Liquor doesn't affect my driving. But the next thing I knew, a telephone pole was in the way and I was tying my long arms in knots trying to avoid it. Which I almost did. I only caught the right front fender. But that was enough to throw Jonah against the door on his side. He had the window open and he was resting his arm in the open frame. He'd just chucked an empty bottle. Old men often walk the ditches, picking up bottles; it keeps the country clean and they make a little money. The three in the back didn't get a scratch, they hardly stopped singing, and all I got was a swollen upper lip from hitting the steering wheel with my face. Also, I was struck in the chest somehow; I have quite a hefty chest. But when I shook my head clear and looked sideways, Jonah simply wasn't there. It was a terrifying experience. He had vanished. The door had swung shut, you see. He was gone. But then we heard him; he was groaning softly; politely, I'm tempted to say. Trying to get his breath back. Trying to rub the dust out of his eyes; that's how he noticed about his arm.

I was drunk, I guess. I kept knocking on the door of the Doc's office, yelling with my fist, could I come in please Doc, could I come in, and the Doc wouldn't answer. Five M.D.'s and a dentist in Notikeewin; six men who presumably could set a fractured arm. And I took Jonah straight to old Murdoch without so much as batting an eye.

I could hear the Doc's voice, low and reassuring, behind the door that lead to his office. He was talking to Jonah while he worked. His voice was resonant in that big wooden house, resonant and firm when I listened, and he might have been talking to me. I could see in my mind Jonah's white face, his hair on end and his upper lip sweating; but the Doc might have been talking to me.

The first-born, he liked to tell me, patting my head. Patting my shoulder, after he couldn't reach my head.

The Doc had warned me more than once. Goddamnit, Johnnie, he'd say, it isn't going to spoil if you leave a little for the next day. And standing there in that waiting room, in the darkness, inhaling the faintly medicinal smell of that reception room, I thought of being an only son. I couldn't find the light switch; maybe I didn't try too hard. On the other side of that door was the Doc, square and pink-faced, white-haired and frowning in the glare of his naked lamps. I thought of all the free advice you get. But more than that. I thought of my old man dead from a shellburst outside a town called Ypres, dead beyond all caring, his regiment covered with glory; and I thought of the old Doc. The young Doc then, patting my head while my mother cried, and he kept saying, you were my first-born.

Because I was. I was his first delivery. He hadn't unpacked when my mother needed him. My old man was trying it by himself, in the name of his belief in self-sufficiency, but after fourteen hours he rode into town on a plowhorse and gave it to Murdoch and pointed vaguely westward—" You'll hear her," he said—and he followed after on foot. I was a tough delivery. From start to finish. My old man was so tired from running those fifteen miles in a pair of shoes with laces that kept breaking, he was half-confused. " Your first one?" he puffed. " You bet your sweet life," the Doc said, proud and flustered. He put a hand to his own genitals, rubbing, touching carefully here and there. "And the first time I rode a horse."

But I had to explain. All my life when things got tough I went running to Murdoch. I had to make him understand. I put my ear to the door and listened; I listened there in the dark, the old chesterfield invisible, the two old armchairs and the magazine stand and the Oriental rug all invisible yet familiar to my mind. The Doc with his needles and stethoscope, on the other side of that door. With his little sticks for making people say ah. I don't have a stethoscope in my office. When they get to me, the heart no longer pounds. Silence is my business, I deal in silence; and its prologue, sorrow. Sorrow and grief. And then I knocked harder. I had to. Not just for myself; for all of us. For all who sat in that draughty room, the sick and the hurting. We wore out the rug and we wore out the springs in those seats. We sat there aching and hurting and wanting to cry; and one by one we went through that door; one went in and the rest of us sat and listened, sat and waited, the lumps in our throats getting bigger.

Afraid of the pain, afraid of the cure.

And it was my boyhood fate to have a body that couldn't be hurt. I got a dozen scars, sure. But the pain was always in my soul.

So I knocked. The great white house rocked to my knocking, throbbed and echoed there in the night's darkness. Little Johnnie B. was knocking. Please let me explain, I was telling the Doc. My fist said it. Your first-born. He caught that train. When he couldn't get a job with the railway, he caught a train instead. He asked you, "What should I do, Doc?" And you answered. "Goddamnit, Johnnie," you said, "this country needs an undertaker who can tell a packing crate from a coffin." And he was stubborn then too, your first-born. Stubborn and hurting. So he caught a train. Instead of swinging a lantern he bought a ticket, with the ten dollars you slipped his mother.

Harvest excursion to the East. Ten dollars cash. Ten smackeroos plus one hell of a long ride. Curled awkward on a wooden seat all night, swaying dizzy to shave while the train lurched eastward, eating bread and bologna and staring out a window all day. But when he got to Ontario he worked like a madman; in all those steaming rich hayfields, he worked like a man gone insane.

Let me tell you why, Doc. He read an ad. On the back of a newspaper that was used to wrap fish. Win your embalming license, the advertisement said. *Win*, for Christ sake! Not earn but win; in some gigantic roll of the dice, some one last crazy shuffle of the deck.

That waiting room; it smelled of cough syrup, of lysol and mercurochrome; and standing there, knocking, I knew also that the door wasn't locked. I sniffed the iodine, the rubbing alcohol. Everything but formaldehyde. Old Doc never locked a door. He told that to his potential voters. The old bear was inside. Inside, as usual, and waiting. I could have walked in and explained. About Jonah's arm. About a lot of things. Like if I couldn't heal I could bury. I was bull-headed, Doc. Always. I was drunk. I was drunk and driving, and one word to your friends in the newspaper office and the victory is yours.

The door wasn't locked. But I stood there knocking, pounding and pleading with my fist, and he wouldn't say those two measly words, come in. He wouldn't say come in and I muttered in the darkness, incoherent and stubborn and hurt and angered. And drunk too, I guess. Can I come in? I kept insisting.

Your little Johnnie B. who would not learn his Latin verbs. *Amo, amas,* whatever. He won no glory in high school. But he was a whiz at repairing the dead. The accidents of mortality, the ravages of pain.

When John did the restorations, people held their breath and sighed. Good grief, they told each other, old so-and-so is more himself now than he was when he was alive. Your first delivery, slapped into life via his purple hind end, he won his license with honors.

But he didn't take the jobs that were offered. No, he shipped out on a laker. Shipped out as a seaman. Little Johnnie Backstrom who was raised on God and poverty. On free advice. On sky and dust.

I skinned my knuckles on the Doc's door. I really did. I put the knuckles to my mouth, sucking the poison out of the torn flesh. And still I had to talk.

In a big black boat, Doc; your first-born shipped out.

And I'll tell you another why.

He couldn't stay away from all that water. When mowing the grass or raking leaves—apprenticeship they call it. Two solid years of respectable lawn and respectable hedge. When driving out into the street to lead a resplendent funeral, the first thing he saw was the lake. The first thing he heard. There on the shore outside Toronto. Young John, a boy from the parklands; after a while it was haunting him: the slap of waves on rock and sand. After a while he had to see every nook and cranny of those Great Lakes; the log booms and the wheat elevators, the whorehouses, the strip joints, the mansions of the rich.

And he had to know what it felt like, Doc—just to be so far out on water you couldn't smell land.

Because I'll tell you something else. I may as well confess. That apprenticeship scared me a little.

I'm not a man who scares easily, don't you ever forget. Look how I drove right up to your door, Doc, with Jonah gripping his arm and gritting his teeth. But that apprenticeship scared me. I didn't just leave the place where I did my stint; I didn't just leave, I ran away. I left everything. My fancy black clothes. My suitcase and matching briefcase, a gift from my mother's friends. My one letter from home. I walked up the gangplank onto that boat with my empty hands in my empty pockets.

And I was clear and running for ten years. For ten whole years; until I was chipping paint off a rail. I was supposed to be taking off paint so I could put more on, but in fact I was reading a newspaper that lay on a deck chair. The high-society page. I was a great reader while on the boats. NIECE OF LOCAL FAMILY VISITS. *Helen P. Murdoch, the daughter of Doctor Duncan L. Murdoch of Notikeewin,*

Alberta, has come east to enroll in a course in the arts and sciences. Miss Murdoch is currently a guest....

For ten years I was free and running. Until I picked up a telephone. I didn't really plan to do it; I believe I'd had a few drinks. My pockets, unfortunately, were brimming with change. I didn't really expect her to answer. The paper was two days old; she might have been gone.

"Hello," she said.

"This is Johnnie," I said.

She might have answered, Johnnie who? She might have said that. Then I might have been okay.

"Johnnie Backstrom!" she said. "Why didn't you write to someone? How are you? We've worried for years! Are you still alive?"

It was practically a miracle.

"How's the old buzzard?" I said. "Old Duncan L., the sawbones?"

I guess we talked for some time.

"How's ma?" I asked her. "Still carting the Doc's flowers off to every pew and altar?"

I guess we talked and talked. I really had been drinking.

"How're the crops?" I asked her.

And then I sprung a little surprise. Maybe it was her voice that caused it.

"Tell me," I said, "do they still need a good undertaker in that burg called Notikeewin, The Wild Rose City?"

Maybe it was a realization that drove me to it. For ten years I was out on the water, and for every day of those ten years I knew we were surrounded by land. We talked, Helen and I.

"Do they need the living expert?" I inquired.

She said, "Yes, they need a good undertaker. But who—" she said, in her beautiful voice, "who, with the kind of drought they're having back West, can afford to bury the dead?"

SUNDAY

JONAH BLEDD and the old Doc managed to
wake me up. Apparently I was sound asleep in the
middle of the floor. I quite often fall asleep on
floors; the very discomfort is somehow a consolation. Jonah got me to stretch out in the back of the
hearse and drove me home, his right arm in a sling;
and then he persuaded me to walk up the stairs,
though he refused, as usual, to accompany me
through the door. I woke up early in the afternoon
with absolutely the worst hangover of a lifetime
that has not been entirely devoid of same. It was
not so much a matter of my awakening as being
awakened. My wife was pounding my knees with
her flyswatter. It seems that nine—I resort to her
word—*strangers,* had arrived simultaneously at the
door of our funeral home. Not, alas, a sudden
outpouring as if the gates of hell had opened, its

bounty to redound forever to my financial relief,
but nine living inquiring souls.

I had plumb forgot. In my initial excitement at being named a
political candidate I had recklessly scheduled a series of three meetings to be held on Sunday afternoons in my funeral parlor. The first
two meetings had attracted a total of seven listeners, two of them my
drinking acquaintances and not cordially welcomed by all members
of my household; five of them, I suspect, spies for the opposition.

And now the remaining and climactic meeting threatened to attract
the magnificent total of nine potential voters. On the twelfth day
before the election.

I should confess that Elaine, having threatened my life and manhood
with her flyswatter, did not immediately mention the matter of the
nine portentous strangers.

It seems she had heard certain details of my previous day's activities before I awoke. Thus she had not attended her religious ceremonies
in vain. I'll have to give her credit, the first thing she mentioned as a
public disgrace was the injuring of Bledd's arm. Before the fender
even. Or the thirteen dollars and some odd cents she had been unable
to locate in my pockets. Or, as I say, the political extravaganza that
threatened on her doorstep.

The hangover itself did not stir her anger; indeed, that phenomenon is generally applauded in our household as a manifestation of
God's essential and ultimate righteousness. She worked through the
list of my sins methodically, making no inquiry as to the wherefore or
why, relying heavily on assertion; but she began with the accident—
that I cannot deny.

Elaine is a fairly compassionate woman. She especially likes cats,
and since I detest cats I sometimes sell her virtues short. Our house is
plagued with cats.

But I made a mistake. Finding myself unable to leap out of bed,
finding myself unable so much as to twitch or wiggle a finger without
a woodpecker knocking in my skull, I begged her, hoarsely, to go
downstairs and invite the aforementioned *strangers* to rush upstairs
and be seated. If they haven't left, I added. And she was about to act
when recklessly I continued. She was standing at the foot of the bed,
her hair in curlers. "Turn on the radio," I continued. "And take that
goddamned aluminum junkyard out of your lovely hair."

It cost me a great effort to speak. But I should have remained silent. Criticism of the sort I had just proffered is a great stimulus to unnecessary repetition.

"Jonah has seven mouths to feed," she said.

"Our guests will leave," I insisted.

"He has five little children." She fingered her curlers, fearful that one might come loose and fall out. "And his arm in a cast and sling. How can he work?"

My wife's first concern about all men. It was a waste of breath to point out that Jonah had no job to begin with.

"That fender," she said, "will set us back ten dollars. The bumper should be replaced."

I tried to explain that I wasn't deaf. "The bumper can be straightened," I added.

But now she was becoming statistical. "Do you know how much food thirteen dollars would buy? Food. You know. Food." Firmly gripping her flyswatter she pointed with her free hand to her mouth, her belly. Perhaps I neglected to mention, my wife was seven months pregnant with our first child. She often repeats herself. "Food," she said.

"Turn on the radio," I insisted. "And ask our guests to bring up some chairs from the funeral parlor." We live over the funeral parlor. It was the intention both of myself and of my assembling guests to listen to a radio program that came on the air each Sunday afternoon. "And tell them I'll be there as soon as I finish my morning prayers."

She snatched the single remaining sheet off my nakedness, not once rejoicing in what her violence did untent, not uttering a single cry of praise. Not so much as acknowledging the contradiction that is man; the mind that wrestles with black despair, the spirit that soars. I kicked a cat off the bed; calm, resolutely, my head erect, I bore my pain and my trousers into the bathroom, kicking another two cats out of the dirty laundry and gently closing the door.

I trust I have explained that my wife, though committed to an iron concept of justice, is not without her dash of mercy. She smuggled the coffeepot into the bathroom, allowing three cats to enter in the process, and while my guests arranged themselves in a semicircle around the Atwater-Kent in our living room I not only shaved, etcetera, etcetera, I drank nine cups of coffee. Swedes and Norwegians are famous coffee drinkers. I am what is popularly known as a big Swede, though I am, incidentally, half-Norwegian in descent. Everything went fine—except that by the time I ventured out of the bathroom, all dressed in black and in my stocking feet because I was unable to bear the mortal agony of bending over to put on and tie my shoes, which badly needed polishing, I found I was host to twenty-three potential votes.

The living room was too small. The heat was unbearable. Now I felt somewhat ill not only from beer but from all the coffee. We had to move, obviously, from the living room down to the funeral parlor. My old Atwater-Kent must weigh a ton, containing as it does four batteries. Lifting would make me either pass out or throw up. But I couldn't let anyone else carry the radio, because, concealed in its complex machinery, was a micky of rye. A precious twelve-and-a-half ounces of bronze and robust rye. And every person in that crowd of twenty-three was obviously of my wife's persuasion on the subject of alcoholic beverages.

So I carried the radio singlehanded in my stocking feet, the holes in both toes bringing no flicker of shame to my wife's ruddy countenance.

"Try not to track up my floors," she said.

An additional eighteen people were waiting outside when I ventured to raise a blind and let the glare of broad daylight assail my scarlet eyes. I had no choice but to let them in. I turned on the radio.

The pain occasioned by the enthusiasm of dozens of female voices rendering a hymn was unendurable. But if I did not turn on the radio full blast I would have to talk, and those forty-odd teetotalers would inevitably and instantly recognize a whisky baritone. My tongue was a dead fish swelling in the heat of my mouth. A wood rasp; it tore at my throat when I tried to swallow; it sawed at my teeth.

I greeted my public.

Stocking-footed I bowed and smiled and signaled and pointed and nodded and unfolded more folding chairs, the clack of each opening chair threatening to explode my pulsating head. My swollen upper lip was a clapper knocking at my incisors. But I did not open my mouth.

The twelve verses with as many choruses of the hymn having been played and sung, we were blessed with a moment of silence. Then, invisible but not unheard, a foot kicked an invisible microphone.

And Applecart spoke.

"That Whore," the invisible speaker said, his voice deep and ringing; sure of itself. "That Who-er," he said. "That Who-er of Babylon. Let us consider this afternoon that scarlet Who-er of Babylon."

He won me over in a flash.

John George Applecart was the leader of my party, the champion; I was his chosen representative. He bore my Christian name, which somehow always made me flinch, but my second initial is J., not G. Inside of two seconds he was Who-ering this and Who-ering that. The whole works of us, we hardly dared to raise our heads. But we listened, by God. We paid close attention.

Sometimes we couldn't exactly follow. But we could understand. Applecart had got it into his head that things can be changed. He pointed out how everything was absolutely wrong: the price of goods bought and sold, the nature of dividends. The cultural heritage itself was threatened. He just ripped loose about everything. It made us all feel a lot better, even me.

I was dying to throw up. I was just hanging on, every muscle in my belly just dying to have one good convulsion. But I couldn't leave that room; I had to listen. Applecart—he preached every Sunday until most of the churches in the province weren't taking enough in their collection plates to pay for the grape juice they were palming off as wine. And at last I was beginning to see. It was the biggest event of the week. Nothing could touch it.

"The first angel sounded," he said, "and there followed hail and fire mingled with blood, and they were cast upon the earth; and the third part of trees was burnt up, and all green grass was burnt up."

He was speaking my language. Everything was gone to the dogs, gone haywire and kaput. He clinched his point. That was stuff I could appreciate. I couldn't have made a beeline for the back porch, even if I hadn't been host to a bunch of teetotalers. I couldn't let on that I was sick, that was natural. But more than that: I couldn't tear myself away.

Applecart was laying it on—without exaggerating by so much as an ell. Our trees and grass were the living proof; you could see which third of the world we lived in. I wish to tell you Applecart laid it on, he made you squirm. Who hears more sermons than an undertaker? But even I was impressed. I knew my micky of rye was concealed in the back of that radio, and moving it downstairs had nearly given me a heart attack. I was dying for one small swig. But all that hard-hitting truth was enough to make a man swear off for life. There wasn't a breeze in the air. The windows were open but the curtains didn't stir. Not a cloud in the sky.

I should confess, I've read the Bible somewhat myself. It's pretty good. How could I help it, living in this country? Besides, my mother read it to me when I wouldn't read it on my own: no Bible, no break-fast. I had no choice. I was doomed. Like the wicked people in some of those stories. Like everybody, I sometimes think.

Talk about a haywire outfit: people couldn't even afford radios. Or batteries for the radios they had. Talk about hard up. Talk about doom.

But more than that, I'd got hold of this idea of study groups. In school I was always stronger in baseball than I was in scholarship; I pitched a no-hitter. But when people are in trouble they like to study, so I sent away to Applecart for some of his free pamphlets, white blue and yellow, and I'd announced briefly that after his talk or sermon or whatever he wanted to call it there'd be a study period. I sent for four hundred pamphlets. I was counting the house.

But just as I was getting into the thirties for the second time, having got lost on the first try, Applecart paused to get his wind.

"Who?" he said. He let his voice drop. "I ask you, who?" And he stopped, he left us hanging. "Who is that red beast of a Who-er?"

The silence in the middle of that lull was blanker than midnight. And just then an old lady with a cane across her lap leaned toward me and whispered: "What day exactly do we expect the rain?"

I damn near died. I might have cried out, but my throat was too parched. My upper lip was too swollen. I pretended I hadn't heard; but every person in that room had heard. The blaze of light came in at all windows as if determined to strike me blind. The heat sizzled into the room which I always kept shadowed, dark. My eyes actually blurred.

I hate to admit it, I was saved from sudden foolishness by the intrusion of my wife. My wife cannot endure a silence of any sort. The gleam of her hair curlers flashed before my blurring eyes. She had spent her initial impulse to be merciful; it had now been annihilated by her most recent examination of the right fender of the hearse. She stepped outside and into the car shed periodically to take another look, fervently believing the fender might have healed in her absence. This, apparently, had not as yet occurred. We couldn't, obviously, afford to have it fixed. Yet—granted that someone must sooner or later die, for my wife persisted in that unlikely notion—how, she wanted to know, "How can you lead a big funeral in a hearse with one fender crinkled and the headlight broken?"

"Funerals take place in daylight," I explained.

Just then Applecart let out a roar. "The Fifty Big Shots," he roared, his voice crushing the silence. "That's who!" he said. "That, I mean to tell you, my dear tormented friends, is who!"

I could have wept for joy.

Those forty-odd listeners straightened right up. They positively beamed.

Applecart was onto the dirty Easterners who were gouging the West. He had built up to that and now he was onto them. He was talking about the Second Coming and the Last Judgment, the final reckoning of the Fifty Big Shots. Just wait, he said. And he gave them a blanket condemnation. "Just wait, and in short order the wicked will be punished and the suffering good will be rewarded." It was a great formula. People looked at me and nodded and smiled. And I smiled and nodded. We were getting the hang of it fast. The Fifty Thieves, Applecart said. You're damn tooting, I nodded.

Then it was time to drive home his point and he clinched her tight: "Come hither; I will show unto thee the judgment of the great Who-er that sitteth upon many waters..."

I worked on the lakes for a number of years, but the thought had never struck my mind; the Whore, it turned out, was Toronto, and all her high-muckie-muck millionaires. He had a magnificent voice, Applecart. He just about tore the top off my old Atwater-Kent. He talked so loud I was afraid his voice might crack the micky of whisky concealed under the speaker. The people loved it. Some of the women cried.

I started to feel pretty good myself. Instead of having two sure votes, one of them canceled by my wife's ballot, I apparently had over forty. That was a big gain for one day.

I was the only person in the constituency who was well enough known to run against Murdoch. Or at least I made this observation to people and a few days later they made it to me; you know how people are. But the minute I remembered how ambitious men must sully their hands to achieve fine goals, I was plunged into another depression. Because those same people who failed to oppose the nomination when Bledd made it—those same people had ignored a simple fact. Old Murdoch helped people coming into the world. I saw them out. And that didn't leave me with a lot of active supporters.

"It's a total wreck," my wife said.

I put a finger to my lips, the tip of my first finger touching the tip of my nose, the thumb unconsciously riding up. The more I listened the more I remembered sailing into Toronto on a dark summer night, off the quiet lake toward the harbor. Applecart had a point. All those lights—the whole city—it was *sitting* on the water. That's a God's fact; squatting on the water. It fouls the water, by Jesus, I thought.

"He has a rotten tongue," my wife said. "That Apple— whatever his name is."

I tapped my raised finger against my pouting upper lip, signifying a dire need for silence. "Who-er," I said, "is a Biblical reference."

"Horse radish," my wife said, a cat just then nuzzling up to one of my stockinged feet and very nearly scaring the pants off me. I have never quite adjusted to living in a funeral home.

Applecart was connecting Satan and all of hell with the dirty Eastern millionaires, the financial racketeers. He was the voice of the prairies speaking. He was ripping into all the betrayers of Christ and His holy principles which, it turned out, had a lot to do with the price of wheat and hogs.

My wife would not go away. She was supposed to be preparing coffee and cake for the guests. She had underestimated the crowd by thirty-five and was having loaves-and-fishes problems.

"How's the coffee coming?" I said.

"His Majesty wants more coffee," she said.

Sarcasm runs deep in the Burkhardts, especially in the women. I did not want more coffee. I was sick from too much coffee, among other things. I got the impression that my wife had intended the original pot to go farther than it did, but this was an inference, not a fact. The Burkhardt women are by and large small and sharp-tongued. Tart-tongued might be a better expression. A friend of mine once remarked that they are fully developed only in their breasts and their mouths. Elaine, incidentally, has supremely substantial and not unattractive breasts, as she is preeminently aware. They were the beginnings of my present vicissitudes and tribulations. Beginnings and endings again.

She leaned over me, refusing to go away, her dress too tight. One of her endless ways of tormenting my sense of decency. "I should go buy a pound of coffee," she said. "The Chinaman will gladly spare a pound."

She was, without being fair or above board, asking for money. Her pause brought a tickle to my throat. I wanted to cough. If you cough in Elaine's presence she begins to make funeral arrangements. It is one of the calamities of my mortal existence that I married a woman who is in perfect accord with my profession. "Couldn't you find a few coins in a pot or bowl?" I inquired. With your cigarettes and matches, I almost added.

A fly was buzzing around my head, setting up a terrible din. I resisted the urge to swing at it wildly. Applecart was shouting. I folded my arms and tried to sit still on the one folding chair in the establishment that had a slat missing. I should have let her answer my first question, but no, all she has to do is keep quiet and I rush in and hang myself: "Couldn't you tap your rich relatives?" I continued.

"They hate to spend money on food and coffee that could be spent on booze."

I swing; she gives my legs the traditional tug.

As I may have mentioned, Elaine is a teetotaler. Her father died an alcoholic, and this seems to have warped her judgment on certain subjects. I was brought up a teetotaler myself, with no bad consequences. My mother would touch nothing but rhubarb wine; she kept the cellar full of it. Every bottle we emptied, catsup, vinegar, syrup, coal oil, blueing, whatever; she filled it with rhubarb wine. She would put wine in anything but a wine bottle, that's where she drew the line.

"Until you win the election," she said, "how are we going to eat?"

Sometimes when in a frivolous mood I answered that recurring question by saying, "With our fingers." But just as I was about to experience another crack on the skull, another fist in the solar plexus—Applecart himself came through with an idea.

He had half that funeral parlor in tears. More than half; some of the men were crying too. God forgive me, may as many people weep at my own departure. It was enough to melt my very bowels. We were going to be saved. We had to pray a little, sing a little. And cast our votes for Applecart.

I should add that I had only recently and on very short notice been named Applecart's candidate in the Cree constituency, running in lieu of his personal choice, who passed away quite suddenly of a heart condition with his personal papers intact in the inside pocket of his new suitcoat. The unfortunate gentleman had been my most recent customer. I personally went and talked to some of Applecart's representatives, acknowledging the responsibilities and sacrifices that would be involved, and his representatives were visibly impressed. I refused to bring up the subject of money. I think I can say they were genuinely moved.

Vote for us, Applecart suggested, his voice hardly able to continue. He was the head of the party. Though it wasn't a party at all, he explained; it was an expression of the people's will, of divine sentiment. Then he continued: "This campaign is solely dependent on your support. This is your campaign. Send your contributions, my dear friends. Send your little sacrifices, your nickels, your dimes, your dollars—"

That's when I got my idea. I have quite a large head, even without a hangover. My hat size is seven and seven-eighths, and then it's usually a tight fit just before a haircut. I have one hat to my name, a black derby. I sometimes wear it professionally. Before those people could stop crying—I turned down the radio just a little. A piano and a guitar were playing a musical number, "O God, Our Help in Ages Past." Applecart sang along himself, in a voice that made you tremble with emotion. I must confess, I cannot sing a note to save my soul. Before those people could finish wiping their eyes, I, quietly, very quietly and with bare head bowed, my wife upstairs feeding her cats for it was their mealtime, passed the hat. "My dear friends," I said, in a voice they had to strain to hear, "we need your support."

You'll never believe it. Even Elaine was impressed. I took in over four dollars. We had a fine discussion of cultural heritage and the flow of credit as the bloodstream of the nation; ideas we got from Applecart's pamphlets. I passed the pamphlets around: no charge. We talked for a good three hours, a number of people becoming very excited, my headache not letting up once, my voice remaining hoarse. I said very little. But I promised that next morning I'd be back electioneering. Everyone insisted. They were so nice I was moved, I was deeply moved. They appointed local chairmen for my campaign. The filling-station man, who ordinarily would charge you for air for your tires, said to come by tomorrow and he'd fill up the tank of the old hearse. I didn't mention a new headlight. "God's light will suffice," I said. "But I appreciate this promise of generosity."

The filling-station man was not provoked to inquiry by my curious statement. "Gas," he simply said, "is easier to find than water."

 MONDAY

GOD'S LIGHT was on before I was up in the
morning; and not a cloud to mar its shining. Not a
wisp of breeze to stir the dust that powdered the
sorry remains of night. Resolutely I marched; down
to where people were to get in line for their handouts. My huge feet rang through the quiet streets;
left, right, I marched, left, right, left, right, trying to
effect a military carriage. Trying to avoid the one
thing that is guaranteed to depress me: an empty
store window.

Eyes forward, I commanded. And overhead a sign: P. HAUCK
MEATS AND POULTRY. Across the street a sign: YOUNGBERG
& SON SALT AND FEEDS. Around the corner a sign: DELMOND
LASSU DRY GOODS AND FOOTWEAR.

And under each sign: an empty window. Torn brown paper.
Mouse turds and spider webs. Dust in which some wit had printed:
ALL CHECKS CASHED.

Resolutely I marched. Apples: finnan haddie: dried cod. Not
exactly what stubble-jumpers dream of. But very good in the way of
vitamins and minerals; Murdoch was always pointing this out,

reminding us that malnutrition was rampant. I use his own unfortunate phraseology. Starvation was a word the good doctor did not know.

I was marching full tilt, and suddenly it was too late to stop. Too late to turn back. I rounded a corner past the Royal Hotel, expecting an open street and more silence. The railway depot awaited me, wooden and red. A boxcar, red and gaping, awaited me; bulging with apples and cod, with potassium and manganese and calcium and zinc.

People stood in line for a distance of two blocks.

I had propelled myself around the corner, the momentum of my initial enthusiasm carrying me into full view. I was exercising, effecting a military carriage. I was obeying the dictates of my partisan followers.

But I hadn't expected people up so early. They had all day to get their rations; why should two hundred people be up before 8 A.M.? I had expected an hour or so in which to study and meditate. But only Murdoch was missing. No gold, I suppose, in codfish.

I recognized people and people recognized me. I had hoped to accept my allotment before the rush began.

Also, I discovered that I was trying to sing. I had been trying to sing, and I simply cannot. I was booming away: our Hope for years to come, our Saviour from the stormy blast.

"What what?" somebody said. "What what?" He was startled. He thought I was speaking. A hardware merchant: what did he need with free food, a man with two jobs? That pudgy-faced atheist, hardware and undertaking. He got three times the business I got, even though he was incompetent. Afraid to charge a decent price. I ignored him.

I had things to say to those people; many things to say. But I found myself speechless.

I called to mind the occasion on which I walked out to the pitcher's mound, a rank unknown, a mere nobody, with people snickering; and I won an enduring fame by fanning twenty-seven men from one of the best teams in the constituency. A victory, I suddenly realized, which would probably cost me many votes in the forthcoming election.

"Hello," I said, to no one in particular.

No one answered.

I had a wild impulse to shake my own hand. But I resisted. I recognized a grocery store clerk, a man I went to school with. A stooped and gaunt man, well known for his large family. "The old codgers," I burst out at him, "have all gone dead. They aren't attuned to contemporary problems." My lip was still somewhat swollen. "They are fat and self-satisfied. Look at Murdoch with his pockets stuffed. Does he line up for an armload of codfish? We need new blood."

"Blood and balls and be damned," the clerk said. "We need free undertaking service. If we could afford it—most of us would be content just to die."

It was bad, I saw, to concentrate on one person. I couldn't think of that clerk's name. Quickly I turned and began to walk up and down, chatting, being neighborly, stopping to shake a hand, asking about a mutual acquaintance. But some people yelled and asked who the hell I thought I was, the prime minister? People thought I was trying to buck the line. So I tuned to those who had got their rations.

One fellow said he only took this stuff because it made good pigfeed. He was abrupt with me, failing to understand my intent. A mechanic raised his pure white hands and said he hadn't worked in a year and a half and offered to kick me in the private parts. If he'd been a foot taller I'd have knocked him flat. Charity doesn't pick up the spirits the way you'd think it might.

There I was, doing my duty, trying to talk to people reasonably, trying to strike up a conversation. Trying to explain why we needed a change of government. "Finnan haddie up the government's ass," a complete stranger suggested, not for a moment hearing what I had to say.

How could I maintain high morale in the face of such opposition? To make matters worse, I wasn't at work twenty minutes when this farmer barged up to me and boomed out so half the line could catch what he said: "Well, Shorty, how's the weather up there?"

Old Walleye again.

I have explained that it was a cloudless day. Not so much as a white streak in the heavens above. But this walleyed farmer had to loaf and kill time right there in the middle of town. It was eight-thirty or so, beginning to get too hot. I was beginning to feel sweaty; the mayor had asked us to restrict our bathing, etcetera.

What could I say?

"At least we can eat—" I said.

That's what started the booing. Apparently people were listening after all. It was quite a shocking experience. People booed me, Johnnie J. Backstrom. An undertaker gets used to being treated with deference. One is deferential and one expects to be deferred to in turn.

You're probably wondering about that J. I never discuss my middle name. Sometimes I sign a J., however, especially on checks. People think it stands for Joseph, probably. Or James. Or maybe Jacob. Or something like Japheth or Jason. But my mother, as I have commented, was a close reader of Biblical texts. She had established to her own satisfaction that Judas had by and large been misunderstood and misrepresented. She felt there was in his fate something more to be applauded than to be derided; he too had a part in the grand design. My mother was a great recognizer of grand designs. She read tea leaves in addition to the Bible, and she had great hopes for her only son. My full name is John Judas Backstrom. Sometimes I sign myself J. J. Backstrom. On hotel registration forms, where no one will ask questions. On my honeymoon, such as it was, I signed J. J. Backstrom and Wife, Notikeewin, Alberta, Undertaker. We received exceptional service.

But the people in that line were very close to being rude. I was wearing my black derby, since I had found it to be of more use than to provide shade, and my headgear became the object of unnecessary abuse. For one thing, it does look like an expensive hat. People said so, and connected me up with various other plutocrats, especially mortgage collectors. It probably was an expensive hat, I got it one night by mistake in a quality beer parlor when someone with an equally large head walked off in error with my one-fifty gray tweed cap. I was disturbed even then, not so much at losing a cap as at finding someone with the same size head. I take a good deal of pride in the size of my head.

Now I realized it was a mistake to wear that particular hat. To make matters worse, I looked fairly good bareheaded; with my head up and my deep-set blue eyes squinted just a little, under my bushy eyebrows. Quite a number of people in that line were wearing straw hats. You can get a new straw hat for a quarter, and most of those hats weren't new. Some of the older men especially were wearing felt hats that had once been quality; hats that now were so stained the sweat band showed through the outside. People like that are apt to become upset. The brims of their hats had become greasy and wilted with handling. I had never in all my life noticed people's hats.

Now I saw that while the men were in old hats, the women by and large were wearing their Sunday hats. It was Monday. Two or three of them even had veils on their hats. They wanted to appear prosperous here, as if they came for the free handouts not because it was necessary to do so but because anyone would be a fool not to pick up something that was free. I had that insight. It was quite an eye-opener. It undermined my confidence. Here I was, a candidate for public office, and I was finding it harder and harder to open my mouth.

And to make matters worse, Jonah Bledd showed up.

It wrung my heart, I mean to tell you. I began to feel terrible. Bledd came around the corner past the Royal Hotel and walked straight toward the boxcar. With his arm in a brand-new white plaster cast and supported by a sling he could make out he wasn't laid off at all, just laid up. He was doing that, I could sense it. I don't believe he saw me. Saving face was something that was always important for Jonah. Sympathy was something he found unendurable. The whole situation was beginning to wring my heart.

I could not remain silent. I resolved to speak out, though my swollen lip would make it difficult to do so for any lengthy periods of time. A politician who couldn't talk. Can you imagine a worse fate? But I resolved to do my best, I would make an all-out effort.

So once again I approached all those people standing in line; people embarrassed at being seen, embarrassed at who they saw. Now the line spilled right across the street and into one of the empty lots that the Burkhardt clan had filled with expensive implements, tractors and binders and mowers and hayrakes and bright yellow manure spreaders; machinery that people couldn't afford to buy. You could tell, the weeds grew through the spokes of the wheels. I walked back toward the end of the line. The government sponsored this handout business. It was a great feather in Murdoch's hat, though as I tried to explain to one or two people, it was done by government agencies beyond his control. Murdoch was only taking the credit, I explained; he was trying to let on that it was part of his efforts to look after his people. I tried to speak and found I couldn't finish a sentence. Everything sounded like a lie. And that damned walleyed farmer, he was walking along the line, passing out literature of his own; probably attacking me, I decided, assailing my character. We had to meet, of course; I couldn't avoid him without appearing to be a coward.

"Backstrom," he said. He wouldn't settle for Johnnie. Or for John J. He had to make sure all those strangers knew who the fool was under the expensive black derby. "Backstrom," he said, "for a man who's going to make it rain, you sure are wasting a lot of time. You ought to be setting up your fireworks and pounding your drums. You ought to be putting on your feathers. And your paint, Backstrom. Your sea shells and your porcupine quills. Hell of a medicine man you are."

Now I am no half-wit Indian who thinks you can make it rain by kicking up the dust. It's hard to explain. It was something else entirely, and this idiot stubble-jumper was completely misrepresenting me. I didn't say I'd *make* it rain. I said it *would* rain. There's all the difference in the world. But try and explain to an ignoramus.

To make matters absolutely unbearable, a swanky new Chevrolet had to pull up to the railway depot. Murdoch's new Chevrolet.

Not Murdoch himself, Murdoch's car—he was nowhere in sight. A woman got out. A simply beautiful woman. The girl I had seen on the platform at the meeting in Coulee Hill. The girl who poured water.

And now I recognized her.

She was maybe five-nine, and built. With dark eyes and dark hair. The kind of beauty that makes your toes curl. She stretched a long bare leg out the door of the Chevy and for a full twenty seconds no one was admiring the car. I curled my toes; I really did. I could feel a hole in the toe of my left sock. It's my big feet, my wife claims; I often have holes in my socks. The Burkhardt girls tend to be small, at least in terms of height.

Helen Murdoch did not even glance at me once. The doctor's only child and beautiful daughter, now full-grown and blooming like a rose, like a saskatoon bush in spring; in the pain that beauty causes I turned to contemplate the flywheel of a John Deere tractor.

Helen, quietly and efficiently, politely, smiling, began to hand out some little green pamphlets. People took them.

I tiptoed along that endless line and borrowed one from an interested reader; I found they were on the relief program and her father's great philanthropy. The reader asked for it back before I could finish reading it myself.

That astounded me. People were impressed. I tried immediately to puzzle out such a peculiar response.

For one thing, everyone was surprised and pleased that a beautiful girl like that, a girl who was supposed to be in the East attending a university, a doctor's daughter, should care about them. Who was I, after all; nobody. They said nice things to her and thanked her and one old man took off his straw hat just to receive that piece of propaganda. And for another thing, that new Chevrolet parked in the middle of the driveway, green and hardly a speck of dust on it, the chrome shining, sparkling in the sunshine; it brought a kind of hush over that crowd as if they were suddenly in a church.

I am not exaggerating; an undertaker gets into a lot of churches, though I personally could go through life without again coming into contact with that coldest and hardest of all inanimate objects, a church pew. The seats of that car were a deep blue-green. If I had driven up in a boat like that there would have been a riot; people would have branded me a criminal, a thief; parts of my anatomy would have been flung to the pack of dogs that hung around the boxcar, sniffing dried cod.

Those people should have expressed their indignation. Instead, they started speculating. One good crop, this fellow said. One decent harvest, somebody answered. Just let me land one forty-bushel crop by Jesus, somebody practically cried aloud. Pretty soon the whole place was humming. I might as well have been a stick of wood. People got out of line to finger the pieces of new machinery. Hopes rose. I believe I could have made my fortune right there, selling raincoats.

But when Helen finished passing out the pamphlets, instead of climbing into the flashy green jalopy, one pretty leg disappearing last before the motor purred—instead of that, she turned from the end of the line and came right at me. At me. Toward me.

I was standing stock-still, stricken dumb, sucking my swollen lip trying to make it look smaller; I was standing speechless beside a team of horses hooked to a car that had been turned into a trailer. A lot of people did that when they couldn't afford gas or license plates. I prayed the horses wouldn't choose that moment to respond to nature.

Even the walleyed farmer was dumbfounded; he walked into the wheel of a manure spreader and nearly broke both legs.

"I'd like to talk to you," Helen said.

She meant me.

Fortunately, she had caught me before I'd picked up my rations. I hate queues. I've got too much spirit. And obviously my hat caught her eye, so I felt better about wearing it. As I say, I am nearly six-four in my stocking feet, and I wore this fairly stylish hat rather well. I have a strong profile, craggy; which is to say, too much nose, too much chin, too much forehead. My wife once said that my own will be my finest funeral, which coming from her is some sort of compliment I take it.

"The pleasure would be mine," I said.

"About Saturday night," she said.

My heart stuttered; it gave a long pause and then a thud that frightened me. My mother died of heart trouble; also the gentleman who preceded me in candidacy for the public office I was so foolishly seeking. I looked around. Jonah had climbed up into the boxcar. He was helping the two men in charge of operations. Or at least he was getting in their way, pretending he was helping. As I say, railroaders are a special breed; they're very close. The two men were letting Jonah help out, with his good arm. They were letting him pretend to help out. As if he wasn't laid off.

"I was supposed to have coffee with Jonah Bledd," I said. That was a barefaced lie. I am not by nature a liar, but the mention of Saturday night and that woman's beautiful mouth were turning my muscles to warm putty.

"Good," She said. "Maybe the three of us can go for coffee."

I was speechless. For one thing, Jonah was avoiding me, I sensed that; I didn't exactly want to face him. But she didn't wait for an answer. She turned toward the boxcar and somehow I found myself following. I followed after, silent and mute.

Standing outside on the cinders by the track, Helen and I couldn't see Jonah, but we could hear the three men. We smelled the fish and apples; I like the smell of apples. And I cannot abide the stink of fish. The heat was a terror. My nostrils quivered in their confusion. I listened: the three voices and the clatter of crates and boxes and the knock of a hammer and the voices again. The rhythm of work, you might say. The other two men were telling Jonah how to make money.

"The price of land is at rock bottom," a voice said. "You could make a good living *without* working. You could buy the whole damned country for a song." And then the same voice to a face in the boxcar door: "How many children?"

"If you could afford the back taxes," Jonah said.

We could see the faces as they approached the boxcar. A woman unfolded a brown paper bag at the open door and again the voice: "How many children, please?"

And then the third voice, inside the boxcar, "I'd like to get me a little grocery store. People have to eat, no matter what."

It's silly to repeat it, they went on like that; they went through carpentering and cement work and house painting.

"Who's going to build a house?" Jonah said. "Four empty houses in my block. Who can afford to paint a house?"

And then: "How many children, please?"

They went through the business of trying to get a truck on credit and setting up as a trucker. Get into business for yourself, they suggested.

"Where would you get the wheat to haul?" Jonah said.

And then again: "How many children?" To a man who didn't look up but raised four fingers. That damned pudgy hardware dealer.

The other voice suddenly thought it was being brilliant: "I know a Rawleigh man makes a few dollars. Selling door to door to women. The markup on spices and ointment, he says, if you can collect—"

I was embarrassed. Eavesdropping is not my way at all. I shuffled my huge feet on the cinders, I cleared my throat. Helen stood on her tiptoes at the door of the boxcar, the skin of her calves looking cool and smooth where the fringe of a petticoat showed. A pile of codfish came out the door, like an armful of firewood, and a big strapping farmer who must have had ten kids let go of his nose and took hold and said thank you.

"Taste as bad as they smell," a man said behind him.

"So do pickled gophers," the farmer said.

"Johnnie and I are ready for that coffee," Helen called.

"Coffee?" Jonah said.

"That coffee, Jonah," I mumbled. I tried to make a face over Helen's shoulder, but found my features completely paralyzed.

Jonah was studying both of us with a look which hinted he had a nail in each shoe and thus could not escape more than half the pain. His tight scalp made it hard for him to look down. He leaned from the door of the boxcar, his cast swinging forward as he bent.

"Going to Wong's," I said. "To Wong's."

We were holding up the queue. Or Jonah, standing in the doorway, was holding it up.

"What's the holdup?" somebody called from behind us. "If you're waiting for the apples to grow, I can tell you we've been here since six this morning, and they ain't getting any bigger."

"Get your nose out of that doorway," somebody called, "or I'll get it out for you. What right have you got in there to begin with?"

People shouldn't have talked to Jonah that way.

"Next thing you'll have your arse in a sling," somebody called.

That brought a round of laughter.

"Coffee," I said to Jonah. "We've got to go."

"I've got to work," Jonah said.

It's funny, but that remark right then made me mad. I can't quite recall why it did. Maybe it was just the heat. Or Jonah's kidding himself that way. I wanted to say, you got your walking papers, Jonah. You got the gate. That terrible impulse to kick a man when he's down. But I didn't. I was partly silenced by the way he looked at Helen and then at me. A walking conundrum of a look.

Jonah was a great family man. He believed in paying his bills and educating his kids. But underneath it all was a streak of the dreamer. That's what made me mad too. We grew up together, Jonah and I; at least, after I moved into town we did. He always figured that one day he'd strike it lucky and things would change. I used to tease him about that. His reckless optimism. For instance, he got that job with the railway over me, hoping to travel. So all he ever did was ride out to the end of the line and the roundhouse in Coulee Hill and back into Notikeewin again. One way: seventy-two miles. Round trip, please. West to east and back again. That's what I used to tell him; I teased him often, and he took it—and when I got finished he'd say, just you wait and see what luck really is.

But right at that moment I was mad. "Okay," I said to Helen. I brought myself to speak. "This heat is too much for me. I'll treat you to a cup of coffee."

I had given my wife the four dollars even, after the collection the day before. I'd kept the change.

Don't get me wrong, I'm a dreamer myself. And a pretty girl was just part of the prospectus. I was dreaming by the time I was big enough to know things aren't what they might be, which out here means before your pockets are very high off the ground. Christ, you have to dream out here. You've got to be half goofy—just to stay sane.

I'm a great one for paradox. My reading of the Bible, I suppose; dying to be born and all that. But really, it isn't an easy place to live. Like when the wind blows black, when it's dry, you drive all day with your lights on. Great electioneering weather. The fish lose their gills in this country. The gophers come up for a bite to eat, and they crawl right into the air.

I won't swear to that—but it's a God's truth, you have to dream.

I was born out here in a farmhouse, remember. The first thing you hear is the wind. And going upstairs, at the turn of the stairs in that first house; a window looked west; and westward in the summer you could see the green of a windbreak, elm and maple and Russian poplar and caragana. Things that don't grow here by nature but have to be planted and tended. And then in the fall you could see through the bare branches out across a mile of wheat stubble; a gradual rise to the horizon, a clump of poplars, a line of telephone poles along a road a mile away, and another farm finally, the closest neighbor. An old man whose wife went out of her mind and had to be put away.

I'll tell you something. When I was really a kid, I wanted to grow up and be a doctor. Like old Doc Murdoch. I wasn't an undertaker by nature, I can tell you. That's a frightening word if you think about it. One who takes under. Creepy. I wanted to heal people, save them, make them whole again. But money was scarce in my family. And maybe brains were too.

But nevertheless, that day I didn't get on with the railway; the Doc called me in that day—into his office. I was all excited. And then he told me the country needs a good undertaker. That hurt me.

I had great admiration for the Doc. I held him in esteem.

But as I may have said, there wasn't a windbreak ever planted that could really stop the wind. It got to the house. I always felt it was trying to say something, and I wasn't understanding. Something very sad. Then it got impatient and banged some rain on the window-panes, just enough to make you feel cozy, and two days later it was sifting the dust past the closed windows onto the sills, making the curtains gray, covering the dining room table so you could write your name on it; John J. Backstrom, M.D., I used to print, with the first finger of my left hand. I guess I know how to dream.

And I've had misery, I can tell you. Watching that damned sky. One day I made a fool remark about rain, and the next day I was getting a crick in my neck. Every time a puff of cloud blew up I fell down laughing and giggling and rolled around till I started to choke in the dust. Then I got up again.

Well, I exaggerate. But I did have misery.

And it got worse that Monday morning when I went for coffee with Helen Murdoch, which performance was, politically speaking, about as reckless a thing as I could do. But I was vaguely mad at Jonah. And partly I was dreaming how things might have been. So we went to the Chinaman's on Main Street by the newspaper office; by that rag of a paper that was backing Murdoch all the way, one hundred per cent. The one that would have made front page news out of my recent mishap: BACKSTROM AND HEARSE HIT POLE. BACKSTROM DRUNK: NO LAWYER WILL DEFEND.

And maybe Helen was writing the story so they could release it. Maybe she wanted to interview me.

We parked her swanky new four-door Chevrolet right smack in front of that run-down tin-covered newspaper office. Helen was a good driver; I wanted her to wheel out onto the highway and just keep going until the gas gauge read zero.

In Notikeewin people often post signs in restaurant windows. Pasted alongside Wong's front door was a yellow poster, the print blotched and black, the paper cheap. It was something about a sale to be held on a farm outside Burkhardt. *Commencing at 11 A.M. Sharp. Tuesday. Free Lunch at Noon Terms Cash one four-bottom plow one five-section harrows one potato digger 2 hay racks 2 bob sleighs.* It went on like that. On and on. Why I stopped to read it with a girl like Helen standing behind me, I don't know. I saw there'd be quite a crowd. *One new Swede saw one wagon and grain tank one 50-ft endless belt miscellaneous assortment of tools too numerous to mention misc harness collars halters 3 complete beds sausage grinder and maker one bath tub...* On and on. One lifetime. There it was. EVERYTHING MUST BE SOLD.

Just as simple as that. One lifetime. That's what terrifies me some-times when I stop to think. It makes me reckless and devil-may-care.

Maybe I just read the poster to kill time while I looked for my tongue. Speechless we come into this world; speechless we go out. What a hell of a state, to be speechless in between.

Wong doesn't get the high-class clientele; the bank managers and preachers and businessmen out conspiring and waiting for the heat to pass so they can crack ice and mix some cocktails—they go to the Queen's Café. It was as if we both admitted without saying anything that we had to keep this on the QT. A little thing like having a cup of coffee. Helen seemed to read my mind. We were sitting there in the second booth from the door, beyond the rubber plant, and instead of starting in about Saturday night she mentioned Ontario.

I was thinking about it myself when she spoke.

"Your wife," Helen said, "she reminded me. You went East on a harvest excursion."

That took me by surprise. When had they met? Then in a flash I guessed it; my wife only went out of the house to go shopping or to go to church. And she hadn't been shopping. So last night at church—I had to smile a little. "You went to church last night."

Helen smiled right back at me, not the least intimidated.

"Just to deliver some flowers from Dad's garden. I didn't stay except to talk to Mrs. Backstrom for a few minutes."

I took a sip of my cooling coffee. A ten-cent beer would have been more than welcome right then, even if I had recently been tempted to swear off completely for life. By God, I will never understand women. Never. Helen Murdoch had absolutely no interest in the United Church whatsoever; both her parents were Presbyterian. So she goes sailing in to see the one person I'd most like to have her avoid. Helen Murdoch's interest in delivering her father's precious flowers was by no means—gratuitous.

No, Helen Murdoch was just plain curious and wanted to have a look. Gall is the best name for it. So she delivered an armful of roses or marigolds or some such thing to the United Church. And what did she decide?

"Yes," I said. "I remember that trip East. I didn't know the world could be so green. I hadn't begun to guess it."

"My father's from Ontario," Helen said. "When I first went to where he was born I couldn't imagine why he left."

"I'm glad he did," I said. And I let loose with one of my big smiles. I have this amazing set of teeth. The job is to keep out a kind of lecherous inclination that creeps into most of my smiles. And then I said, "And why did he?"

"It was so beautiful," she said.

"That's probably why," I said.

"No," she said. "I mean—those huge trees. Instead of little poplars and willows and balm of Gilead. Those rivers and streams all over the place, and grass up to the cows' bellies. Corn that was taller than I was. And fruit on trees instead of in boxes. And the big lakes. I couldn't understand."

She had all this dark hair, and when her big dark eyes lit up I wanted to find her an orchard, so I might guess the original look of surprise.

"You're out of school for the summer," I said.

"I graduated, finally."

"Time flies," I said. And then I had to go on. "What're you doing here? Why haven't you got a fancy big job in the East?"

That was a mean thing to say. I was being nasty, in my own quiet way. All of a sudden I had to be nasty; but silly as this may sound, I was having an actual moment of fear. "Something soft and cushy," I said. Sometimes you speak a sentence and somehow it just leads on to the next one, which is even more incriminating.

But Helen didn't let on. "I got a phone call," she said.

"I was pretty well lit when I phoned you," I explained.

Little Helen Murdoch smiled; a gentle, amused smile that should have made me wary. Little Helen now standing five-nine, and fully developed. H.P. we used to call her. Because her name was Helen Persephone. What a hell of a name to stick on a beautiful woman.

She smiled and I couldn't keep my mouth shut. I had to talk. Sore lip and all, I was feeling much better, I had to sound off. I had to tell her about my trip to the East to work in the harvest fields. The smell of clover rich and sweet, scenting the whole air. The grass falling heavy and green when the sickle hit it. Water—so much water in the air and grass and ponds and brooks, it blurred the whole world a blue-green; and the old snake fences that spoke of tremendous forests; and sausage makers and cheese makers and creameries in all the dozens of little towns, turning out good food, absolutely delicious food. I remembered—she mentioned trees—I remembered a tree so big, one day I counted fifteen cows sleeping in its shade. Holsteins, not Jerseys.

"Eden," I said. By God, I just burst out. " The green lush old Eden." For a minute there I felt really good. I forgot the blinding sun outside, out there past that rubber plant and the Venetian blinds; I forgot that vast empty glare of sky that was waiting to humiliate me once more. Just for a minute I felt really on top of the world. " That was A-1," I said. "Once I got a whiff of that country, I had some idea of what heaven must be like."

"But Dad left," Helen said. "And another thing—you went there, but you came back."

That brought me up short. People always do that to me, right when I'm enjoying myself. I had to think for a minute or two. I was in the East for twelve years all told. That's a fact. Why deny it? And during all that time I don't think I gave two thoughts to all those damned dirt roads running nowhere in straight lines. To all those telephone poles with their burden of wire, trying to hold the horizons together.

Or the sky. That was one thing I managed to shut out of my head. Nature can be so damned unnatural. That red Who-er of a sky trying to suck you up into its own cursed hollowness. I could give you a whole damned sermon on that sky. And every day and always the sun, it comes bulging out of the dawn, stunning those few little plants that have somehow overnight peckered up their leaves, their petals, their stems. What a blue-eyed bitch of a country this is.

And then it came to me. Sure I went East. And the big thing I learned back there was undertaking. I stood out in my class when it came to restoration work. I was a whiz at that. At practical embalming itself, I was less than perfect. I was no great shakes. I was wound up all over again; I saw the way clear to defend myself. "Hell yes," I said. "H.P., sure I came back. If you're in the undertaking line and there's a place that needs a good undertaker, what do you do?"

She laughed that special laugh of hers again. "Business is brisk," she said.

"Business," I said. I waved both hands. I might have been a millionaire, dismissing her trivial worries.

Helen had a fine sense of humor, I could see that. Sometimes she made me laugh. But my misery, to tell you the truth, was getting worse the more she laughed. With that beautiful mouth of hers, as I mentioned.

I am no stranger to dreaming.

She was so damned beautiful that first my stomach began to feel upset. It had nothing to do with Wong's coffee; Wong makes pretty good coffee for a Chinaman. Then the muscles of my legs began to feel the way they do when you walk out to pitch the last inning of a no-hitter. Then I had that urge just to snap my jaws open and shut a few times.

"Business is so brisk," she said, "that you try to create more by smashing a hearse into a telephone pole."

That was anything but true. That was an insult to my personal integrity. "You are entirely mistaken," I said, serious now. "Who would get killed first in any accident? Johnnie J., that's who."

"No, Johnnie," she said. "You don't quite believe in your own destructibility." She fiddled with the brim of my hat, which I had balanced on the catsup bottle. "You don't believe in it, but just to make sure you have to keep meeting death."

I have always been a sucker for women who see through me, I really have. They intrigue me. I can listen to such women for hours. I'm fascinated to find out what they learn, what they recognize. With such women I am like the proverbial moth; I am worse, for I know what the flame will do, yet I fly straight into its charming light. My own wife has had a number of insights, though she is less than a flaming brand.

Helen went on: "Jonah met it just once and he is terrified."

"You misunderstand Jonah," I said.

"You probably weren't watching the road. He was, I'll bet."

"It was an accident," I said. "I'm a pretty careful driver. I've driven thousands of miles."

"Careful," she said. "So you went straight to Dad."

I nodded my head. "Sure. You see right through me. I wanted to confess. Is that what I'm supposed to say? I had to run to his office. I wanted him to call a cop. Or better still—just a newspaper reporter."

"You left one thing out."

"Is that so?" I said. I was studying her beautiful eyebrows.

"You knew he wouldn't do it," she said.

I was about to make a stout denial, but she went right on: "You had to hang around making a drunk fool of yourself. You knew he could put you out of the race. And then you had to rub his nose in the fact that he wouldn't do it." She stirred her coffee for the second time. "That's why I came home."

"The Doc," I said, "could and would pronounce me dead without interrupting his golden smile."

"You knew he'd pat your head again. Johnnie, you knew he'd forgive."

I had to clamp my mouth shut; for I almost asked, did he forgive? I cannot stand forgiveness. That is one concept I find intolerable. I'd sooner she had punched me in the teeth. I'm a man who hates his enemies. "You knew you could have it both ways," she said. "It doesn't matter to you that he has to go to bed at night and lie awake. He can't sleep at night—people starving, people without jobs. People sick who won't come in because they can't pay. People ashamed to ask for charity. It doesn't matter to you that he might just *love* you a little bit, Johnnie."

She was upsetting me. Do I sleep at night? When my wife isn't reading the Bible she's snoring. "The Doc doesn't miss any sleep over me."

"He phoned me," she said. "He phoned in the middle of the night. 'I've got a new political opponent. Remember Johnnie?' he said."

"You must have had a good laugh," I said.

It's crazy, but I felt a pang of jealousy. I had misunderstood about the telephone call and finding out we have misunderstood always makes us embarrassed and mad. Ordinarily I try not to feel involved. But there for a split second I envied the old Doc; no woman like that ever crossed a continent for me, though I might say a number of them have been obliging in other ways.

"He just said you are his opponent," she said.

"You came home to witness the slaughter," I said.

She stopped fiddling with her spoon. Her long fingers became inactive and I wanted them to discover me, to slide on past the coffee cups, to come alive again to my own crumpled fists.

To my own brute appetites and hunger. Imagination is a terrifying thing. That woman in her silence could not begin to read my mind.

"Johnnie," she said. She didn't meet my steady gaze. "He's getting old—from plain hard work he's getting old. Couldn't he just win one more election?"

"It's killing him, the work," I said.

"It's what's keeping him alive," she said.

I was having trouble with my upper lip. "I haven't got a chance."

"I saw you in Coulee Hill," she said. "You were—" She hesitated. "You were exciting."

I tried to come up with a little scoff. But now my stomach was churning and seething. I dreaded one of those really thunderous growls; I have this capacious stomach, flat-bellied though I may be. I wanted that woman to think highly of me; and yet I had to hurt her. I didn't dare pick up my thick cup; I knew I'd begin to tremble, my giant hands flinging the cup like a shuttle.

"H.P.," I said. "Your old man needs you. You're damn right he needs you. Because I'm going to give him a run for his money."

I was trying to protect her. I really was.

"Johnnie," she said. "When he said it was you—I knew he was in trouble. He was sort of laughing and sort of hurt—but even while he spoke I remembered that other man who phoned me. I told that man it was hopeless to come back West—so he caught the next train."

"I was on a three-day toot," I said. "I was pretty well loaded."

"And the first thing you did," she said, "was ask about him." She waited. "How can you do it, Johnnie?"

She looked at me, and those big dark eyes of hers—instead of being angry, they trusted me. So help me God. They said, Johnnie, you were drunk when you phoned, but I believed you then. In wine is truth. *In vino* something. I can believe you now, if you'll just speak honestly. You came back, Johnnie. And I came back. People are suffering, and we came back. They said all that, those eyes. And then they added—we both love him, Johnnie. We both love that old man.

"He almost sees you as a son," she said.

I hated her innocence.

I hated her goddamned innocence. She had no idea what a brute animal man can be.

My misery was complete. I am absolutely fascinated by innocence. I felt I should make a clean breast of it, just spread out my giant hands and say, look, don't trust me like that. Men quarrel. And I am a ravening lusting beast. I cannot resist beauty and innocence. I cannot contain the hungering of my own flesh. I must foul and stain beauty wherever I find it. I must corrupt and destroy.

I should have made a speech right there. I could feel the vein on the left side of my head, the left temple, beginning to throb and hammer. I should have cried out: do not, dare not. That woman, pleading, was all loveliness and passion. Speechless, I should have posted a sign: trust not, believe not, hope not, love not.

I dove my hands into my pockets. "Let me get this," I said.

But she had already brought a coin out of her purse and was preparing to pay. I picked up my hat, the hat her hands had touched. She was leaving, and I was shaking so badly, I was unable to find a penny of my change.

I guess it was six hours later that word came about Jonah Bledd; I was in the pool hall. I had been there for hours, despite my promise to get busy campaigning. I really wanted to leave, but people thought I was winning, so how could I gracefully depart? I am usually unbeatable at snooker. Only Jonah could beat me; in fact I wondered at one point if he might not pick up a little money as a pool shark, the minute his arm got better. For a while I was actually three dollars ahead; but when the phone call came I was losing and my last dime was on the edge of the big green table.

I had been wrestling with my oversized conscience; it was spoiling my shot, especially my bank shot—I was getting the angles wrong. I had thought of about one million excuses to go drop in on Helen Murdoch at her father's home; and every excuse, I recognized, was motivated by my unprincipled lust.

Old Doc and I were sent for together. I rushed out of that pool hall as fast as my legs would carry me. Somebody found Jonah's boat near the lower end of Wildfire Lake. The little skiff was drifting and empty. But somebody else near the upper end had seen Jonah set out to do some fishing. The river that runs through Notikeewin, the Cree River—it takes a long swing south and then up, making a kettle of the constituency, and down at the southern extreme of that long curve the river gets wide enough for a stretch of a few miles to be mistaken for a lake.

People go to Wildfire Lake to swim and fish. But it's dangerous. There's a current, for one thing, even though you wouldn't guess it, looking at the surface. And the bottom is mostly mud and weeds, except that in one place it's what we call bottomless.

Bledd loved fishing. With that arm of his in a cast, and no job, he had not a thing to do on a Monday afternoon. He bummed a ride down to the lake. It appeared that the anchor rope gave way; people figured he must have lost his balance.

As I say, old Doc and I were sent for at the same time. People do that around here sometimes; they send for a doctor and also an undertaker. It's a strange custom. We arrived at the little dock almost simultaneously, though I had left town before he did; me in the old hearse, the Doc in his spanking new Chevrolet. The Doc had a great reputation for being a wicked driver.

By the time we got there the police were at work with their dragging equipment and some other men were helping and quite a few people were present to watch. Quite a few people didn't have jobs or anything, and this was something to do, a way to kill time; a lot of them rode down to the lake in the backs of two or three trucks. But this was no outing. You could tell by the way they stood in little groups, just stood. They were looking.

The Doc drove up before I had time to get out of my hearse; he parked on my right. He was there before he recognized me, I suspect; or maybe not, I don't know. I respected the old Doc. I wanted to show him I bore no ill will. Before he had a chance to move out of his car I jumped out of mine and walked around to the right door of the Chevy.

The door was open by the time I got there. Somebody came up to the Doc's window to report there was no luck yet. "No luck yet," this guy said, that was all, and touched his straw hat and turned and went back down to the beach.

The Doc turned to me. "No luck yet," he said.

The Doc and I, we understood each other. There was a lot of emotion in that little speech. I didn't know where to begin. On that long drive out there, I'd had too much time to think. I was trying to keep my own emotions bottled up: I cry very easily.

"She's a bitch of a world," I said.

The Doc was striking a match. I gave the car door a slam. "Doc," I repeated, turning down the window, "she's a dirty bitch of a rotten world, you mark my words."

The Doc was lighting a cigarette. "Jonah was four days younger than you. I brought him into this world."

My bitterness welled up inside me. I had held it in check as long as I could, driving alone on the way out from town. "You spank them," I said. "I plug them, Doc. Between us we cover the field."

"Take it easy, Johnnie," the Doc said. He patted my shoulder. It was getting pretty warm in the car, even with the windows open. You couldn't touch metal without getting a burn.

"I'm taking it hard," I said. "I keep thinking."

The Doc brushed the white hair out of his eyes. In a whole lifetime he hadn't quite solved that problem. Sometimes he brushed at it even when it wasn't in his eyes. "Watching you and Jonah," he said. "With all your high spirits. You don't know how good it was for me." He brushed at his hair again. "Every time the phone rings and I hear the word accident or injured or killed—after a while you start getting a little catch in your breath, waiting for the name."

Old Doc was a pretty decent guy. He liked me. People are taken by me, sometimes; especially women. But I was upset that day. "I'll never do anything again as long as I live, foolish or wise," I said. "What the hell's the use of making an effort? Why try? Why struggle when the odds are ninety-nine to zero?"

"You've got to buck up," the Doc said.

"Buck up all right," I said. "You bend over, the hobnails get you in the arse. You straighten up, they get you in the balls. It's a fifty-fifty proposition."

"Now wait," the Doc said. "Jonah—You should consider—"

"Consider indeed," I said. "I considered, and I'm done and finished with considering. With feeling. With worrying. With trying to solve the problems of the damned world. With trying to make ends meet. With women. With politics—"

The Doc stubbed out his cigarette, only one-quarter of it smoked. I could never do that; if I started smoking I'd have to smoke the butt on a toothpick or just simply learn to burn my fingers. As generous as I am, certain kinds of economy obsess me. Someday I'm going to murder my wife for the way she peels potatoes; she throws away more than she uses, by God, time after time. A man should keep hogs.

"I was pretty hard on you," the Doc said, "out there in Coulee Hill that night. You took me by surprise; and I'm ashamed to say it, I wasn't just politicking—I was punishing."

"Doc," I said, "if I had drowned instead of Jonah it would have been no loss. It would have been a blessing. A great benefit to all concerned; especially to you. I am ready and begging to cash my chips."

The Doc touched my hand for a moment; he touched my fist, I had clenched my fists. "Johnnie, lad," he said, "you're going to stay in the fight. I hope you'll never be a quitter. Fight to the bitter end. Nothing is easy, Johnnie. I want you to stay in this damn battle, it'll be an education for you. You've been a little rash. But in some fool way I'm proud of you. Even if you don't land a single vote, never let it be said—Johnnie Backstrom quit."

"Doc," I said. "I'm beat and I'm down."

"The hell you are," the Doc said. "I brought you up better than that."

"I am whipped and broken," I said. "The count is ten and I haven't stirred."

"The count is ten on Jonah," the Doc said. "He was afraid to get whipped."

If anyone else had said that, I'd have been under obligation to bust his jaw. That was an odd remark, coming from Murdoch. I always thought he was a kind of levelheaded guy who knew when to keep his hands in his pockets. "I don't get you," I said.

"He was afraid to be a fool. So he was a coward instead."

The Doc was being a harsh judge. He was condemning a friend of mine, and I couldn't make the usual defense. My back was to the wall. So I had to speak out. "With two good arms he might have survived," I said. "And he didn't break his own arm. Maybe nobody told you, Doc, but I was driving that night."

That accident of mine was another thing on my conscience. In a way it seemed to me that I had killed Jonah. I glanced away from the Doc, out the window on his side, and there was my hearse, smashed fender and all. There it was, waiting for a customer. My best friend. The only basically good human being I'd ever met; he was good right to the core. I'd joked about needing a funeral and he hadn't laughed.

I was sorry now I'd made the joke—in some beer parlor or other, getting polluted and being irresponsible.

"Jonah said he was driving," the Doc said.

"I was at the wheel," I said. "I had a pretty good jag on. I was drunker than a skunk. I was three sheets to the wind. What a bagful. Right to the gills."

"Jonah said he was driving," the Doc repeated.

"He was a liar as well as a coward," I said, letting my voice be a little sarcastic.

"He reeked like a brewery," the Doc said.

The Doc was not himself a heavy drinker.

"Jonah was sober as a judge," I said.

And that was hardly untrue. Jonah and I drank together from the time we sneaked into a beer parlor at the age of sixteen, both of us passing for twenty-one, and I don't believe he ever quite got loaded, and I don't believe I ever quite failed. That Bible training took a firm hold on him. Sometimes I think I wasn't as far gone as I thought I was. I was a little bullheaded; if a big ox like me couldn't be as sober as Jonah, at least I could be four times as drunk.

But it was more than that. When you guzzle the way I sometimes do, and chase around after women, you start hearing a voice. Not the DT's. I mean, there's a voice criticizing every damned thing, saying why don't you make something of yourself, why don't you straighten up? Jonah was busy holding down a job, and then he got married, and then he had children one after the other. And he started paying for a house. Sometimes when things weren't too smooth in the Burkhardt domain I'd slip over to his place. I could hardly believe my eyes. There he'd be with his huge noisy family, and he'd make me feel relaxed, contented. He was so relaxed and contented himself, sipping away at a beer in his wife's presence, a brood of kids climbing all over him while he pretended to read that rag of a local paper. I don't often feel relaxed; I'm high-strung.

"Jonah Bledd was the soberest man I ever knew," I said.

"Let's get some air," the Doc said.

It really was too hot in the car, hot and sticky; he was right. We got out to stretch our legs.

We walked along the shore of the lake, on the narrow strip of beach where people go swimming. Wildfire Lake got its name when some homesteaders had to plunge into the water to escape a prairie fire; the lake saved them. We walked beyond the sandy beach; the snipes and killdeer saw us coming and flew and walked again in the mud, making neat funny patterns with their toes. No one went into the water, though the day turned out to be another scorcher. Little kids, the few who showed up, seemed afraid of the water as soon as they heard the news, and the grown-ups were either helping with the dragging operations or watching. You could see; they were sweating, they were pouring sweat, but they thought it would be wrong to go in.

Once I said to the doctor, "Why don't you run on back to town, Doc? Get out of this heat. It won't take an M.D. to pronounce Jonah dead."

He shook his head; and that sort of pleased me. I was afraid I had been rude. We were standing on shore, where the mud was caked hard enough to hold us; we watched the flash of oars. I hate to admit it, but I would have felt alone out there without him. The Doc was always good company, you could count on that.

People were deferential to me and Doc, so we were left to ourselves. We sat in his car again, and we talked, the way men do sitting in a car that isn't going anywhere—that kind of easy, personal talk. About marriage, how it isn't what it's cracked up to be but being single is worse. About his garden. My mother's funeral, which he still remembered. Baseball teams, and how they aren't as good as they used to be, especially the pitchers, they can't throw a fastball. The prospects for a good hockey team. Everything but the weather.

And you know something, it's a funny thing; I was sitting there talking, and all the time I was feeling as if *I* had drowned. That's a God's fact. I was so certain I had drowned that a lot of things that once bothered me didn't seem to matter. I felt cleansed; I wanted to clear up the record. "Doc," I said, "that daughter of yours grew up to be an attractive girl. A real prize."

"It's great to have her back," the Doc said.

"You've got a fine daughter there. You're a lucky man."

"I have reason to be proud," the Doc said.

I tried to give a chuckle. "And reason to lock the doors at night," I said.

"She's a good girl," the Doc said. "She brings life back into the old house. It reminds me—" He looked out at the lake; the sun was low enough so the glare didn't hurt our eyes. "It brings to mind the way it used to be when your mother was alive. She'd drop by, laughing and talking, and that whole house would be alive. She loved flowers."

I wanted to talk about Helen. I really wanted to explain to him how a man can have a sudden wave of desire that makes him irresponsible. But the Doc couldn't say enough about my mother, I didn't get to open my mouth. I was left with nothing to do but stare at the boats, at the men rowing back and forth, back and forth. There really wasn't much to look at.

People brought us something to eat; nothing elaborate, the coffee was cold, but it served to wash down the jam and peanut-butter sandwiches. The Doc got out of the car and talked to everyone; I just sat in silence. I should never brood, but I did.

After a while you could touch the body of the car. Sundown came, and they still hadn't located the corpse. The men who were rowing the boats looked shrunken and dark on the water. The people on shore leaned on each other. Darkness came, and the police said they'd have to quit for the night rather than risk another accident. They said for all of us to go home.

Those people who had stood motionless for hours were suddenly in such a hurry they were a threat to each other's lives. The doctor walked me to the hearse, as if the hearse was a mile away instead of right next to his Chevy. I climbed in behind the wheel and still the Doc didn't go away, so I didn't start the motor. He was leaning in the window of the door where Jonah flew out.

"Drive carefully," he said.

I didn't quite know how to reply. For one thing, I can't accept advice graciously; no matter how I try, a peculiar note creeps into my voice.

"And look," he added. He brushed the white hair off his forehead, bumping his head on the window frame in the process. He was beginning to sound exhausted. "Let's keep it a secret, just between you and me."

I didn't quite know what he was talking about. Or to put it another way, I wondered if he knew what he was talking about. But my heart started to pound. "Yes," I said. I should have said what, but I said, "Yes."

"I still think it was cowardly," the Doc said.

"He couldn't swim a stroke," I said. "Maybe he actually—"

"And he was more at home in a boat," Doc said, "than he was on dry land."

"I guess that's true," I said. Jonah used to tease about my working on boats. I was always scared to death of boats.

"We wouldn't want to embarrass his family," Doc said. "So let people blame it on his arm."

That put me in a very bad light.

"Yes," I said again.

The old Doc was gone into the darkness. I heard the engine start in the Chevrolet. Then the lights came on, shining out over the lake for a moment, making the dark water even darker instead of light. The lights swung in an arc as the car backed up, for a moment blinding me where I sat, making me look away.

I reached to turn the key in the ignition—and again I couldn't do it. I sat there by the lake in that hearse until I was the only person left on the beach. It got to be sort of spooky, I don't mind confessing.

At first I heard only the slap of waves, sleepy and unconcerned, against the muddy shore. I heard the breath of wind rustling the poplar leaves. Poplar leaves have their special way of moving; that's why the tree is sometimes called the trembling aspen. Or is it quaking aspen? And listening to all those sounds, the waves, the wind, somehow all of a sudden I knew that for a long time I had been thinking about Jonah; he had come out of the water and was rapping on the rear window. At the back of the hearse. I who am seldom speechless, I sat asking myself, what are you going to say to him, Johnnie Backstrom? If you let on that you are aware, what are you going to say? I sat motionless, not even glancing aside, my eyes looking and not looking, my ears hearing what I was trying not to see, hearing the obvious question: How did you do it, Johnnie B? How did you grow up to be such a useless son of a bitch? Such a no-good useless loudmouthed blowhard son of a scarlet bitch? How did you single out the two people who mean most to you in this wide world, how did you single them out to hurt and injure and destroy?

I had to answer. I had to. I turned up all the windows and still I could do nothing but hear. The waves. The wind on the leaves. The tapping, tapping. An apology would not be enough. No easy apologies. I'm sorry would not do the trick this time. A reformation was in order, a genuine attempt at a new beginning. I positively had to answer.

I'll tell you the God's own truth—I sat there and I cried. Hot tears scalded my cheeks. Because, and this is the reason, I knew where Jonah was. I had known all afternoon, in a sort of unacknowledged way I had known, and I hadn't been able to say; I just simply could not bring myself to tell those coppers, drag out there where the lake has no bottom. Where she is bottomless. They searched where the fishing is good, where a man could get tangled in the weeds; cops are apt to think that way. And all afternoon I had known where Jonah was, out far, far out, with the anchor rope around his middle, in the one place he was sure to choose.

He wasn't rapping at my window. I knew that too. And I knew it wouldn't matter a good goddamn if I answered questions all night. I knew all that, as I say; I was perfectly aware. But I sat for a solid hour, I had to, listening, thinking, terrified of little sounds, me, a huge man, nearly six-four in my stocking feet. I sat and the tears rolled down my cheeks.

TUESDAY

THEY DIDN'T FIND JONAH next morning
either. I was on the dock ten minutes before the
police arrived, the sun already pushing itself free of
the horizon. I sat in the bow of Jonah's skiff,
watching the water, wanting to tell the police
where to look; but I couldn't bring myself to speak.
They'd not only find Jonah, I knew; they'd find that
rope around his middle. A compulsion to talk was
storming inside me. It wasn't the fact that the
family couldn't pay that bothered me; not that at
all. It was lots of things. I'd been awake half the
night. Then, at ten-thirty, I remembered the
auction sale to be held on a farm outside the town
of Burkhardt, and like a drowning man clutching at
a straw, away I went, driving so hard a cloud of dust
a mile long hung out behind me like a tail. I had

promised myself a reformation; actions, I had told
myself in the middle of the night, actions not
words answer the hard questions. Dust be damned,
the need to do good was rife within me.

Partly I went to the auction sale because I knew there'd be a big crowd. I like crowds; but further, virtue like salt serves best as a seasoning. People enjoy auctions, even if they can't afford to buy a single thing. There's always the chance of a real bargain. I suppose every man there had a secret suspicion that he was going to pick up a couple of unused tires or a cream separator for a nod of the head and the change he had in his pocket.

I didn't know until I arrived; it was the walleyed farmer selling out. An old drinking pal, you might say. I hadn't recognized the name on the poster. He was making sale to beat a mortgage company; they'd served notice Saturday evening, while the poor man was listening to Murdoch's spiel. They were seizing his crop, which didn't give them much to take hold of, if the field beside the lane was any indication. The gophers had to kneel down to get a bite to eat. And by Friday when the high officials arrived to seize his possessions, they'd find an empty house and a barn and a couple of other buildings that were too big or too rickety to move on skids. It was a cash on the barrel head sale, take your purchase and run.

I got there at noon, just as some neighbors' wives were getting ready to dish up the free lunch. It was quite a spread; potato salad until I thought I'd burst, and pork and beans in big pots, bread and biscuits and lots of scalding hot coffee. None of the usual finnan haddie. Everybody seemed to be having a fine time.

The auctioneer was having to work, though; the busiest pair of men in the whole constituency were Svenson and Left. I'll tell you, Svenson was sweating to get his bids, and it was sweating weather. Not a cloud in those miles and miles of pale blue sky. He stood on a table and that noon-day sun really got at him. The sky was more chrome than blue. His arms were scarlet from sweat and sunburn when he held up a neck yoke or a horse collar for everyone to see.

The farmer recognized me at first glance. He must have, he didn't look my way at all. He was walking around, trying to pretend he had something to do, not saying too much but staying away from where the actual bidding was in progress, as if he didn't want to embarrass any of his neighbors. They were helping him out, in a way, by coming to buy things, but they were looking after themselves too, keeping an eye peeled for bargains; thus the need for a man of mediating conscience.

Old Walleye stepped up behind me just when I was lighting into my third plate of potato salad. A man my size tends to be a big eater. He caught me just as I was settling down on an old rocking chair. I was at a certain disadvantage, having this man talk down to me from where he stood while I was eating his potato salad.

"Well, my old friend, Shorty," he said, tapping my shoulder with a huge wooden spoon. "How's the weather up there, Shorty?"

I was, of course, sitting down. That remark will someday produce in me a spell of madness.

"I trust," he said, "you came out here today to set loose a cloud-burst so everyone will have to run home before the sale is over."

A lot of people who were standing up to eat began edging closer. They saw they were in store for a little excitement. The farmer wasn't exactly in the best frame of mind. My mouth was full and I was unable to speak, so he just ignored the arm I was waving and went on, "I'm making a sale just so you can get a big crowd together and do some electioneering."

A number of people tittered.

This was in front of the house where all the furniture and kitchen utensils and everything was stacked in rows or piles on the bare ground: bedsteads and mattresses, empty sealers, a butter churn, winter clothes, an old organ, a shoebox full of postcards, extra leaves for a table that didn't seem to be present. The womenfolk were serving on the porch. Once in a while you got a glimpse of kids' faces in the bare windows—the farmer wouldn't let his kids out of the house, though there wasn't a stick of furniture in the entire building. I went and looked in while I was waiting for the food to be served; that's when I noticed the front of the house had been painted in the last few years, but not the sides and back.

"I thought I might talk politics a little," I said, "if you have no objections."

"Hell no," the farmer said. "I'd like to see a good rain, so when the mortgage company comes in to harvest they'll make a real mint."

"I mean to talk politics," I said, "not rain. And the first thing we've got to do is change the law so these mortgage collectors can't throw a man off his land on such short notice."

The farmer hit his own head with the wooden spoon that would still be his for another hour or so. "Maybe you could make the interest rates higher, so a fellow wouldn't be tempted." He winked around with that peculiar eye of his. "At only twelve per cent, by Harry, I was unable to resist."

"That's what I mean," I said. I was starting to get warmed up. The juices were beginning to flow. But trust my luck, something had to collapse, buckle or bend. What happened right then was a perfect example of why every human effort is a waste of energy.

"I imagine," the farmer said, "a politician only gets a one per cent cut. It seems to me you're being robbed."

I was all warmed up and ready for action. So out of nowhere this little unwashed geezer had to butt in; he was five feet tall, dressed in a heavy overcoat. On a day like that one. He practically came right out of the farmer's armpit.

"I am the prophet," he said.

I simply blinked. "Excuse me?" I said. I turned an ear toward him, the better to hear his recantation.

"You have sinned; you are a sinner," he said.

Swedes and Norwegians are in general very clean people. This little heap of rags had not seen water in his whole life, you could tell at a glance. You could tell without glancing, if you had half a nose; and I am well endowed in that vicinity. His beard was caked with dirt; the kind that blows off summerfallow, black and pure. He looked like a human dust storm. Right there at the auction sale.

"Backstrom," I introduced myself. "John J." I shifted the plate of potato salad to my left hand and reached without standing up. In a crowd like that one, if you gave up a chair you'd spend the rest of the day trying to get it back.

This black blizzard presumed he was going to administer a blessing rather than shake hands; he raised his right arm, his old overcoat slipping back to reveal a dirty bare wrist: "I am the prophet," he announced again.

"Elaborate," I invited, hoping we might all get a few laughs.

He was only five feet at the most, maybe five-one. "The sinner shall suffer for his sins," he said.

I must say in all honesty: that little prophet stank. If hell has an odor, he was it. He ducked in past the farmer and stood right in front of me, completely protected from the wind. I quite often have a plugged nose, but right then, unfortunately, it was clear. That prophet was absolutely the dirtiest human being I have ever laid eyes on. "Certainly," I said. I rocked a little in the rocking chair, out there on the bare parched ground in that chaos of furniture and household goods in front of the farmer's empty house.

"Absolutely," I said. "That's why He sent this poor innocent man a plague of Eastern moneylenders."

"God is just," this little crook said.

"When those Eastern hogs get finished in the trough," I said, "there's nothing left for the rest of us. Look at this poor man having to hold sale, a man who never did wrong in his life. Where is the justice?"

A lot of people were listening close now. You could see them scratching around in their empty pockets, getting a little riled up. That fool of a prophet ought to have known when to keep a tight lip. "The punishment," he said, "is coming from Heaven." He slammed down a fist in his opened palm, and I couldn't judge which was dirtier: "The sinners are doing the suffering they earned."

He held a very high opinion of himself, that sawed-off windbag.

"We didn't do anything," the farmer broke in, "but try to make a living and keep our noses clean."

The prophet let out a maniacal squeak of a laugh. "You didn't do anything!" You could tell, he should have been under lock and key. "That's right," he said. "You get punished for being innocent." He felt obliged to explain. "Oh that is a ripper and a honey! You get punished for being innocent!"

By this time we had a better crowd than the auctioneer. This little prophet had a squeaking voice; but it carried. And people were gathering around, half of them amused, half of them irritated. I sensed all that and I didn't stir out of my rocking chair; I sat still, trying not to rock, trying to look indifferent and just a little irritated at having my meal interrupted. That walleyed farmer and I seemed to be joining forces, or at least we both knew who the enemy was. "By Harry," Walleye said, "this is my auction sale." He didn't like that talk about sinners. Without intending to I remembered beating Jonah out of a few odd cents to pay for a beer I'd ordered, and I thought of stealing my poor wife's grocery money. Stealing is one of the worst sins. You'd think some of the wealthier Burkhardts would have helped us out in a time of such vicissitudes and tribulation, but no sir, not a penny of cash. Hand-me-down maternity clothes for my wife was all, and nothing for me but a curt nod. And there I was with my hearse smashed up, my means of livelihood threatened.

"So the innocent don't suffer?" somebody was asking.

But the farmer was worked up about his auction sale: by-Harrying this and that. "Do you suppose I'm selling out and leaving just for the hell of it? Do you think I *want* to take my family out on the road with no place to sleep, by Harry? Do you think for a minute I *asked* that mortgage company to do what they're doing?"

"You're lucky," the prophet said. "You're probably the luckiest man alive."

I had to straighten up a little myself; I wanted to hear what could possibly follow that comment. I discovered I was rocking like a madman in that rocking chair.

"I sure am," the farmer said. He tried to make out he was laughing. "I'm a blessed and fortunate man, by Harry."

"The world," the prophet said, "is coming to an end tomorrow. Get rid of your earthly possessions. Prepare for the final judgment."

"But there's a stampede and dance in town tomorrow," somebody said. "Couldn't you make it the day after?"

That brought the place down.

"Tomorrow," the prophet said. He didn't crack a smile. "You'll dance all right. I should say you'll dance." He brushed at his beard as if he'd just noticed on it one small particle of dust. He was positively delighted at his own remark; he hopped up and down a little himself, his feet almost coming out of his old boots. "Oh ho, oh ho, will you ever dance!" He damn near chuckled, but that would have flaked the dirt off his face. "I guess you'll dance!"

I couldn't resist; his conceit was too much for me. I hate conceited men. "God is merciful," I said.

That little prophet smashed down both grimy fists on a dresser and nearly broke the mirror. The mirror was directly to my right, and for a moment I wondered if the old geezer wasn't busy watching his own performance. But no, he had hardly taken his eyes off me. "Remember," he said. "And he that sat on the cloud thrust in his sickle on the earth; and the earth was reaped."

He slapped one of his overcoat pockets; which act, aside from raising a cloud of dust, was supposed to indicate that the lump in his pocket was a Bible. I might have brained him right then. He wasn't the only person who read the Bible. By God, my wife brings it to bed while she does her hair. He was getting my dander up. Predicting the end of the world like that; it hurt business. Nobody would believe that kind of talk. But I could see myself, people were getting serious.

Why put a lot of cash into a secondhand tractor or a binder if the world was going to end sometime the following day? I was really getting mad; but again that farmer saved him.

"I'll tell you what," the farmer was saying. "If you've got anything you want to dispose of by the end of the world, why don't you just leave it with me right now?"

People laughed. They thought the little old guy would be stumped by that one. But no sir. He pointed across the yard, that dirty wrist coming out of the overcoat once more; he pointed to where a dusty unwashed Model-A was parked next to the water trough and the windmill. "That's mine," he said. "That chariot of corruption over yonder. You take it. I see no reason why I can't walk from here to sometime tomorrow."

Well sir, you could have heard a pin drop; if the auctioneer across the yard over by the water trough hadn't been shouting: "Two and a half, two and a half. I got two and a half—" He held an old white horse by a short halter. "Two and a half. Going. Who makes it thirty thin dimes?"

"You're joking," the farmer said.

"I'm in dead earnest," the prophet said. "It's yours. Don't just stand there. I've been looking for some fool to take that jalopy off my hands, and it looks like I've found him." He came within an ace of cracking a smile. His teeth were nearly as dirty as his face. "You might have to get yourself a gallon of gasoline somewhere before you drive too far."

It was no great shakes of an automobile, I'll have to say that. But on the other hand, my old hearse wasn't exactly in top shape either. I sort of wished that if he wanted to believe the world was coming to a dead end he'd at least have given his chariot to me. And that wasn't an entirely selfish thought, for the farmer broke out, "I've got one headache on four wheels already. I don't need another one."

"It's yours," the prophet said. "And if you don't mind, I'll have a sample of that potato salad."

He'd been watching me eat most of this time. A path opened in that crowd as if a cannon ball had gone through. And it led right straight to the potato-salad bowl. The elderly lady who was dishing it up looked as if she was going to keel over, from the smell or what I don't know, but she scooped up a spoonful of salad that would have fed a thresher and she plopped it right down in the center of an empty plate. She did the same thing all over again. Then somebody gave that little prophet a fork, just before he started in with his bare hands.

But that farmer wasn't the sort of fellow to be cowed by the end of the world. He strutted across the yard, beating time on his knee with that wooden spoon he wouldn't let go of; he walked right bang up to where the auctioneer was hollering himself hoarse in vain: "Mr. Svenson," he said, "that Model-A is my latest acquisition. By Harry, here I am trying to get rid of things and instead I'm collecting more. I want you to drop everything and sell it for me right now, before somebody changes his mind."

That farmer was no fool. If ever a crowd of people listened to an auctioneer, it was that one. I was never so completely ignored in my life.

And that's when I got my insane idea. I half-wanted that old Model-A, because driving around the country in a hearse wasn't exactly the best thing for my electioneering. But more than that—I felt guilty about Old Walleye. Rain or no rain, I wanted to show him I had it in me to be decent. I wanted to prove to him I wasn't such a bad guy. That's an impulse that gets most of us into trouble sooner or later. I wanted to help him out.

So I got up from my rocking chair and put down my empty plate on the dresser the prophet had pounded, and I maneuvered into a position where I might be able to do a little quiet bidding if things didn't get out of hand.

The bidding was slow to begin with. People were half-afraid there was a catch somewhere. But pretty soon a young fellow in yellow cowboy boots walked up to the car slowly and then he lashed out all of a sudden with a quick firm kick at a tire. He went to another tire and repeated himself. Now a number of people kicked the tires with no hesitation; they seemed to be okay, except that the tread was generally thin; the spare was missing. I watched closely. Another young fellow opened a door of the car and took a pull at the steering wheel while the rest of us watched the front wheels; they moved.

Pretty soon there was a lot of talk going on, a lot of speculation; the auctioneer could hardly make himself heard. But he was a game fellow. Auctioneers work on a commission. He tried to pretend it was all some sort of a joke. "I've got ten," he said, though he didn't let on where he had it, "who'll make it twenty?"

He said that a few times and then a voice somewhere chipped in, "Twelve." I couldn't see who it was.

"Twelve," the auctioneer, Mr. Svenson, said. "I've got twelve for a car that's worth fifty if it's worth a cent. Who'll give me twenty bucks even?"

"Fourteen," another voice said.

That's the way it went. Pretty soon you could feel the excitement in the air. Instead of nobody wanting that car, pretty soon everybody was after it. People just had to have it, you could tell. Right before my eyes, people started making up stories about it, guessing where it came from, what kind of speed it was good for. "Doesn't run on gas," somebody said, "runs on water." "Where would you get the water?" somebody asked him. "That old coot is well over a hundred," somebody said. "Shouldn't be driving to begin with." Then an argument developed over the prophet's age; some people insisted, give him a bath and he'll look like a young man. "Give that car a good scrubbing," somebody said—he bent and spat on a fender and rubbed the dirt—"and it'll look like new."

I recognized that that would be a great automobile for a man with political ambitions. People couldn't stay away from it.

The auctioneer had stopped joking too. Pretty soon you could see he wasn't going to part with that car for fifty dollars. The sun had just about broiled him, but he waved his bare arms, he unbuttoned another button on his shirt, he talked and shouted and pointed and practically stamped his feet through the old table he was standing on; twice he had to be steadied.

My first bid was for fifty-two dollars. I didn't speak. My throat was too dry for that. I just nodded. The auctioneer was saying, "I've got fifty—fifty—going for fifty—going for fifty—" And I nodded. Or at least, I felt my head nod. My huge head which no one could miss. I didn't have much to say in the matter. My head just ducked down forward and back up, the muscles in my jaw so tense they were beginning to ache a little; but the auctioneer saw it, apparently, for already he was at it again: "I've got fifty-two, who'll make it fifty-four?"

That's the way it went. Pretty soon, though, my throat was dry; the palms of my hands were wringing wet. And my fool head kept nodding. Just bobbing down and up and down and up and down and up. I could no more stop it than tell you now what I thought I was doing.

But Jonah Bledd was on my mind, for one thing. A pain was pressing within me, and I had found a way to let that pain out. Each nod of my head was a hiccup of the soul, letting out a gasp of pain. End of the world be damned, who could believe such crap? Sinner be dammed, who was a sinner? Was the water guilty that drowned Jonah? Was the wind guilty; the wind that turned the fields to dust?

Was the sun guilty? Why should I answer questions? When did I get to ask questions? The sickle be damned and the reaper be damned. Who was the judge in the first place? A man is free. Each man is free. And I wouldn't be pushed and shoved and stepped on. I have my rights. Words were in me, knocking to be let out. Pain was in me, and I let out the pain. Seventy, somebody said. I nodded my head. Judgment be damned and mercy be damned. Eighty, somebody said. I nodded my head. My soul had hiccups and my head was nodding. A hundred and ten, somebody was saying.

I got that dusty Model-A for one hundred and twenty-eight dollars. When the auctioneer said sold, that crowd just plain went wild. The tension was killing them. You'd think a condemned man had been pardoned. They shouted and roared and pounded me on the back and wrung my hand until I thought I was coming apart. People said I was great guy. The farmer himself was absolutely beaming. I felt pretty good.

I felt so good I wanted to thank that prophet for providing me with such an opportunity. "Let me shake the hand of that old prophet," I said. I started toward the porch and the potato-salad bowl, elbowing my way, staring in every direction.

But the prophet was nowhere to be found. There wasn't hide nor hair of him to be seen. "Where is he?" I said; I was practically desperate.

"He left," somebody said. "I believe he left."

"Where did he go?" I pleaded.

"I believe he left." That's all that anyone could report.

It was very disconcerting. It really was. I needed Jonah there; to tell me I was a meathead a fathead and a shithead. And a horse's ass to boot.

The way the auction was set up, you had to go into the barn and pay Mr. Benjamin Left, the clerk, before you could take your purchase home. The terms were strictly cash. I walked around my new Model-A a few times, kicking the various tires and looking closely at the windshield and the paint job. I even lifted up the hood and about twenty of us looked at the engine for maybe ten minutes and talked a lot about rings and spark plugs and pistons. By then the auctioneer had moved on; he was trying to sell a threshing machine to a bunch of farmers who were sure they could thresh this year's crop with a Chinese fan.

As I say, you were supposed to go into the barn and settle up before you did anything with your purchase. I noticed that my hands were still sweating. The sweat was rolling down my back under my shirt. There wasn't a cloud in the sky. The heat was horrible that day. Something fierce. I felt I might pass out. I had to go sit in the shade by the barn for a while. It was a big old barn that had once been red. The sun had moved far enough to the west to make a little shade. Those who weren't listening to the auctioneer were gathered around the Model-A, talking about it, talking about me too. They speculated on where it had come from; for one thing, they noticed, there were no license plates. But now they didn't call it the prophet's chariot; they simply said, Backstrom's Model-A.

My old hearse was sitting clear across the yard on the other side of the house. Back of the house, with a lot of cars and other rigs. The womenfolk were still hanging around the house, feeding a few stragglers and doing up the dishes so they could be sold. The farmer would need every cent he could lay his hands on. Somebody said he was striking out for the Coast in the morning. He was going to sleep the night with some neighbors and then he'd leave before sunup, in case the mortgage people expressed any undue concern. The bankers who were throwing the man off his land.

I began to feel quite ill. One hundred and twenty-eight dollars is a pile of money. Especially if you are an undertaker with modest means. Or a farmer with all kinds of mouths to feed and no land to call your own. There were hundreds of votes at stake. A lot of people were impressed with me; with my courage and generosity and my style. You could tell by the way they looked over at where I was lying stretched out in the shade, trying to appear nonchalant with a straw in my mouth. They liked my style; style is something a politician must have.

I felt terrible. I really needed to throw up. My stomach felt as if it was bursting with potato salad. Some of it must have gone bad in the heat; I could taste onions.

That goddamned little turd of an unwashed sawed-off prophet with his end-of-the-world malarky. I've never liked people who don't have enough self-respect to keep themselves clean. It was my first impression, the minute he opened his mouth, that I should knock his dirty teeth down his dirty stinking throat. I'm a great believer in first impressions. But I am basically not an extremely violent man, though I have been in a few fights, all of them against stupendous odds, none of which I ever lost.

It was a miracle that Helen Murdoch didn't come driving in right then. To hand out silly pamphlets on her father's philanthropy; to wow people with that flashy new Chevrolet. What would my new car look like beside hers? She'd probably drive in and with her unerring instinct park right smack beside Backstrom's Model-A.

That barn started to feel like a cliff that was about to crumble into a landslide. An avalanche. I clung to the hope that I might be swept away. JOHN J. SAVES HUNDREDS WHILE PERISHING ALONE. Or the barn might blow over. TORNADO DESTROYS ALL HOPE OF RAIN: BACKSTROM DEAD. Or a simple earthquake might topple the structure, swallow me up into oblivion. J.J.B. DIES HEROICALLY IN MONSTROUS CALAMITY: OUR JOHN SOLE VICTIM OF CATASTROPHIC QUAKE.

Only that calamity and catastrophe had been preceded by an even worse one. I felt in all my pockets. With my huge hands, I practically ripped the pockets off my body. I slapped my pockets, I counted them and recounted them, mentally and literally. On the sly and shrewdly, I turned six of them inside out. I assembled all the contents of my ten pockets in one pocket. I was in possession of sixty-four cents, borrowed from my wife's purse the previous night while she in innocence knelt to move her lips in evening prayer; another crime, incidentally, for which I was bound to be summoned to a reckoning. My dear wife had waited up for me, in solitude and misery, until nine minutes to midnight: the statistic is hers. Two quarters, two nickels, and four pennies, one of them a large penny and surely worth more. Plus two buttons, which for a delirious moment I mistook for dimes. I slapped at my pockets as if a mouse had run up the leg of my pants. I would have thrown the buttons away right then but Elaine had asked three times what I did with those two missing buttons. Where are the buttons from your fly? she asked; I could never produce them upon demand. I racked my brain. I ripped at the striped silk inside my old black suitcoat, hoping against hope a coin might have slipped from a pocket into the lining. I turned down the cuffs of my trousers and I kicked wildly in the air, pretending all the while that I was chasing away a torment of flies.

I found I had to urinate. That was another calamity. For the obvious place to urinate was in a rear stall in the barn. The womenfolk were using the outhouse; some humorist, perhaps the farmer himself, or that dumb clerk who guarded the barn door, had put a sign on the side of the outhouse: LADIES AND CHILDREN—TODAY ONLY. Very funny. Hilarious. I was in one hell of a pickle. My conscience tormented me. I have what is basically an uneasy conscience. My bladder was bursting.

I tried to figure out why people had stopped bidding at such an unlikely moment. I'd promised myself that if I forced the bid up to one hundred and thirty dollars I'd stop right there; I'd have done my duty by that poor farmer. I'd simply stop nodding my head and rest on my laurels.

I reasoned with myself. Coldly and calmly I went over the whole thing. I exercised my judgment in relation to all the apparent facts. Maybe people felt I really needed that Model-A. They felt it was I who had desperate need, so they stopped bidding against me. Out of compassion and the milk of human kindness. They just stopped and let me have it.

I was in a terrible predicament. Maybe, I thought to myself, I am temporarily insane. I actually groaned aloud several times. I tried putting a straw in my mouth, only to find a moment later I had chewed it to shreds. It tasted faintly of the barn into which I could under no circumstances enter. I was trying to look nonchalant. I reasoned with myself all afternoon, until I had a severe pain in my head as well as in my jaw muscles and my stomach and bladder. But it was of no use. I reasoned and I reasoned; but it was absolutely of no use whatsoever.

THE way I got out of it was: I drove away. In my hearse. I said I'd be right back; I don't believe anyone heard me. I stayed until nearly six forty-five, pretending I had fallen asleep, the shadow of the barn growing longer and longer, and by then a lot of people were leaving; they had to go home to do chores. While I am quite a large man, I did manage to stray over to my hearse more or less unnoticed: I pretended I was looking for a pen to sign a check. I got in and drove away, joining the line of cars and wagons and buggies leaving via the lane. But I became impatient with the line-up, I pulled over into the ditch and charged past everyone; when I got home I hid myself in the funeral parlor.

I turned on the old Atwater-Kent, and I listened to music. I find music very soothing, especially some of those sad cowboy tunes that speak of betrayal and futile love; Wilf Carter is my favorite singer. I pretended once again I was sleeping, stretched out on a couch, and my wife didn't enter my sanctuary. She was a little relieved, I suspect, at not having to hustle up a meal at such a late hour. She's always in a hurry to get to church. She sensed my mood when we exchanged a few words through the door. Some of her cats had got into the funeral parlor, against my express orders; their dust makes me sneeze and one sneeze could ruin a service and hurt the clientele I have built up, though as my wife once observed, in defense of a cat that had six kittens in the forbidden room, I don't get many repeat customers.

I love music, yet I am not indiscriminate; and just as the twilight turned to dark, over the airwaves came a chorus of voices: "O God, Our Help in Ages Past."

A song to which I have mixed responses. But I was in difficulty, and I expected great things of Applecart. I thought he might put me back on my feet, as he had done once before. Out of the gathering darkness came his big voice, assured and reassuring.

"Friends," he began.

"Applecart," I said, "I've messed things up."

"My dear dear friends," he said.

"Applecart," I repeated, "I've been messing things up all my life, okay, I admit it, but today I hit a new low."

"The campaign is going well," Applecart said. "We are making commendable progress. I have encouraging news to report."

"How come?" I said. "Why, Applecart, do I have this gift for the wrong action? Why must I bungle and flub every human gesture? Why must I forever, swinging as vigorously as I do, hit my thumb not the nail?"

But Applecart wasn't listening too carefully to me. He was reading off twenty-six names and addresses of people, of kind souls, he called them, who had sent in contributions of over five dollars.

"Midas," I said. "Applecart," I corrected myself. "I appeal to you, man to man. I am hardly a born winner. Yet, Applecart, does every move in the right direction have to be a total loss?"

"But for all the good news," Applecart said, "we must not relax from our striving. The enemy is upon us like a vulture from the sky. He would compound our ruin and woe."

"You're telling me," I said. "Applecart, you are stirring the dust of a ruin. You are speaking to woe itself."

"Follow me," Applecart said. "My dear friends, follow me. Despair not. Follow me. Despair is the wages of sin, victory is the wages of virtue."

I should have felt cheered up: but that's when my depression really took hold. Everything got jumbled in my mind, my wife, the cats, my high ambitions, Applecart himself, the hearse, the auction sale—as things are prone to do when one resorts to alcohol. I had this micky of rye concealed in the back of the radio—I may have mentioned that my wife abstains—and I set out to kill it. The insides of a radio confound my wife and she never looks in. She hates to be confounded.

I don't like it too well myself. I sipped at the micky, having dropped the cap of the bottle into an air vent; but when Applecart started in on the wages of sin is despair, I resorted to longer pulls. There isn't a great deal of rye in a micky. Pretty soon I forgot about the radio, and pacing around in that funeral parlor I began to address myself to Applecart in person. I had hoped he would soothe me; Applecart, my guide and champion. The man who had inspired me on an earlier occasion. The only man who might appreciate my predicament; he too had been compelled to seek financial aid. But this time I was forced to argue. He was talking so damned grandiose about delivering people from hard times and the drought, I finally couldn't stand it—I shouted: "Do something! For the love of bloody Christ, don't just talk! *Do* something for a change!"

My wife, by this time, was gone to church. On Tuesday nights they get ready for Wednesday nights.

Applecart just went on droning straight ahead, ignoring me completely, I who was the epitome of man with his back to the wall. He said grandiose windbag things about the present government ignoring its sense of moral responsibility.

What the hell did that mean? I asked him what that meant. "What the sizzling smoking hell, Applecart?" I said. I was waving the micky. Applecart is a teetotaler himself, or claims to be, and he never smokes. I don't smoke myself. I find it a filthy habit. My wife pretends she doesn't smoke but sometimes when I come in unexpectedly I find her fanning her apron around the kitchen. She says something about the stove smoking. Sweet Caporals, I am tempted to add.

Applecart came right back at me with more of his promises. He kept saying, we are plagued. "We are plagued," he said. "We have been plagued. But we shall be delivered from our plague and pain, for out of pain comes deliverance."

"I guess so," I said. I very nearly spilled some of the micky. "If you are ever in doubt," I said, "consult your local undertaker for time and place."

"Out of the destruction will come—"

"You bet your sweet life," I said. I didn't let him finish before I interrupted. I was wound up. "The old dualities. Always the old dualities.

When you're in a tight fix: mind and body, right and wrong. Fill the old grab bag with something for everybody. When you're cornered: good and evil, black and white, up and down, damnation—"

Then I caught myself. Election all right. In ten fleeting days. With everybody casting a vote, for John Backstrom, against John Backstrom. Yes or no. Thumbs up, thumbs down. The glad hand. Or the inevitable goddamned hobnailed boot.

"But what in the Christly hell will you *do*?" I shouted.

Applecart wasn't listening. He was a voice blasting away into the darkness. He didn't seem to have ears. He was one big blabbering mouth. Follow me, he kept saying. Follow me, my dear friends.

"The world is full of big talkers," I said. "Full of expensive blowhards. But where's the justice? Where the hell's the justice of it all? That's what I want to know."

I went on like that. Sometimes I was hardly listening myself. I got off on the subject of dualities. I said, "Yes sir, Mr. John George Applecart, let me tell you about dualities. I've read the Bible a little myself. And I've lived a little too. And here I am," I said. "I consume and I consume. Chapter and verse. Newspaper columns that bulge with advice. The want ads. Food. Hats. Socks. Gasoline. Women. Beer. Hardstuff. I have a large jaw and mouth, my appetite is healthy. My eyes are twenty-twenty and so eager they hate to sleep. My ears are wax-free and larger than normal. I consume and I consume. And yet in the end, where does it get me?" I waited. "In the end," I said, "I am consumed. That's all, that's all. Consumed."

"The fourth angel," Applecart said, "poured out his vial upon the sun; and power was given unto him to scorch men with fire. And men were scorched with great heat—"

"You're damned tooting," I said. "You tell them, buster. You're hitting on all four now. If you need a witness, just send the doubters to John J.B."

"And men of passions," Applecart said. "Men of evil passions. The men of burning passions shall themselves burn."

"Water!" I shouted. "Water! No, no, Applecart! Goddamnit, no!" I said. "You are a flatulent windbag!"

I shouted at the tiny pinpoint of light; the solitary red pinpoint out of which boomed a voice that filled the funeral parlor. I jumped up and down. The floor itself, which usually only creaks, was vibrating. It was very spooky. It was a wonder I didn't turn gray on the spot. The day I met Elaine Burkhardt I sensed her poor old mother's house might make an excellent funeral home; thus, again, another in a long series of failures of perception. The whole house groaned and shuddered; I was delighted to have that micky of rye, just over twelve ounces, my favorite brand. "By the mortified testicles of Abraham and Absalom," I shouted at that booming voice, "you, Applecart, are a swindling Pharisee."

I went to the closed door and listened. If my wife had been home she'd have barged in at that point, in anger and feigning tears. She's very troubled about my language. She has taken some oath at church to improve my language, a promise the irony of which needs no explaining. "You are," I shouted, "a goddamned two-bit shifty faker."

I was embarrassed at my own outbreak of shouting. Ordinarily in a funeral parlor you never raise your voice. But there the radio was standing, a console model, where I usually put the coffin, and the voice was coming out full blast. Eerie, I found it. Thank God I have no superstitions. I had to shout. I went and turned up the volume as high as it would go, I asked no quarter, and I shouted back at it: "Explain! Explain!" I shouted.

Follow me, is all that voice would say. That hollow voice. Send in your contributions. "Send in your nickels," Applecart said, "your dimes, your precious dollars, my dear friends." He paused; and I heard the gurgle of water. "For remember," Applecart said. "Remember that promise. Do as I ask you. And there shall be no more death, neither sorrow, nor crying, neither shall there be any more pain—"

"A pig's arse!" I shouted.

That's when I lost my temper. I'm a fairly strong man, standing as I do nearly six-four in my stocking feet. And with long arms. I've got to make a living too.

I struck that old Atwater-Kent a blow that would have brained an ox. Ordinarily I don't resort to violence. But I smashed that radio with one blow.

The voice went off. That little pinpoint of light went out. That pin prick.

By that time it was pitch dark. I couldn't see my own hands. It was too dark even to feel. I just sat down in the middle of the floor right where I was; I spoke to that deafening silence.

"And the kids with hungry bellies?" I said. " Those women today, who should be nubile when instead they're skin and bones? Those people lining up at 6 A.M. for rotten apples and dried cod? Those people fired and laid off? Those people put out of their homes, sleeping in ditches?"

And I stopped and listened.

That's when I heard myself crying. I didn't know up until then that I was sobbing away like a baby. For the second time in as many days. Ordinarily I consider it a bad sign if I cry once in two years. An undertaker is the last person in the world who should cry. My whole body shook. It was all I could do to steady my lips around the neck of that micky so I could take a swig. But it turned out to be empty.

Everything was against me. I burst out at myself in wrath and anguish. I vilified myself. "You phony bastard," I said. "You pretender. You walking clip joint. You know it won't rain. It can't possibly rain. You slippery two-bit gaseous fraud. It's never going to rain again. You overgrown shifty big faker. You lying son of a bitch. Why don't you get up in front of all those people you're fooling and just be an honest man for five minutes? For five minutes of your miserable sniveling existence, get up in front of people instead of behind them, and speak the unvarnished truth. No more of your measly little promises, your chiseling lies. Get up and tell everybody, speak out, stand up straight like a man and shout, tell the goddamn truth for a change. Just for five minutes tell the goddamn truth."

WEDNESDAY

I MUST HAVE FALLEN ASLEEP. I had a bad dream, a terrible dream. A regular nightmare. By God, I dreamt that it poured rain. Endlessly. It got started and wouldn't stop. It was terrible. The crops started to rust. You could see the rust at the bottoms of the stalks, and then you could find it in the heads of wheat and barley, the heads appearing, finally, but no kernels in them. Hulls and no kernels. You looked at a field and you could see whole patches that were rust-colored—dying from rain. Then the soil wouldn't soak up anymore water and the crops began to turn yellow and drown in the low spots. Flooded out. Acres and acres turned yellow and then black. And then, after days and days without sun, the crops on the higher ground wouldn't ripen, and there was a danger of frost. That would mean everything lost. Everything. Now if the sky did not clear, everything would freeze and turn black, ruined. And for all this, people blamed me. They said, Johnnie Backstrom did this. Just to get a public office. For money. To stuff an old tin cash box. Indemnity, he calls it. The walleyed farmer was everywhere, in the pool halls and restaurants where people went to keep dry, in the hardware stores and grocery stores and filling stations and egg-grading stations and machine shops. Wherever people got together. He ruined all of us, the farmer said. But he's making big money now. And Jonah Bledd was there too, not saying anything; just watching with his hair on end.

Men stood in doorways of barns and looked out at the rain. Women sat at kitchen tables and stopped looking at the catalogues and watched out the window at the rain. The chickens looked wet and sick and bedraggled out in the mud. They huddled together under the caraganas or up against walls and didn't eat and didn't lay. The cows, driven in from the pasture against the endless mist of rain, were mud up to their tails; their udders were mud and had to be washed. Their dung was pure liquid. Everybody blamed me. They said, Johnnie Backstrom did this, and now he's sitting in the Parliament buildings, warm and dry and drawing big money. He turned it on and now he can't turn it off.

When I woke up I expected all the culverts to be flooded and the bridges washed out. I expected the rain to be pounding on the window-panes. I was stiff and aching from lying on the hard floor and I got up slowly onto my hands and knees, carefully, trying to leave my head where it was, and then carefully I mounted to my feet, and I went to the window: there wasn't a cloud in the sky. It was the false dawn. Not a streak of cloud anywhere to behold.

I felt pretty rough. But I was mad too. Not just about the sky. I was still mad at Applecart for all the crap he had poured into my head in his pitch for faith and belief. My wife would be furious about the radio; she had some soap programs she listened to every morning while her cats lapped up a fortune in milk. That's when I decided to go to the stampede. Everybody would be there. I'd stand up and tell people the straight goods, no holds barred.

I was still in a hitting mood, though. At 4:30 A.M. I went out to the car shed to fix the fender of my hearse. I went to work on that damaged fender with a hammer.

Body work, if you are given to parables, contains quite a message. You make a dent smooth by hitting it. But I wasn't entirely successful. While I am in general a gentle man, on that particular occasion I could not restrain myself. I hit too hard, for one thing. I am left-handed and at one time threw ball for Notikeewin, losing only three games in as many years. Four games; we lost against Burkhardt in the fourteenth inning when one of my curves failed to break and the opposing pitcher hit a home run. I began to pound with that hammer where there were no dents, on the theory that to wash a spot out of a tie, say, you have to get the area wet around the spot. Actually, I did make the damaged fender somewhat better. But in a temporary seizure of wrath and anguish I started in on the good fender, the left one. I'm quite a heavy man, and I swing a hammer with considerable force; I hit the fender just once, but powerfully.

You have to understand. Maybe you've had the same experience. Something comes over you. Something wells up inside. A film comes over the eyeballs. The world was getting too warm before the sun had left the horizon; I found it positively stuffy there in my car shed, surrounded by all the junk I had accumulated in the name of matrimony; worn-out tires that I couldn't bear to part with, and stacks of old magazines, chiefly *Ten Story Western;* cardboard boxes that might come in handy, a pile of used boards from a door I drove through, two shovels, a wheelbarrow, a rake with a broken handle from which I had twice got very bad slivers, a suitcase full of a disman-tled electric motor, two dozen empty shotgun shells, a broken rocking chair I meant to repair in my spare time. That mysterious thing seized me; that longing for the old chaos. That old earth, without form and full of the void. The car shed rang; it rang with the din of my anguish, but inside me was a worse din. I stopped pounding a couple of times and straightened up, to try and gasp some air into my lungs, and still I was being deafened; still the din and the roar.

Sometimes it seems that chaos is the only order. The only real order. To hell with mealtime and bedtime and worktime and churchtime and thinktime. I was tempted to throw in lifetime with the lot. Add them all to that accumulation in the car shed. I needed chaos, the old chaos, and that hammer and fender weren't enough.

So as I say, I went to the stampede. In my hearse with its matching fenders.

Mine was the first car into the stampede grounds. There on the outskirts of Burkhardt, home of my wife's illustrious forebears, most recently an alcoholic father and his nagging wife. I was honored by being let in free. I could see there was going to be a monstrous crowd. The first event was bareback bronc riding. At least three hundred people were present and watching at 11 A.M., pressed to that pole and hogwire corral when the first chute opened. The rider didn't stay on that big reddish-colored bronc for five seconds. You could see a grain elevator between his chaps and the bronco's back. The cars and wagons were lined up for nearly half a mile at the gate on the highway, each driver paying a quarter to get in. The men at the gate wore carpenter aprons and cowboy hats; they ignored the people who were shouting and cussing at the delay.

By half-past eleven, the food booths were all set up and covered over with roofs of fresh-cut poplars. Somebody had cut trees and stuck them in the ground in rows as if they were growing, and already in the morning heat the leaves weren't quite fluttering the way they should. The Catholic Women's League and the Elks and the United Church women and a dozen other groups were starting to boil wieners and setting up little clumps of catsup bottles and saltcellars, pouring mustard and relish into dishes they'd brought from home, tearing the green off cobs of corn that must have been shipped in from somewhere else; and every time another car or wagon drove through the gate a woman or girl jumped out and ran to a booth with another cake or another couple of pies. I saw chocolate cake with thick white icing and chocolate cake with fresh sticky chocolate icing; angel-food cake and marble cake and ginger-looking spice cake and three-layer cake and every kind of cake you want to think of. But it was the pies that caught my attention. My mouth began to water; I had to keep swallowing, dry as I was after all that micky of rye. I've always been a great man for fresh pies.

And for a man who hadn't eaten supper or breakfast, this was a sore temptation.

I was the first customer at the C.W.L. booth, and I am not one who gives money easily to Catholics. But some of the best cooks in the constituency are of that denomination. Also, they were open first. Those C.W.L. ladies, getting in each other's way as they settled into a routine, finding and mislaying things, unpacking this and repacking that, greeting each other and yet hustling—they were a pleasure to behold. Especially with every fresh bright plank of their makeshift counter simply buried in fresh pies, every pie representing a personal sacrifice. It was a miracle how those women could spare the butter and eggs. But they smiled and hustled, lifting somebody's kitchen cups out of layers of the *Free Press*, making coffee in a big pot on a camp stove, trying to get the soft drinks into the washtub before all the ice melted, Orange Crush and Big Orange and cherry soda and lime something. And busy as they were, they paid attention when I introduced myself; they said they'd heard of Johnnie Backstrom, candidate for the Legislative Assembly, and they were very cordial.

So I felt compelled to linger around. I teased those ladies about their liking to see men eat, and I told a joke. The one about Pat and the Jew and the Blessed Virgin. Pat and Abe went out fishing and their boat turned over.... A very clean story. I studied the rows of pies, and I especially complimented whoever it was that made the flapper pie, which is my favorite. But I didn't slight my three second choices: Dutch apple, sour-cream raisin, and saskatoon. Those ladies were so flattered they gave me a bottle of Big Orange. They wouldn't take a penny. It was no great feast for a man who had missed breakfast. I have never been much on carbonated beverages to begin with, but I think I got a lot of votes right there at the C.W.L. booth.

The Wednesday half-holiday doesn't begin until high noon, so by one o'clock the cars were really rolling in, from up and down the line and from everywhere. People came in wagons also, and buggies and trailers, and they tied the horses to the wheels and put out hay, as if the horses themselves should join in the celebration. A bunch of Indians showed up from some place, a whole tribe with all their ponies and little kids and the men with their hair braided and the women with papooses. Cowboys swaggered around in pairs or maybe three together, or maybe one of them with a cowgirl or a guitar, which always drew a lot of attention. The whole place was a whirl of dust.

You could have a good time just sniffing the air; corn on the cob in melting butter, those dying poplars, ice cream going soft before it was eaten, wieners boiling, hamburgers getting overdone; and you could smell cowboys too, or the stuff that makes them smell like cowboys, coming from the main corral and the smaller corrals behind the chutes where they kept the bucking horses and steers and the calves for the roping events and the cows for the wild-cow milking contest. And I'll tell you something. I'm not ashamed to say that somehow or other I enjoy the smell of horseshit once in a while. It's wholesome-smelling.

I killed a little time talking to a man who drove up and parked his car beside my hearse; other drivers had avoided it until I was nearly offended. He had just sold a fine big steer for three dollars cash so he could bring his kids to the stampede; they were tickled to death, the whole raft of them. Then he started dividing up the two seventy-five that remained after he paid a quarter to get into the grounds, and when I saw he was making a mistake in mathematics, he wasn't figuring himself into the divisions—then I walked away.

I went over to watch the wild-steer riding. A lot of the local boys were taking part in that event, not just the professional riders, so the whole community wanted to observe. It was the big event of the day for a lot of people, and I mean to tell you, there was more to look at than high-heeled boots and forty-dollar saddles. You should have seen the faces pressed to the hogwire that surrounded that pole corral.

They were having trouble in Chute Number Three. The animal wouldn't hold still long enough so that a rider could get down off the fence and onto its back. You could see that much through the big heavy gate on the chute. But all of a sudden a cowboy yanked open the gate and took one jump for the fence.

A boy came out on a monstrous black bull. That was one of the things that really got the crowd, having someone ride a young bull. It was more dangerous. And this bull didn't like the prick of spurs.

The boy riding him looked to be about sixteen, wearing yellow boots and a new green silk shirt; but he was good. Maybe he wasn't good; maybe he just needed the prize money. Or maybe he was showing off; I never found out. He took off his hat with his right hand and started fanning it, he hung onto the bellyband with his left hand, and his spurs were raking the bull from the shoulders to the flanks. That boy was a great crowd-pleaser. You could actually see the blood he drew.

And then the cowbell rang and the crowd started really cheering. The time was up. The rider had stuck it out, making points all the way for style. The judges up in the judges' booth were all writing notes.

But the bull wasn't finished. He kept bucking and turning. And the boy who had been riding so grandly suddenly looked scared. His hat was too new, that was a bad sign. He had got onto something and he didn't know how to get off. He'd planned on being bucked off, I suppose, and here he was riding the worst animal of the lot, and he wasn't losing. That was his trouble.

Two pick-up riders started out to try and crowd in on the bull from both sides and pick the boy off. He was using both hands now, pulling leather, and his hat was somewhere on the ground getting its first stains. But before those cowboys got to him he just let go of the bellyband and fell. That's when the bull turned.

The clown was there in a flash. He caught the bull's attention. That was his job. Whenever someone got thrown, especially a local boy, the clown would run out in front of the bull or steer in his gaudy outfit while the rider scrambled out of the dust and manure and hightailed it for the fence. The clown had a barrel he'd jump into. He was good at it; he would run and jump and never miss. Sometimes a really ornery steer would take a run at the barrel with its horns and send the barrel spinning and rolling and everybody had a good laugh. Especially when the clown's head would pop out of the barrel with that black derby on. He'd look around, always in the wrong direction, and then just in time he'd glance and spot the steer bearing down and he'd duck again and we'd have another laugh. Or a lot of people would have a laugh.

This clown was very exceptional. You don't often see a big clown. Not really big. This one—well, I might as well be honest—he was crowding six-three or six-four. He almost didn't fit into his barrel, which I suppose was part of the joke. I enjoy a good laugh as well as anybody else; but this was very painful for me to watch. For one thing, he was the funniest clown I've ever witnessed. I've always been attracted to clowns.

He stepped in between the boy and the bull, as I say, and turned and stuck out his rump. The boy was slow at getting up. The bull saw the clown's red-and-yellow behind and snorted. The crowd roared. The clown started his quick sidestep.

But he was just a split second late. The bull must have tossed him thirty feet in the air.

The funny thing was, the crowd all thought it was part of the act. They roared and applauded. They thought the clown would jump up and run for his barrel. But he didn't. He tried to get up but wasn't moving quite fast enough, and the bull was on him again.

I guess I closed my eyes for the next few seconds. But I was seeing it just the same. The body mangled and ripped by those gouging horns, the innocent figure mutilated, rolled and trampled in the stinking dust. The spirit struck into frantic despair; I saw it all right. Without so much as peeking, I saw and I saw.

When I opened my eyes one of the pick-up riders was crowding his horse between the clown and the bull. But the clown didn't get up. He was lying twisted. Two men ran out and bent over him; one of them signaled toward the chutes.

Don't ask me why, I simply took that high fence in one leap off the hood of a parked car; I raced for the center of that arena. Three or four cowboys tried to stop me, greenhorn that they took me for, but with no success. One of them was knocked flat.

And then I was bending over the clown. His bulbous nose had come off, showing a human nose that wasn't painted or anything, except that blood was coming from it. He was bleeding pretty freely somewhere beneath his torn clown's costume; the red was stained a cleaner red.

I guess those cowboys wondered what hit them in the next two minutes. For as soon as I made it, a couple of hundred people did the same thing; boys and men and even women got into the corral. And nothing could stop us. We were all crowded around that clown lying motionless, and someone in the middle of things was shouting, "Get back, folks. Let him have some air. Give him air."

Other people took up the request. A dozen people, maybe, were repeating, "Let him have some air, folks."

But it didn't do any good. I can't explain why. That clown had captured all of us. We wouldn't move. Now someone had gone for a stretcher and they were hollering to ask if there was a doctor in the crowd. It was plain the clown couldn't be moved until a doctor looked at him.

Another thing I noticed, the clown was very thin. His costume was baggy and had billowed when he ran, but he was skin and bones. The only thing that moved on him now was his eyelids; they kept opening and staring in a sleepy confused way, and all the make-up, the white paint and the black and yellow, was smudged with sweat and dust and the blood from his nose. Then he tried to say something. His mouth moved small inside the smile that was painted on his face. He kept trying to say something to me, a perfect stranger, but he couldn't make it. He tried to raise a hand and point but couldn't and I wanted to point for him but didn't know where.

"The kid is all right," I said. I thought maybe that was it. "You saved him," I said. "Just a sprained ankle."

But that wasn't it, apparently; he kept trying to point, kept trying to tell us all something.

Anyhow, to make a long story short, young Lipinski, the newest doctor in Notikeewin, happened to be on the stampede grounds. In a few minutes he had the clown lifted onto a stretcher and four cowboys went running with it toward the gate. They're used to things like that, I suppose.

But the whole crowd of us—we didn't move. Four hundred people by now. Or at least—everybody saw I didn't move and nobody was big enough to move me, so they stayed too. I was a leader right there. And that's where I made my speech, my first major speech. I'm not bragging when I say it was a good one. It was a great one. All my pain came out of me right there, and I spoke to a lot of people.

For one thing, it was a real scorcher of a day. And there in the corral it was simply blazing hot. No wind, nothing; not a breeze. We were all thinking about that clown who had stood up to a wild bull.

I didn't so much speak as roar. I raised my left hand.

"And I beheld another beast coming up out of the earth; and he had two horns like a lamb, and he spake as a dragon." That must be from the Bible. As I say, I nearly wore out my eyes on small print, sometimes against my will. But it stuck. Those words just came to my mind and I boomed them out. I have a fairly powerful voice when I'm wound up.

The crowd fell silent. They're mostly a bunch of Bible-pounders themselves around here. They knew what I was saying. "Yes sir," I said. "A beast came out of the earth and that clown stood up to him."

"Amen," somebody said.

"He stood right up to that beast. And the rest of us ought to be paying attention."

They were listening now. I heard somebody say, "That's Johnnie Backstrom." That little remark gave me confidence.

"The lesson is an easy one," I said. "We've got to stand up. For six years now we've been down on our knees, flat on our bellies; we've been shoved and mauled by the high-muckie-mucks."

"Amen to that," somebody said.

"By the plutocrat millionaires from the East. For six long cowardly years, we've groveled in the dung and the dirt, the dirt and the dung."

"Yea, yea," somebody shouted.

"We've been pushed and shoved—and I'll tell you why. Because we haven't got the guts to stand up for our own rights and principles." I raised both fists and shook them. The sun was just hammering down from the sky. "If you *enjoy* sucking the hind tit, you prairie chickens, then close your ears. Pretend you didn't see that beast. Run over and suck on a bottle of Big Orange. If you still have a nickel—after six years of being rolled in the dirt and dung by the plutocrat millionaires." I paused and licked the sweat off my lips. "But if you *don't* enjoy it—then crowd a little closer. And don't be afraid to push and shove a little yourself."

That made them sit up and take notice. I could have reached out and touched twenty different people without taking a step. There must have been five hundred people jammed into that corral, and more coming.

"I myself don't like this business of sucking the hind tit. I don't like slaving from morning till night for the big-money interests. The beast is upon us. The beast is here and charging. We are being gored and gouged by the charging mad beast. The big-money boys, the grabbers from the East. The high-muckie-mucks that never worked a day in their lives. Those high-muckie-muck gougers from Ontario that wouldn't know grade-one hard northern wheat from a bowl of corn flakes." I paused again. "Yet they harvest your crop. They do the harvesting, not you, you stubble-jumpers. Oh sure, sure—you get to do all the work. Lucky for you. All they do is the banking."

People were crawling up on the corral rails to hear me better. They were standing on car fenders and car roofs, just to get a better look. Johnnie Backstrom was wound up and going. Even the cowboys were listening. The very bucking horses and the wild steers were listening, by the lovely Jesus.

"The Fifty Big Shots who milk the country dry," I said. "The grabbers from Toronto who never worked a day in their lives. They'd throw us in the jug for stealing a dollar: so they steal a million right out of our pockets—and then they get credit for being fine people. The cream of the crop. The top dogs. They throw big booze parties and tell each other what a dandy crew they are. Yes sir, believe me, folks, I paid a short visit to the East, and I know how you get to be a high-muckie-muck. By stealing and robbing, that's how. To hell with other people's rights and principles. Steal and rob, steal and rob. And to go on being a top dog you have to go on stealing and robbing. From the poor. From innocent bystanders. From the farmers and the hicks out West."

There was a real roar from the crowd on that one, a deep growling roar.

"Oh sure," I said. "They send us a few apples and some salted codfish. And some of the apples are rotten to the core; and worms have beat us to the codfish. But show your gratitude. All they want in return is our farms. Our land and our businesses and our flesh and our tears and our blood. That's all." I gave a big grin to show I was being sarcastic. I have this magnificent set of teeth. Everybody laughed. "We'll get along swell with the mortgage owners. Just don't move their hands out of your pockets. Just be willing and grateful to go on sucking the hind tit."

People were getting riled up. I saw it was time to drive home a few points.

"And now, folks, just so you can show them how grateful you really are, I have a special request to make. Remember this. Old Doc Murdoch, M.D., is a friend of mine. I know him better than most of you will ever know him. I happen to know he comes from the East himself." I paused to let that sink in. There was quite a bit of hooting and hollering; and some of it, I must confess, was in favor of the old Doc. "And of course Easterners," I said, "being the fine square shooters that they are, given any kind of a chance, will look after nothing but our own best interests." I had to break into a grin. "So I have this special request, folks. I want you all to vote come the election. Please get out and cast your votes—for the doctor from Ontario, Murdoch, M.D."

Well sir, I guess they rolled in the aisles. Or they would have, if anybody could have found room to lie down in that huge corral. There was one hell of a mob of people present. They were still crowding in, pushing and using their elbows. They were in stitches. They split their sides laughing.

I was wound up. I mentioned that the one thing worse than a high-muckie-muck is a minion of same. I guess there were a lot of Murdoch supporters in that crowd when I started. I mentioned a few more things about fine old Doc Murdoch, like his big white freshly painted house and how to afford a swanky car. "What are you driving?" I said. I pointed to this man and that man. "What are you driving? What are you driving? Don't tell me a swanky big Chevrolet."

I was wound up and going. Those things came from my heart; they really did. I was mad. I said something about old Doc bringing you into this hellhole mess, but what was he doing to get you out of it? I worked up a sweat.

It was while I was mopping the sweat off my bare forehead that more of the Bible came to my mind. Just like that. "And the fourth angel poured out his vial upon the sun; and power was given unto him to scorch men with fire." I shook my fists at that blazing hammering sky. And then I dropped my voice. I let the hush fall. "We are afflicted," I said. "Afflicted and plagued, my friends. But remember. Let me repeat: remember. If you feel—if you feel in your heart and bowels that the heat can no longer be endured. If you know that the burning must cease. If you agree that we must have back our self-respect, our sense of decency, our hope, our pride—maybe then you should vote, my dear friends—you should vote for the clown."

I blinked against that roaring blaze of sun. I was bareheaded. Hundreds of people were waiting, all quiet, all listening. Farmers and merchants, elevator men and truckers and men with no jobs at all. Men wanting work in the harvest fields. I have this strong profile; craggy. I swung my head this way, that way; I paused as if to listen to myself. "Yes, my good friends. I'm the first to admit it. Johnnie Backstrom is a clown all right. I'm the first to admit it. But at least I can add this. I'm a penniless clown. I haven't been sitting up there in Parliament for twenty years, making clowns of my neighbors and friends." I shook my head. "I've been trying to *earn* a living, like the rest of you. And I haven't done any great shakes of a job. Just ask my wife."

The chuckles were intimate and warm, like those of old companions forgiving a foible. They understood about wives and foibles. Maybe that's what worked on me—that touch of intimacy. That little touch of genuine mercy.

"So I'll add something else," I said. "And a penniless man hates to say this. You'd be bigger clowns yourselves for voting for me—unless it rains by election day."

I choked up in my throat. I've never been quite sure I intended to say that. I got carried away. Everybody kind of choked up. I guess they'd heard about me, word gets around. They'd all had a few laughs at my expense; and they could have another good laugh, if they wanted to, out there in that dusty hot corral where a clown had just been injured, gored by a mad bull.

Not a one of them could laugh, however. I let the silence hang for nearly a full minute. I was glad my wife wasn't present; she would have had to speak up. Then I said, "My dear, dear friends, if I might call you that, I want you all to have a great time today. Because inside of one week from this moment you'll all have your noses to the grindstone, getting ready to harvest one Jesusly bumper of a crop."

That place just went wild. I'm a big man, standing nearly six-four in my stocking feet, but that crowd picked me up as if I was a bag of feathers. They carried me around inside the corral, shouting and whooping and throwing their hats or whatever came loose, and they busted through the corral gate and carried me out to where all the good food was piled up and the booths were set in rows. They threw me in the air and damned near broke every bone in my body when they couldn't hold me coming down; but they set me up on my feet and somebody whipped a micky out of the rags he called his trousers and said have some pain killer, and, may all teetotalers roast in hell, I had it. I was dying of thirst after all that talking. I was half-embarrassed to return the remains.

But I almost got knocked over again by people pushing more bottles at me.

"That hind-tit speech of yours," a fellow said, "was the best speech I ever heard in my life."

"Amen," somebody said.

That's what they called it, my hind-tit speech. They all agreed it was a ripper.

Then the cowboys let a dozen wild cows into the corral and the milking contest was on, one man trying to hold a wild cow's head while another tried to get a little milk into a pail. Everything was getting into the pails but the milk. There were some people caught in the corral along with the cows, and their big job was to get out alive. You might say all hell and damnation just busted loose.

"Follow me," I shouted as loud as I could. Just those two words. That whisky was delicious. I was dying of thirst. I was standing there in the middle of a crowd that was so packed I couldn't budge an inch. "Follow me," I shouted.

"We're following," somebody shouted back.

For some reason, people started handing me free food. I have no idea who got stuck for the bill. I was given a whole graham-wafer flapper pie, not a slice missing, which I lit into right on the spot. It was a tribute to me, a sign of affection. I couldn't resist. After that talk, I was starving. The whisky and the pie and the cobs of corn all went down together. I consumed. Yes sir, I consumed—pineapple squares and strawberry shortcake, Dutch apple pie and hot dogs with raw onions and whisky and ice cream and sour-cream raisin pie and affection and love and saskatoon pie and generosity and deference and admiration and adulation. I consumed and I consumed. I have a huge capacity, there was no filling me up; I was starving and I ate. I was bottomless. I devoured.

And let me tell you the saddest part—in the end it was the same old story once again.

HOWEVER, I am not the sort of man who would let on that he is undergoing an ordeal. I demonstrated verve and zip. I ate with obvious relish. That stampede had been standing still compared to what it was doing now. I was good for business. I simply could not remain motionless, I had to begin walking; people followed along to listen or just to get a look. Bad manners or good, I occasionally spoke with my mouth full. I was agitated and occasionally took great strides.

Men were pitching baseballs at six bowling pins set up in a pyramid. " Triple your money," the barker said. I was dying to pick up one of those baseballs and really hurl it; a fellow handed me one ball. With one deadly pitch I cleared the table of pins, and unless you are a rube you know the pins are deliberately placed so as to make that feat practically impossible. "Keep your money," I said. When the applause began I raised my hand; it stopped and I walked on to the dart booth. I picked up a dart and flung it; pop went a balloon. Another dart; bang, another pop. I accepted the kewpie doll; I cradled it in one arm, people smiling, following me as I walked: I handed the doll to a man who was guarding the handle of a sledge hammer. I swung the hammer. Gong went the bell. More applause. I gave the cigar to a lady who had let out a little shriek. More laughter.

And then the egg-throwing—my God, those people hurled eggs at the face sticking through the stained old bed sheet as if they expected to destroy Satan himself. I passed up the chance to give it a try; I might have killed that old man. I refused to toss baseballs into a tub. I might have dropped rings onto coins on a table, but people were telling me their difficulties. I found myself listening. The men at the crown-and-anchor wheel—the wheel went spinning hard and then it slowed down and made a clicking sound and stopped, jumping one more notch at the last second, and the silent old woman swept the coins off the crowns and anchors and diamonds and clubs—and the men looked at me as if I should do something. But I don't gamble. I stopped when I got married. I stuffed a hot dog into my mouth hardly bothering to bite it in half.

All those people were paying attention to me, watching and sometimes talking, telling me their problems. And I actually found myself listening; I who am not the world's best listener. I heard about wells going dry; about the slough holes drying up and leaving the cattle without water; the land starting to blow in the slightest wind, whole farms drifting off to Saskatchewan in the wind. It was frightening to listen.

A lot of people wanted to treat me. Both that and talk to me. We were very busy there in the middle of the stampede grounds, making arrangements; a lot of people wanted me to come give talks in their local schools and dance halls. In skating arenas and churches and curling rinks and barns. To study groups, even. Everywhere. Some men right on the spot organized a committee. I was flooded with requests and needed assistance. I was making a list of places to go during the next week, on a little pad I carry, and at the same time I was trying not to refuse any drinks, which would have appeared discourteous and somehow a betrayal on the part of a man of such great appetites. I was very busy.

So when word came that the clown had died, I was pretty well loaded. But I wasn't drinking simply for fun; anything but that, I can assure you. Dr. Lipinski sent for me. He sent word via Helen Murdoch, of all people; he wanted me to handle the funeral arrangements.

I was extremely busy. So I had to send word back, via Helen Murdoch, whose quiet face showed no emotion, suggesting that he contact the other undertaker.

Taking great strides, as was my wont, I came to the gate; I didn't turn around. The men at the gate, their cowboy hats all dust now, stepped back and nodded. Perhaps they'd left the gate to come listen. I went striding out through the open gate and onto the highway and made a right turn. And still a lot of people followed; I was genuinely surprised. The finals were beginning in the big corral; the main events of the day would soon commence, with a lot of prize money at stake.

I went straight to the beer parlor. It was a relatively short walk, but a long enough haul for a man as lonely as I was. Yes sir, I was suddenly lonely. I hustled and hurried, taking great strides, but I had time to notice the six grain elevators standing empty and tall in a row along the railways tracks. The boxcars off on a siding, waiting for grain, their doors open so you could see clean through. Clean through to the empty sky beyond.

I expected to find a lot of company in the beer parlor. One usually does. And what happened?

That goddamned walleyed farmer was the first person to greet my eyes. The one person who should have departed. He was supposed to have departed early in the morning, while cops and mortgage fore-closers are sound asleep. People were saying good-by already when I left the auction sale, that's how I got away unnoticed, and here he was again. It didn't seem decent. I should say right off that he was drunk.

Money wouldn't buy a chair in that beer parlor. It was jammed to the rafters; the tables almost disappeared under heaps of bodies. Smoke shut out the light, and the stink at first was breath-taking; the stench of spilled beer and cigarettes and sweating people, some of them cowboys; customers jam-packed into a swarming room. It took your eyes a minute to adjust, after the glare outside on the sidewalk. The noise was deafening; I don't know how I managed to hear that farmer when he spoke. He was all dressed up in new blue denim bib overalls with not a patch on them. He had got a haircut; all that was really familiar was his crooked eye.

"Bring this man a beer," he said, meaning me, obviously; he was speaking to a slinger. To one of the four slingers trying to maneuver loaded trays of beer and tomato juice through that utter chaos. The slinger made his way to the table and bent close and the farmer said he wanted to buy me a drink. I had my chance right then to escape; I'll never understand it; somehow I was drawn to that farmer's table. A lot of people following me couldn't get into the beer parlor at all, it was that crowded. They were shouting about it at the door, trying to get past a fat guy who just pushed his belly into the doorway and stood there.

Yet the farmer waved one arm, and as if by magic there it was, an empty chair right beside him. I sat down. "Bring this man a beer," the farmer said, shouting this time, right into the slinger's ear. The slinger still cocked his head as if he hadn't quite heard; he was trying to hear and balance a tray of empties at the same time.

The farmer cupped his hands to his mouth. "I want to buy every-body a drink."

I must have looked astonished; I know the slinger did. I was watching his face. The place was absolutely jammed. But the farmer dug into his new overalls and pulled out a roll that wasn't big, but at least it was a roll. I had forgotten that money could be anything but folded. He peeled off a twenty and pushed it into the slinger's free hand; the slinger was gone like a shot.

The farmer waved his fistful of loot under my nose. "I'm spending the money I made on that Model-A."

Sarcastic bastard. I felt like telling him what to do with his free beer; I should have told him. But my throat was parched. After my big speech, I was a walking drought.

"You are a horse's petunia," he said.

"Now wait a minute," I said.

"A fake and a fraud," he said. "A cheap chiseler."

"I'd like to explain," I said.

"A meathead," he said. "And a farthead."

"A fathead," I corrected.

"A farthead," he said, "by Harry."

That was too much. I cannot abide that word. My patience was stained to begin with. "You were lucky," I said.

"The luckiest man alive," he said.

"Consider," I said. "Just think about it. What if that little unwashed pipsqueak comes back for his car? You'd be in a hell of a fix, wouldn't you, if he showed up on your doorstep demanding his automobile?"

"I haven't got a doorstep," the farmer said. "The goddamn prophet hasn't come back."

"You don't know how I argued with my conscience," I said. "It was a steal—getting a car in that condition for such a good price. But I couldn't do it. Goddamnit—" I just stopped talking. It was hard to talk in all that noise. I tried to let the matter rest.

I wanted to forget the whole subject. I really did. Because I'll tell you something. This is hard to say: but I wanted that Model-A. I wanted it badly. I mean, I wanted to be extravagant once in my life and get away with it. Like a stampede clown, I wanted to duck into my barrel, just in the nick of time. Just once I wanted to say, well, that was fun. That was great sport. But no, instead of that it was the old misery and woe again. No wonder I turned out to be an undertaker; I was born headed in that direction. It was my fate.

"Goddamnit," I continued, "that little bugger of a prophet had it all wrong. She didn't end. The old world didn't end after all."

"The world didn't end," the farmer repeated. He straightened up and put away his money; then he leaned toward me again. He was visibly impressed. His mouth puckered in puzzlement. He was astonished. "It's remarkable," he said. "You know—when I think about it—by Harry, I believe I thought it would."

"Common sense," I said. "My common sense told me the world wouldn't end today."

The slinger was banging down glasses on the table, slopping beer everywhere; he was in a great hurry. The farmer and I raised a glass each and clinked them as if we were trying to smash them to bits.

"Here's to the girl on the hill," the farmer said.

I had already started to drink, so I nodded. I took one mammoth swallow and as usual found nothing in the glass but its bottom; up above my nose, there it was, the old glass bottom, chipped and stained.

"It didn't end," the farmer said. He was staring into his own empty glass. "By Jesus, wouldn't that knock you flat on your can." He caught at the slinger's white jacket. "Give us two more, bud."

That farmer was a liberal spender; he shelled out another twenty cents. But he didn't lift his full glass. "Maybe it should have," he said. "Maybe it should have just stinking well ended."

I was moved to compassion. I had to say something nice to that man. "I hate to see you go," I said, "you're an asset to the community."

"That mortgage company," he said, "will be scouring the woods." He shook his head and paused to consider. "I have a lot of friends here," he added.

I had no choice but to reply: "I owe you for that Model-A," I said.

"Forget it," he said.

"No," I insisted. "Could I sign an IOU or something?"

"Forget it," the farmer said.

We were both quite drunk. Also, I think some people were under the impression that I had bought the round for the house; beers bought in return began to arrive at our table. We were pretty well corked, that farmer and I. To state the bald truth, we were stewed to the gills. But still I was sober in a way. I was sober enough to want that farmer to say something nice, something consoling.

Hell, I'm only human. I argued with him. I wanted forgiveness. Pure and simple, I wanted that farmer to forgive. Forgetting and forgiving are two different things. "I'm the kind of guy," I said, "who never forgets."

"Just once," the farmer said. "Forget the whole stinking mess. It was a mistake."

"Never," I insisted.

By this time the farmer was bent to within a foot of my face. "You persistent ox," he said. "By Harry, I somehow remember—"

Just then a new keg was tapped. It's a sound I generally applaud. On this occasion, everyone applauded. It's a great sound. Especially in hard times—it has the rush of prosperity about it. Whoosh—

"To Johnnie Backstrom!" somebody shouted.

I raised my hand briefly. I should have felt elated. But I was mortally depressed. It was unbearable. "It's unbearable," I said to the farmer. "Did you see that clown this afternoon?"

He was arranging our free beers in columns on the table.

"Funniest guy I ever saw," he said.

"He sure was," I said.

"Wasn't he a scream, though?" the farmer said. He pushed me another beer, watching my face with his strange look. I glanced away: the whole beer parlor was a shambles and chaos, the drawer in a perfect fever, pulling his chrome handles, setting up the beers; the slingers sailing away with loaded trays, the customers waving and shouting.

"He was a scream," I said.

"A shame he got killed the way he did," the farmer said.

"Looked like a young guy," I said.

"How's that?" the farmer said.

You couldn't hear yourself think.

"I said, he looked like a young guy. Maybe in his thirties."

"Sure did," the farmer said.

It was entirely unbearable. That clown was something I couldn't forget. The place was so noisy we both gave up talking for a while. Silly things came to my mind—like whatever happened to his hat? Or what will they bury him in, not in a clown's costume? Professional problems came to my mind. I'd lean back in my chair sometimes, a habit which I have probably because of my size making me feel cramped, and people were talking about either me or the clown. I don't know which of us created more excitement. Hundreds of people had seen that clown get killed, and they were one up on those who hadn't; the people who missed it were kicking themselves.

I became completely depressed. A great deal of time had gone by. Also, I was nearly incapable of standing up; but I made it to the men's only and back, and just as I was sitting down the farmer suddenly bounced clean out of his chair.

"I've got it!" he said. "I remember. Now I know it. I finally placed you, by the old Harry."

"I'm Backstrom," I said, "candidate for public office—"

The farmer grinned. He sat down in his chair again, carefully, as if it might try to dodge him. "You pitched ball for Notikeewin."

"I certainly did," I said.

"You pitched a no-hitter," he said.

"You're telling me," I said. For a rare moment I felt expansive. "I could have played that game with nobody out in the field. I could have played with the infielders blindfolded."

"I was the last batter," the farmer said. "The twenty-seventh batter."

I seldom remember the faces of the men I pitched to. Their knees and shoulders were my concern. "Then you should know," I said.

"You were damned lucky," he said.

"I was dammed good," I said. "I was on that day. Nobody could touch me."

"Until the last batter came up," he said.

"Last batter hell," I said. "I was sent for that day."

"Until that curve didn't break," he said.

"That last pitch was my fastball," I said. I helped myself to a beer. "That was my steamroller. My cannon ball. That was my waltzing tornado."

"That was an inside curve that didn't break," the farmer said. "I could have pounded it out of the ball park."

"You should have," I said. "You'd have tied the game."

"You're damn right I should have," the farmer said. "I might have taught you a lesson. But I kind of liked the big dumb scared kid who was out there on the mound, throwing his heart at us. He was goddamned good—up until the last pitch."

"He was goddamned good all the way," I said.

"I should have swung," the farmer said. "I damn right should have swung. I nearly broke both wrists holding back. But I had watched that blushing big hick kid for nine innings, scratching his crotch and kicking his toes against each other, and by then I was on his side. So I let the umpire yell, strike three."

"You were fanned," I said. I slammed down my beer glass. "Strike three all right. You couldn't see it. You didn't see that damned ball go by. You stood there waiting for the pitch. Lucky for you you could hear. That was my sidewinder special, my invisible whiz. You stood there blinking. You were still waiting for the pitch when the umpire yelled, 'Strike three, you are out!'"

Apparently I threatened to hit that farmer. At least, some people got that impression; they were sitting on the other side of my table. Five or six men grabbed me and tried to pin my arms back.

I could have whipped that farmer with one hand in my hind pocket. I really could have.

Maybe I had been a little loud. I had been drinking. I had been pouring it into my capacious belly, picking up glasses off the table, one in each hand. No one could possibly keep track; the slinger himself, the man who came over to see what the ruckus was, he said his damned arms were aching just from hauling it.

"This horse's petunia," the farmer said. He motioned toward me. "This farthead is trying to buy a car off me. He wouldn't hurt a fly. He couldn't possibly fight his way out of a wet paper bag. Just let him go and he'll fall down."

I sat in my chair; what else could I do? I am a big man; a big man gets no credit for whipping his inferiors. I had to endure that kind of provocation. I had to pretend I was a friend to that liar and thief. Pick on your own size, people would say.

"I wouldn't buy a car from you," I said, "if you were giving away Cadillacs at a dollar each."

I shouted a little more like that. But the fact remains: I had to pretend six men could hold me. That's why I put my head on the table; I cradled my huge head in my own arms. Maybe I slept a little, I don't quite recall. Maybe I brooded on my new knowledge. I was a beer bottle flung into darkness. A cob bereft of corn. A peanut shell. Maybe I brooded on my grief, I don't quite remember. But the fact is undeniable: I did not stir.

THANK God for the dance, that's all I can say.

Along toward 10 P.M. I opened one eye; the eye that was higher as I lay on my left ear. My neck was getting sore. Three figures were addressing me. At first I took them for three old ladies; you could hardly see for smoke in that beer parlor. Three old ladies, bobbing and smiling. But that mistake, unlike every other one I've made, didn't last. I recognized the three men who rode in the hearse with Jonah and me, in from Coulee Hill. Oh show me the way to go home, I remembered. I'm tired and I want to go to bed.

They shouted all together, the three of them: they made me understand I was being sent for. They were a delegation. They elaborated: people wanted me to come dance the opening dance. People were waiting. The orchestra was waiting.

I can say in all modesty that that was quite an honor. Just like the bride and groom at a wedding dance—though at my own, alas, I was pronounced unable to perform because of something I had unwittingly consumed.

I had no choice but to head full tilt for the community hall.

My wife, as I may have mentioned, did not accompany me to the stampede. She was, in addition to being very pregnant, slightly upset about the two fenders and my pounding like a maniac at four-thirty in the morning right below our bedroom window. I was alone when I entered that hall; I couldn't go out on the floor and do a jig by myself. I would have looked utterly ridiculous.

But as I walked into the hall I noticed Helen Murdoch in the crowd, clinging to the arm of What's-his-name Lipinski. I walked right across the open floor, not once hesitating, across the new sprinkling of corn starch, and I bowed and asked her for the first dance. I have this instinct, sometimes, for just the right thing. Everyone applauded. I looked like a really good sport, offering to dance with my opponent's daughter. I looked big-hearted, generous; a man without rancor. She could hardly refuse.

I guess that's how it all began. You know—beginnings and endings. The old confusion.

For one thing, I am no slouch of a dancer. In fact I am pretty good at just about anything from a schottische to a French minuet, in spite of my ungainly size. But the dancing of Miss Helen Murdoch, daughter of my worthy opponent, made me grope for a descriptive term; I came up with heavenly. And I am not a man who uses language in a reckless fashion.

The heavenly Miss Murdoch, though unable to attend in person, had heard about my speech in the stampede corral. She had been informed, or, more accurately, misinformed. "What kind of underhanded lies have you been telling about my father?" was her way of opening the conversation.

There I was, just beginning to revive in spirit, just beginning to straighten up, and a boot in the knackers again. I twirled her around once or twice, my eyes trying desperately to focus while I twirled. And I said to my eyes, why focus? Why focus, eyes? I said. What indeed do you get to see when you focus?

What do I see in this world, a man six-four in his stocking feet? Consider. Balding heads, mostly. Dandruff, that's what I see. Some day just spend a few hours looking down on the tops of heads. Hair thinning, hair falling. Hair chopped and burned and greased and dyed. Hair combed sideways over bald spots. Human vanity at its worst. Human dreams thwarted and gone. That's what I see, all around me. I am cursed; a man with a fine head of hair of my own, all I get to see is the various and sundry afflictions of the human scalp. That's what I saw as I twirled. I'm a great twirler when I dance.

But I had to answer. I am certainly not a liar; but I chose not to dwell on the obvious.

"A man had been killed," I explained.

"Did my father kill him?" she said. "Was he anywhere near? Did you have to make a speech?"

"We eulogize the dead," I said. "It's a fine custom."

"Why did you attack the living?"

"I merely pointed out a few flaws in the whole rotten stinking setup. A man had been killed. He didn't just die, he was killed dead."

"Did my father kill him?" she said.

"A poor innocent clown," I said, "had the life ripped out of him by a black bull." And then I burst out unexpectedly: "No, Helen. No. Your father didn't kill him. At least not all by himself. And nor did the bull, H.P. Because we all killed him. All of us there, wanting to be amused. Wanting to be entertained. All of us wanting to be tickled and rubbed and scratched in the armpits and vastly titillated. We all killed him, just as sure as he is stone cold dead."

She actually missed a step for a second or two, and I've been told I'm very easy to follow. I'm a good leader. The orchestra was playing a lively piece, the pianist bouncing on her stool, the drummer drumming with his whole body while people tapped their toes; I'd estimate a crowd of four hundred and fifty, with people still flooding in, men women and children surrounding that dance floor and watching in something that resembled rapture.

While I had nothing to do but suffer. "Wouldn't it be nice," I said, "to turn a knob and shut off the human mind? But no. I have to go on thinking. I remember, and I can't forget, H.P. Not just the clown himself. But the crowd watching. The crowd that killed him. Oh, dance on, young lady. Kick up your happy heels. Yes indeed. Yessiree. That clown danced too. He danced for that crowd. Not for the bull. For the crowd, he danced. And we're dancing too, Helen. You and me. For the crowd. We're kicking up our heels, showing our spirits. Make the bastards laugh. Make them giggle and grin. And if you really want them screaming, remember something else: the dead kick up their heels too."

"Johnnie, Johnnie." She was shaking her head.

I thought for a second I was twirling her too hard. I started to apologize.

But then her whole lovely body yielded up close to mine. Her living body, soft and firm.

Great smoking balls of fire.

I mean—somehow I got the feeling that a lump was in her throat; she wanted to smile and cry at the same time. It left her speechless.

I know the feeling. It's a terrible feeling, I know. We were out there in the middle of a dance floor with nearly five hundred people watching and she raised her head and gave me a confused generous warm loving smile that would have bowled over a bigger man than John J. Backstrom, Undertaker.

Her eyes were sad and shining at the same time. Her lips, that beautiful mouth; it wanted to smile and it wanted to talk.

My indignation at all the world turned right there on the spot into lust. Pure lust. I have read enough chapters and verses to recognize that phenomenon when I meet it. I held her in my powerful arms; I had to refrain from crushing in what was almost an embrace her full high breasts, her perfumed hair, so glittering dark, her ribs—Words fail me.

I wanted that woman.

Helen Murdoch is over five-nine and just a shade what most men would call on the voluptuous side. Mary Magdalene be remembered, my throat strangled up tight, my chest contracted. I should have held her a yard away, just to avoid embarrassment; but instead my right hand was within an ace of seizing her buttocks. "What," I said, "did that young punk of a stethoscope-lover mean, sending you to talk to me about the corpse? His idea of a joke?"

Women sometimes like a man to act possessive. I twirled her around, almost lifting her up.

"It was my idea," she said.

"Your idea?" It was my turn to miss a step. I could count my missed steps on the fingers on one hand, but that was the worst. I swear I heard a few people giggle.

"I drove Dr. Lipinski's car to the hospital when he had to ride with the clown, and then after—I knew you hadn't done any business in a few days."

Lipinski is one of these young punk good-lookers with lots of expensive suits and the ink still wet on his diploma. I've never liked him; I prefer men of experience. The school of hard knocks, I always say, is the only real school. It's the only teacher.

"I'll get by," I said. Her point was irrefutable. Business had not been brisk. I felt very guilty about not taking the job; it would have been a cash transaction. "I'll win this damned election hands down, with all due apologies to your father. Who needs money?"

"You're beautiful," she said.

How does a man reason with that kind of logic? It was a non sequitur. I opened my eyes and there were hers, maybe nine inches away, not seeing anything but my silly craggy face. After that I could find absolutely nothing to say.

Sometimes I know beforehand that I'm going to utter a remark, something I'll live to regret, and yet I go ahead and utter it. I had the identical experience when Elaine Burkhardt of the great Burkhardt clan, implement dealers, told me that she, as she so cleverly phrased it, had not fallen off the roof. A reference, apparently, to the malfunctioning of her menstrual cycle. Elaine Burkhardt, on that memorable occasion, did not bat an eye while John J. felt an overpowering need to burst into tears.

"Not me, you," I said. To Helen. "You are the most beautiful creature in all of God's creation."

So of all things, she stopped smiling. Little H.P. And before I could crack a joke or anything, the music ended. The orchestra was suddenly playing its signature, shave and a haircut, six bits, and before I could decide what to do about what could become an embarrassing situation, the crowd was applauding. Helen stood near me; before I could speak another remark, something about another dance later maybe, the music began again and four hundred and fifty souls, nearly five hundred, began trying to dance in an area that was meant for seventy-five couples. And something like two hundred men were asking Miss Helen Murdoch for the next dance please.

I was left standing alone in the middle of the floor, dozens of couples swirling around me, dozens of heels snapping at me like the teeth and jaws of a pack of dogs. And I deserved it.

Old Murdoch meant well; he always meant well every time he gave me one hour's worth of free advice on how to avoid failing Latin or how to do better by not playing baseball night and day or how to stay out of an early grave by not terrifying fathers about the condition of sundry maidenheads. He meant well. He always tried to joke when he counseled me; as a result his counsel always sounded funny.

I stepped outside briefly with a couple of strangers who said they had a micky in their car, which they did. We killed it; and I excused myself. Then, at eleven-thirty, just before midnight supper, a caller stepped up onto the stage with the orchestra and shouted, "Fill up the floor for a square dance."

I was in a corner talking politics to an elderly gentleman who had said to my face that the man wasn't alive who could beat Duncan Murdoch. I was contradicting that same gentleman when I became dimly aware that the caller was adding: "Ladies' choice, folks. This one is ladies' choice."

That's a custom in this vicinity; one dance in the course of the evening is ladies' choice, and generally it's a worthy custom.

I have quite a flair for square dancing. I once picked up three dancers while doing swing like thunder—you know, when the caller says, Ladies bow and gents bow under, hug 'em up tight and swing like thunder—and I swung them all off the floor and turned around three times without putting them down. I might confess that I had a sore back for a week; but the people who witnessed the performance never forgot it. My wife claims they were petrified with fear.

It took a good five seconds for the avalanche to begin. They claim in the mountains you can do that; you can start an avalanche by shouting. The caller shouted through his megaphone, silence followed, and then the buzz and rumble began.

As I say, I was in a corner talking to this old gent who wouldn't listen to my logic. I turned when I heard the peculiar noise; and already it was too late. It was too late entirely. I had no chance whatsoever to escape. People who say I made no effort to escape are entirely mistaken; I saw it was vain to try and escape.

First of all a mere dozen or so women approached me, middle-aged women, asking me politely if I'd care to dance. That's what you say when you approach someone at a dance in Burkhardt or vicinity. Would you care to dance? Or, This dance, please. One or the other. These women in general were saying, Would you care to dance?

But I hesitated to choose, confused as I was by the embarrassment of riches. The wives of men prominent in the community were now asking me, Johnnie Backstrom, to dance a square dance. And even as I hesitated another sound arose; the sound of an additional thirty or forty women who had also, apparently, heard that I was an A-1 dancer. The wife of the mayor of Burkhardt, along with a bank manager's wife, found themselves elbowed in the back by three or four younger women. Women my own age or perhaps younger, some of them single.

It was all well and good, this show of interest, but they had me in a corner. These fifty or sixty women were laughing and shouting now. Raising their voices:

"Johnnie Backstrom, dance with me."

"Please, Johnnie, me," some of them were saying.

"Let it be me, Johnnie."

"Will it rain tonight, Johnnie?"

And laughter.

"Will it pour rain tonight?"

I was in a corner, as I say. And the more those women shouted and pushed, the more I became uncertain as to whom I might select as partner. I immediately perceived that any particular choice would turn a lot of other women sour. I saw I couldn't act rashly.

They were screaming now; maybe sixty women were pushing, waving to get my attention, calling, trying to get past the women in front. The women in front were hesitating, somewhat embarrassed, but the women behind them were pushing and pulling at each other, getting red-faced and rowdy. Somewhere in the background the caller was calling as loud as he could, "One more couple over here in the corner."

The policeman must have been out having a drink with some of his friends. I'd noticed a policeman in attendance earlier. I wanted to shout for help to some of my acquaintances, but I could see nothing before my eyes but women. Over their heads I could see, distantly through the smoky air, the stage and the caller and the pianist beginning to bounce on her stool as she tried out an unheard chord and the drummer turning a little knob or something and drumming with one hand and trying to listen.

Just then a woman touched me. A woman reached out and caught my little finger. As she did so she was yelling my name, Johnnie Backstrom, as if I were a good mile away.

And all of a sudden twenty women were grabbing at me, not too careful where or how they took hold. I had a terrible impulse, an embarrassing impulse, to cup one hand over that part of my anatomy which I least wanted to see mutilated.

I have these huge hands. But they were useless. Once I raised a fist to push back and I immediately punched a very large breast. I didn't quite know how to go about defending myself.

Obviously, I was in a tight predicament. A woman jerked at my tie, threatening to choke me. My best tie. Another woman, her blouse having become unbuttoned during the activities, got hold of my belt: I couldn't be certain whether she intended to pick me up or to take off my pants. It was a nip-and-tuck situation.

I yelled. What was there to say? I yelled just as loud as I could.

The women yelled right back. They were laughing and screaming and waving now. They had hold of me; I could hardly move. I yelled and they yelled right back, one hundred women or thereabouts drowning out my cries for assistance.

I kept trying to see over their heads. Standing nearly six-four as I do, I was able to see over their heads in spite of their large numbers. I felt I was the last man left on the face of the earth. But at least I now spotted a friend. I saw Helen Murdoch standing just inside the doorway. And then I saw she had her left arm hooked into the arm of that pale grinning idiot, What's-his-name Lipinski. They and three other couples had formed a square of their own. I saw them all watching me, especially my friend Helen, and her miserable excuse for a partner.

I suppose what happened was, I panicked.

I've never lost a fight in my life, not even against insurmountable odds. One night in a whorehouse in Buffalo three colored gentlemen tried to roll me and I pitched all three of them one by one through a third-storey window. I panicked now, as I say. Suddenly I was charging, taking great strides, dragging after me a dozen women who had hold of my coat, my shirt, my arms, my belt, my tie—whatever they could get a grip on.

I don't believe I exaggerate. I was somewhat confused at the time; that I confess. But I believe to the best of my knowledge I recount events as they occurred.

I got to Helen Murdoch and on an impulse I picked her up in my arms, a drowning man clutching at a straw. I held her up in my hands over that crowd. It was no use trying to speak. I held her up and all those women could see I had chosen.

I thought they might all fall back; but that was not to be the case. They had got started screaming and they didn't want to stop.

"Johnnie Backstrom!" they screamed. At the top of their lungs.

"We want Johnnie!" they kept shouting.

They were chanting now, voices falling together here and there. "We want Johnnie! We want Johnnie!"

I turned and went through the door, preceded by my large feet, forgetting to put down Helen before I departed. The darkness came as a welcome relief. The first shock of night and the sudden silence. For the darkness arrested those shouting women. They looked out from the doorway, past the two unhinged doors, and they might, judging from the way they stopped, have come to the edge of a high cliff or the shore of a deep ocean.

Like when you stand on deck at night, on the deck of a laker, and know what lies one step beyond: one step beyond out into the hushed darkness.

Suddenly the noise was gone. I put Helen down. We looked around, our eyes adjusting, finding a detail here and there. Cars were parked on both sides of the street and angle-parked in the middle of the street. In one car a cigarette glowed; a girl stalling for time. Let's have a cigarette, they say. In another a match or a lighter flared. A car door opened and closed somewhere in the yielding darkness as if no hand had been called upon to act. But people, I knew, were drinking, necking. Fumbling in the back seats of cars, saying no and meaning yes, struggling to make the old contact, moaning in the darkness and lying still and feeling comfort and joy and guilt and sorrow and shame and fear. Having a good time, as I had recommended.

And then we were walking, Helen and I. Perhaps we had been walking for quite a while. But not for too long, for the voice of the caller found us now, came clear from the hall: "Allemande left to the old left hand."

"Lipinski will miss you," I said.

That was a foolish thing to say. But Helen had the good sense to avoid a reply.

We kept on walking.

"Birdie in the cage," the caller was shouting. But already his voice was beginning to fade. The sound of the piano was gone; only the cry of the fiddle persisted, and the fainter throbbing of the drum.

As I say, I sometimes say something foolish and then compound the folly by adding further foolish things.

"That square will be incomplete without you," I said.

Then I noticed that we could see the stars. Which shouldn't have surprised me, I suppose; there were no clouds to hide them. But we kept walking, my arm around Helen, and then Helen's arms sliding up from my belt, her hand touching, softly touching my back. The pandemonium faded behind us. The wooden sidewalk drummed dully beneath our feet and then we came to the end of the sidewalk and our feet made no noise and distantly, distantly the caller was calling through his megaphone, "Birdie fly out and crow fly in," and then a moment or so later, trying to make himself heard over a noise we could not hear, "Crow fly out and give birdie a swing"; and then another moment later you couldn't hear the caller at all and Helen and I, we were alone on the edge of town, the first odor of fields assailing our nostrils, the first hint of dust and sage, neither of us speaking; and we turned without speaking and walked, taking long strides together, striding strongly; and we entered the stampede grounds free of charge, the booths empty, the poplar trees stuck in the ground in neat dead rows, the grass pulverized, the steers and the bulls and the calves for roping and the milk cows for milking not too far away, giving off a faint hint of their presence, the old cows softly lowing, the horses unseen pawing the ground; and Helen still hadn't spoken and my hands, my huge fumbling hands, were touching her breasts, then touching the flat of her belly, her pretty behind, and I believe she was saying something; I picked her up in a great hug and her lips touched my ear, my great hands not ever satisfied; and I kissed her mouth and her eyes and her dark hair and everything, I had to kiss all her beauty, I had to and didn't ask and she let me, her hand touching my head and my face and lips while I kissed, her skin musky, warm in the cooling night; and we were on the ground, on the dry broken grass, and the dust and nothing mattered, not the grass sticking to my face, not the dust on the knees of my best pair of pants, not that one cry I gave, not the stars; nothing at all mattered; nothing.

WEDNESDAY
FOLLOWING

LET ME SAY I was a roaring success for the six days from that stampede to the following Wednesday. For six days I was a busy and laboring man indeed, shaking hands until my arm ached, talking until my whole esophagus cried out for drink. I was in demand. But Wednesday came, as predicted, the second last day before the election. Wednesday came, but the inevitable rain did not.

And late on Tuesday night the police abandoned the search for Jonah Bledd's body. Grappling hooks and pike poles and dynamite had not undone the water's close embrace. The cops had sought but had not found. The little kids, tired of waiting, went in swimming again. They squealed at each other, "Guess what I stepped on?"

"A foot," somebody said.

"A thumb," somebody said.

They'd shout and scramble for shore. They scared each other by naming the parts of the human body, which was something I did not understand.

"A kidney."

"An eye."

I may have neglected to mention, Jonah was an R.C. His funeral mass was Wednesday morning. Jonah turned Catholic to marry a quiet lovely girl of that denomination. A woman who struck him as a vision of potential happiness led him to his conversion, and while I counseled against it, plumbing for the sacredness of bachelorhood, he never regretted his conversion. Just as I never abandoned my afore-mentioned position. We enjoyed many a good discussion of the subject, usually over a beer, one of us arguing for joys lost, the other arguing for joys found. Jonah, as you may have guessed, held to the latter position. I personally have always held bachelorhood to be a natural and desirable state, so, as follows, I plunged into matrimony. My own principles have forever been the last thing to offer me guid-ance in life.

Helen Murdoch made me understand what Jonah had done; Helen who comes of Presbyterian antecedents but who on Sunday morning reads the Toronto *Star Weekly*. Finally I saw what that vision was and what it could make a man do, alas. Up until then I had no idea. Up until then Johnnie Backstrom, a born heller with women, had in a sense remained a stalwart virgin. That's a fact.

Her father and I met at the Mass for Jonah Bledd. It is odd that we should have been at a Catholic service, at a funeral for a body that wasn't there; but life is a peculiar medley.

If you have ever attended a funeral at which the body is absent, then you have some idea of how I felt. I was upset. Existence itself had earned suspicion. Tough questions were raised.

The Mass began at ten sharp in Our Lady of Sorrows R.C. Church; Protestants and Catholics alike, a good sampling of the population of Notikeewin, The Wild Rose City, were crowded into that relatively modest wooden structure, that fancy little box of a church. After five days of hard electioneering, before packed audiences in schoolhouses and barns and skating arenas, I was hardly able to contain myself when I saw more than half a dozen people within shouting distance of each other. And here I had to maintain a stoic silence while a young punk of a priest who shaved with a washcloth could say what he pleased.

Sitting in church is a very discomforting experience for me. So I practically do it for a living. For one thing, I have no excess flesh on my posterior, I am muscle and bone. But during a funeral the under-taker can usually hang around the back door; he can go out for a while and stretch his legs while the sermon is on, he can walk to the graveyard and take one last look to make sure everything is in order. Or in my case, sometimes I tinker with the hearse or arrange flowers, if they aren't the kind that make me sneeze. I have to be careful, one sneeze can make a very bad impression. Flowers and cats, especially, bother me.

But on this occasion I had to sit and stand with everyone else; I refused to kneel, I look silly kneeling, I'm too big. It hurts my knees.

The usher had put me in the second-last pew on the right beside old Doc Murdoch. I got there a shade late and apparently the usher didn't know what he was doing. Fortunately, Helen had arrived earlier and was seated about six pews ahead of us. My own dear wife had feigned an upset stomach, a headache and morning sickness, but in fact was not there because of a blind prejudice against the R.C.'s. She is of the opinion that that denomination is much too lax on the subject of bottled spirits. Her father, I may have explained, fell out of an attic window while under the influence and broke his neck. I have always been of the opinion that he pushed himself, to achieve a little piece of mind, be it ever so illusory; but a half-empty twenty-six of Scotch found clutched unbroken in his arms is used as evidence against my often-reiterated proposition. He had very expensive tastes, and left his beloved widow and only child somewhat less than well-heeled—another of the many discoveries I made late in life.

I entered the church, as I say, with head bowed and blindly following an usher, and before I knew it, was seated beside Doctor Murdoch, minion of the Eastern high-muckie-mucks and front for the Fifty Big Shots.

Many were the audiences I had stirred to wrath and indignation at the crookedness of our oppressors, the various tycoons; at the evils of grasping man. And now I was compelled to hear out a priest on the subject of goodness.

I was not the only person who viewed Jonah Bledd as a basically good man. It was a generally shared opinion. He had done everything the recommenders of morality have ever recommended. He lived by the Ten Commandments and when drinking sometimes recited them in lieu of song; he obeyed his wife and children as well as higher powers, paid his debts on time if possible, took care of his health when necessary, enjoyed, as much as is feasible, going to work—and there he was in the middle of the aisle. Or there he wasn't—for he was represented by a catafalque, an empty frame covered over with an expensive black cloth calculated to look like a coffin but fooling no one, least of all an undertaker. I reflected the minute I walked in: if the R.C.'s keep this up, undertaking as an art will vanish from the face of the earth. Undertakers will themselves starve to death, one final refutation of the proposition which is killing them.

There he wasn't, Jonah Bledd, a good man, and a fellow human being in black was solemnly saying his praises. "He was a model for the rest of us," the priest was saying. That much I did hear. I'm not the world's best listener. "A model among men; a model for men." You could tell just by listening; here was a green priest who hardly looked dry behind the ears, celebrating to the best of my knowledge his first funeral.

I'm probably mistaken here in my choice of verbs. A priest celebrates a Mass, that much I know. But does he celebrate a burial Mass? Very odd. But perhaps he should. Perhaps he should. I wanted to poke Murdoch in the ribs and say, I, too, Johnnie Backstrom, am much given to celebration. How would I do for a model, Doc?

To tell you the truth, when I entered that church I saw the usher was going to seat me where I ended up sitting. I saw it coming, and I did nothing to prevent it. Obviously, I wanted to be placed right beside my political opponent, Duncan L. Murdoch. And I wanted to begin the conversation by saying, Well, old Doc, another one got away from you. Another one fled this life you are so determined to maintain. You're slipping, old Doc. They're dying like flies on you.

That would have been an exaggeration, as my finances could bear witness.

"He was a model in his daily life," the priest was saying. A young priest with a white handkerchief stuffed up one sleeve as if he expected any moment to break into tears, either of nervousness or pity. The widow was disconcerting him with her crying. Goodness, apparently, was not much of a consolation. "Let us contemplate his living and his dying," the priest said.

The back of Helen's head, six pews forward, was forever engaging my attention when I should have been looking at the catafalque and the priest and the altar. Helen's head was beautiful, under the silly little black lace scarf balanced so precariously on top of that coiled and lovely black hair.

Black lace was somewhat of an affectation with Helen. I was, the first time, frankly surprised. Generally I have found that women who wear lacy black garments are trying busily to fool themselves; but Helen was an exception. I looked and could not help looking, and again it was misery, not simple joy.

Why? I was asking myself. What? How?

For what reason could a beautiful girl like that be interested in a dumb ox like me?

As I say, sitting in church, I find time to think. I hate the whole process.

And then a frightening answer crossed my mind.

Women have a way of liking undertakers. And maybe—I shuddered so hard the old Doc glanced aside at me—maybe it's because, I've done it, they can say. The ultimate risk. That's a fact. Even when I worked on the boats, a girl would ask me what I did, the way people ask, What do you *do*, and I always said, I'm an undertaker by profession. You're kidding, they'd say. I'm dead serious, I'd say. And instead of fleeing they'd perk up and say, It must be odd. Or they'd say, You don't look the type. And I'd say, What did you expect? And they couldn't answer. They'd say, Well—and they'd pause. At most they'd start saying something about black, and then they'd notice I was wearing black. I always wore something with a little black on it, if it was only socks or a shirt. And their eyes would begin to change. Their touch changed, it really did. An excitement came into the deadest voice. And for a moment there in that church I was afraid I knew why. I've done it, they could say. I've kissed him, I've laid a hand on him, touched him where he lives, gone the limit with him. They could assure themselves after. They could laugh. How horrible; they could laugh aloud. The undertaker. The taker under himself. The most terrible courting.

Think how that insight made me feel. Depressed. But I thought of one or two of the lucky women, and then I began to feel better. Especially a girl in Toronto who was somewhat given to theological speculation. Also a Baptist I met on the back seat of a bus. I was quite a heller in my time. I thought of Helen. There I was, sharing a pew with her father, elbow to elbow with him in the morning, elbow to elbow with her at night.

I felt a stirring right in church at a burial Mass, a return of the old longing, and I was almost embarrassed. Stiff in life; stiff out of it: how can we win? I tried to think of a prayer; I knew praying would help. When we were kids in church, the Lutheran, before my father was killed, and the place was packed with girls all smelling of the perfume they weren't supposed to wear and walking slowing up the aisle, dreaming by Jesus of matrimony, how to avoid a futile demonstration of desire was one of the major problems. I remember, Jonah and I and some other boys had a big argument one day in the outhouse at school. Jonah said praying helped. Pray be damned, I said, let it rage, let it roar. Let it send the buttons flying. I was that way sometimes, I had to disagree with whatever Jonah said.

But this time I would have prayed if I could have thought of a prayer.

, Tear loose all right. Send the buttons flying. Now, I guessed, Jonah's whole body would be tugging at that rope and anchor down where Wildfire Lake was supposed to have no bottom. While the kids far above joked about stepping on a toe, an eye. There it was, cool and light and safe on a hot day like this. A flower in full bloom, the arms and legs like petals rising and moving and falling in the liquid air, the white of the plaster cast a conundrum to perch and pickerel alike. The hair on end.

It was getting stuffy in church, in spite of the gloom. The gloom made it worse. The candles themselves almost guttered out in that box of a church, as if the heat was getting them too. My whole great body was an aching stinking reminder of my own ultimate doom. That depressed me. I hadn't had time to bathe before Mass. Not even down to the belly button, as I sometimes do when in a hurry. I was never getting a decent night's sleep. I had shaved and rushed to church; I hoped the old Doc wasn't being offended. I crossed my arms, trying to hold in my own decay, my decline. My reek.

Good God, life is short. Life is short, short, my body cried. So live, it said. Live, live. Rage, roar.

Undertakers can't think these thoughts. If you once start thinking, you're finished. I thought so hard my erection practically went away. But not quite. It was in that state halfway between heaven and earth when the slightest unknown quantity can tip it in either direction.

Old Doc was breathing heavy beside me. He was tempted to get a little sleep. The talk about goodness wasn't exactly wringing him out. Here I was stung and stabbed by the priest's words, and the Doc took everything in its turn. He didn't flinch at anything.

Well, I thought to myself, the old Doc wouldn't snooze at one of my sermons. He'd flinch and squirm a little. Just let me get up on that altar, young fellow, and I'd have this audience running a finger between its necks and its collars. Let me get into that black outfit of yours, reverend, and you'd hear a sermon for a change. By God, if there's anything that makes an undertaker's life unendurable it's the sermons he has to overhear, and after a while you start having a few ideas of your own. I'd raise both arms up sideways from my body to command silence, the big sleeves falling back to leave my powerful fists bare-knuckled in front of the altar. Bare-knuckled and white with my clenching. And then when the silence came I'd drop them. I'd spread all my fingers, gently, as if to touch a baby's hind end—

Death, I would say. Death, my dear brethren. In the name of the Father and so on. You must die. You *deserve* to die. I deserve to die. Then I'd hesitate. Let that sink in. And after, in a stronger voice, my hands threatening to rise again, threatening to close but not quite making it: but why must the good die? Models be damned. Who wants models? Give them a few tough questions. Why must the good be ripped out of this happy existence? Out of these present joys. I ask you, I ask you. Away from the joys of the daily dawn. Back into darkness, away from the sheer joy of seeing it's all there again, the warm old bed smelling faintly of your own comfort, the open window, the fresh morning sky. From the sheer blissful joy of just stretching a little and then having a quiet scratch. Yes, my dear brethren, I scratch in the morning, I'm human, and my wife shortly thereafter in her limited vocabulary reprimands my humanity. My manhood. But I rise to cups of fresh coffee. To the smell of toast, burnt or otherwise, to gobs of melting butter and strawberry jam and to the question, Why must the good be hammered and nailed into oblivion? Into darkness away from family and friends? From the little children they support and the people they love? By God, that widow wouldn't be crying alone up there in the front pew with five little tots too small to know what was going on. She wouldn't be alone. That congregation wouldn't be sitting there half-embarrassed because a woman was crying her head off. Why? I'd say. I'll tell you why. You and I deserve death. We who will not govern our passions. We who shilly-shally with the temptations of the flesh, the pleasures of the bottle. The useless daily pleasures of bragging and swearing and sleeping late and avoiding work. The jerk-offs. But what about the good man? Then I'd pause. What about the good man? I'd let my arms go slack, my shoulders sloping in a gesture of despair. He doesn't deserve to die. And then in a rising voice again, my shoulders squaring under that black outfit, my basic toughness showing through from under that disguise. But he dies—he is *forced* to die—that one good man is forced to die by a conspiracy of greed and selfishness, by the betrayals of his dearest friends, by the connivings of the constipated rich, by the collaborations of the deceived poor. I wanted to shout in Murdoch's ear; I wanted to jar him out of his old slumbering. He is forced to die, that one good man—he is forced to die—in pain and anguish and misery—he is forced to die by the stinking unholy minions and tycoon high-muckie-muck—

But a bell was ringing. A bell rang, a bell saying, gross, gross, gross. Three little sounds that dinned in my head. Dinned and roared. The old din and roar again.

Gross, gross. My appetites. My longings. My dreams. My deceptions. My fantasies. My bottomless gullet. My grasping huge fists. My insatiable hunger not just for something but for everything. Gross unto death.

And then we were standing. Joints and benches creaked. There I stood, me, Johnnie Backstrom, staring again at Helen Murdoch who stood not six but five pews forward, I counted. I could take them in one leap, I told myself, one mighty leap. There I stood, thirty-three years of age, a full-grown man with an erection in church. Nearly six-four in my stocking feet; my mother's pride and joy. Would we never sit down? Would those hymns go on forever? What could be more useless than my accomplishment of that moment? Consider for one moment.

I had too much time to consider. The organist, somewhere above me, was pedaling hard in a losing fight.

Nothing could be more useless.

And then I remembered something else. I had to buy contraceptives. I hate that job. All my life I've been buying them by the half dozen and hating myself. False economy, for one thing. Why didn't I buy a gross when I was seventeen and avoid a lot of grief? Or a great gross. It's so goddamned humiliating. Holy old terrified testicles. But I didn't have the money. The small buyer is always penalized. The Eastern thieves jack up the prices till a man can't even afford to screw. Consider, by Jesus. I creep into a drugstore, my huge hands beginning to sweat in my pockets, my neck choking in my collar. Imagine, a man my size marching up to a pillar of the community and asking: six French safes please, plain. Sometimes I try to say contraceptives, but I begin to stutter. A very difficult word. Rubbers sounds so crude. Sometimes I wait for a second clerk to appear, the first one having paralyzed me into silence with a glance, and I wait and out comes a gawky pimply kid who has probably been in the back room where they keep them, fondling the merchandise and having dirty thoughts. Or out comes a sweet old lady with an angelic smile. How can she know about such things? Imagine. With a voice like mine, in which it is impossible to whisper. Everyone knows me, to begin with. I'm practically a legend. They look at me, complete strangers, and you can hear them guessing in their little minds, that must be big John Backstrom, what could he want? What could ail a man like that, the picture of health? I get flushed. Scarlet. I'm naturally fair. I feel my throat going dry. My scalp feels too small. Sometimes at the last minute I get buckfever and ask for tooth paste or shoe polish. Always one or the other. My medicine cabinet, all my life, has been full of shoe polish; and I am a man who hates the messiness of shining shoes. Shoe polish or tooth paste. Name a brand and I've got a tube somewhere; my wife once asked me about it. Why all this old tooth paste? she said. I shook my head; and for two days I did nothing but brush my teeth. And all along I wanted contraceptives. Rubbers. Other boys carried them for months on end and I never had any. Or when I get them I'm just as bad. What if I had an accident on the way home, I used to wonder, and got killed with six contraceptives in my pocket? Explain that to your mother. Explain that to your wife. Or five in my pocket. That would drive my wife crazy. I positively hate having to make that particular purchase, yet I am driven to it time and time again by the contingencies of lust and practical necessity. The one time in my life when I said to hell with it, an archangel couldn't get this one pregnant, my bravado was the occasion of an even greater calamity. But on that particular occasion, to tell you the truth, I had not anticipated my own marvelous success. I was caught unprepared. Or actually, I may have had an old one in my wallet, which was in a pocket of my black suitcoat which was lying in the back of the hearse, but I had created the impression that I wasn't the sort of man who would carry that sort of thing, let alone interrupt the good tender natural inclinations of my slightly inflamed love to begin unpackaging and unrolling and disposing of boxes and wrap-pers. A life that becomes a choice of evils is hardly worth living.

I was nervous. The rustle and clatter of life went on endlessly around that empty catafalque. I began to wonder if the Mass would never end. Catholics are usually pretty good in that respect, they know when to quit. But this new priest was slow. You could see the altar boys carrying books around and answering and genuflecting at a terrible pace, but the priest went on as if he was reading Latin for the first time.

I took a prayer book, a daily missal, out of the little wooden rack on the back of the pew in front of me. I checked in the table of contents and flipped to the burial service to make sure the priest hadn't lost his page. My posterior was aching. I had a cramp in my neck; the muscles in my neck and shoulders were beginning to seize and bunch. Also, I was out of position generally on a badly designed church pew amid the knots and ropes that gird the human form beneath the general heading, underclothing.

I who had trouble learning Latin, there I began to puzzle out words of my own free will, without prompting. It was time for the final absolution. The priest came down off the altar with two altar boys and holy water and incense and everything. That moment always moves me. I choke up. What a great thing, final absolution. Just imagine, to be forgiven the punishment due for your sins. What a boon that would be for me. If I thought for a minute they'd grant it to me I'd turn Catholic in a flash, my wife be damned. Something like that makes my dearly beloved's little streak of mercy look like peanuts. Also, she is more forgiving to cats than she is to humans; for humans she believes in a strong dose of justice. Castor oil for the bowels; justice for the remainder. Would she cry at my funeral the way Mrs. Jonah Bledd was crying? I guess not. Not very likely, I can tell you. Don't place any bets, my dear brethren. Your husband has passed away, people would lament. He has kicked the bucket, she would say, and a good riddance. I'm sorry to hear the news, people would say. He had it coming, she would say. Mrs. Johnnie J. Backstrom would rejoice her eyes out. No more combing the house at odd hours in search of hidden mickies and twenty-sixes. No more repairing of damaged fenders outside her window at 4:30 A.M. No more kicks and blows and foul language echoing after her dear cats through the corridors of that warped old edifice she was forever referring to as my dear mother's house. Oh, she could get pious about that dear old mother who had been so slow and reluctant to go to her precious Maker and silencing grave—

But the old Doc sitting beside me had to chime in when I was feeling most strongly. I hate being interrupted when I'm feeling strongly. The Doc raised his head toward my ear and automatically, out of good breeding, I bent down.

"But he killed himself," the Doc said.

I felt stubbornness well up. "He's forgiven," I whispered.

"Except there's nothing under that black cloth to forgive," Murdoch whispered.

I glanced sideways and saw nothing but the Doc's gold teeth. "It doesn't matter," I said.

"What doesn't matter?" he said.

"The catafalque's being empty."

We were whispering.

"The hell it doesn't matter," the Doc said. "He's supposed to be a model."

"He was," I said. "And he's forgiven."

"For committing suicide?"

I began flipping through the missal. I had just seen the relevant passage. The priest had just gone over it, I wanted to read it to Murdoch. I wouldn't show him the English, I'd show him the Latin only. Wipe away, it says—cancel out, scratch off the sins he may have committed through—*per fragilitatem carnis*, it says. I like that. Through the fragility of the flesh. That's good. I who had trouble with Latin. Imagine me trying to study medicine, with all those unlikely names. But the fragility of the flesh, a doctor should know about that. I used to page through the Doc's medical books looking for pictures, and after a while I ended up looking at names. That's a funny thing. That's probably what kept me out of the field, along with certain other problems. I couldn't have given a name to what I knew.

"He is absolved," I said. I couldn't find the passage.

I'll tell you something; my erection was completely gone. That is another of the miracles of this world. I felt shriveled; I felt old. Almost dead, you might say. The Doc was a great fellow, but I felt the way I used to feel after he gave me a lecture on how to live a better life and how to make something of myself. It was that damned square granite face of his.

"He shouldn't have done it in the first place," Murdoch said.

"You can't blame him," I said. "He was so self-satisfied and rich he couldn't contain himself."

The Doc didn't think I was funny. "He had five kids."

"And no job," I said.

"Can he help them now?" the Doc said.

That stopped me for a minute. The priest was about finished; he had to sprinkle holy water right there in front of my eyes, making me feel guilty; he was making a little rainstorm of his own. I glanced at a window; all I could see was colored glass. A man couldn't breathe in that place. It could have been raining cats and dog outside for all you could tell in there. If that priest brought on a rainstorm it would reflect badly on me. "Doc," I said, "you're a great guy. The greatest in the world. But sometimes I'm tempted to say to you, you've got a lot to learn for such a great guy."

"He didn't deserve forgiveness," the Doc said.

I was genuinely surprised at the Doc's attitude. "Go tell the priest," I said. "Maybe it's not too late to cancel the absolution."

"It's our secret," the Doc said.

It's a strange thing. He held out his hand, right there in church, and I shook it. Sort of on the sly. But even while we shook he said, "I don't have to approve. I never will."

"He couldn't take it, I guess," I said.

"Couldn't take what?"

I let go his hand. He had a big hand, like the paw of a bear. "He just couldn't take it," I said.

The Doc gave an impatient snort.

"He couldn't," I said. " The guff, Doc. Jesus, you've been on easy street all your life."

The Doc sort of laughed in my ear instead of saying anything. That patient tolerant insufferable laugh of his. When you own half a bank your laugh changes. I wanted to tell him something. When I was a kid, for instance, I had a recurring dream. I had it over and over. It took a lot of different forms but always ended up the same way. Somehow or other, in each dream, I got hold of some coins. I found them or I won them or I had a job or somebody gave them to me. Or I stole them. I had the dream so often that pretty soon when I dreamt it I knew I was dreaming, so I got wise. I'm going to hang on to this cash real tight, I thought, and when I wake up I'll have it. Morning after morning I woke up with my fingernails cutting the palm of my hand. I woke up with my hand clutched so tight, sometimes I had to use the other hand to open it. "Doc," I said, "did you ever open your hands and find them empty?"

"I never opened them or closed them to use against myself," he said. "Not to tie a knot or to throw an anchor." He brushed the hair out of his eyes. "Not to injure."

I stuffed my hands into my pockets.

The priest was winding things up. There wasn't going to be a last glimpse of the body at the door or a procession out to the graveyard.

Not a chance here for an undertaker to shine, quietly efficient, incon-spicuous. Nothing like that. Just raw old death. Sheer absence.

"Doc," I said, "I hope you aren't above doing a little forgiving in a really exceptional circumstance."

"I'm an honest man," the Doc said. "I only try to be honest, with myself, with others. In my profession. With my friends. In politics."

That was a dirty cut. I wished I hadn't even mentioned the word forgiveness to him. "Defeat is nothing to sneeze at, Doc," I said. "Don't be so proud of yourself."

People were leaving. That young priest had kept us too long, you could tell by the way people hurried.

"I'd never blacken another man's good name," the Doc said, "no matter what he did to me."

We were locked in combat right there, the Doc and I. We were locked in mortal combat, and I swear, that's the first time I realized it. "Doc," I said. "The good die young. The rest of us die messy and hard."

"I'm disappointed," the Doc said. "Johnnie, you've disappointed me. I always think of you as a son. My first-born. I can't help it. I loved your mother deeply. She was a beautiful woman, in her own strange way. So strange, so strange, Johnnie. I guess it is my fate to forgive: but I'm disappointed."

I didn't want to be misunderstood. I could have accounted for everything. But he turned and was out of the pew, going out at the far end. I went after him. To explain, to plead with him; a man some-times has to say things he isn't quite sure he means. What can we be certain of? Doc, I was arguing. I pushed into that crowd and almost ran over three men like pious old ladies, trying to get their fingers into the holy-water fount. Doc, I was yelling in my head, it was all a necessity. The pain is what does it, Doc. I hurried, I shoved.

I elbowed my way, but that crowd was too much for me. They got jammed into the doorway and felt they were outside, apparently, because the menfolk started putting on their hats and nodding to each other, the women started to gossip.

Suddenly I burst through, into the blaze of sunshine just outside the door. The glaring light and the heat. I could feel my whole body wither. It needed moisture, my skin, and it got more sun. My eyes were half-blinded. I reached, I groped for the Doc. I had to explain. And maybe I had to do combat too.

But just as I got hold of his left shoulder a stranger, an elderly man in rags and a few buttons, who obviously hadn't been to church, got hold of the other arm.

"Doc," I said. "Listen."

"Gunn," the other guy was saying. "Remember?"

The Doc didn't hesitate. "Hello, Amos," he said.

"It's my wife," Mr. Gunn said.

"How's she doing, Amos?" the Doc said.

"Not so good, Doc. I think she's failing."

"At her age," Doc said, "it isn't easy to carry a child. You've got to make allowances, Amos."

"No," Mr. Gunn said. "I'm allowing. But something is wrong. My wife won't let on. But she's failing. I drove to town; I need repairs for the pump. But I came to see you, Doc. I've been waiting out here."

"You should have come in," the Doc said.

"Not me." Mr. Gunn looked down at his shabby clothes; he smelled just faintly like a pigpen.

"Let's get out of this crowd," the Doc said. I knew he was supposed to go have dinner with a bunch of lawyers and people like that. He was supposed to address a dinner luncheon in a place that bragged it wouldn't let me in the front door, the stuck-up bastards. I secretly hoped the Doc would have to miss his engagement. "What's the matter, Johnnie?" he said. I was still holding his shoulder; I have such a powerful grip sometimes I don't know my own strength.

It's funny; I didn't answer. I just let go as if I had taken hold of his shoulder by mistake; as if I recognized that this was the wrong man and I was embarrassed.

"Could you see that Helen gets home?" he said.

He disappeared toward a car Mr. Gunn was pointing out with the old straw hat he held in his right hand.

I turned away abruptly; I looked back toward the church, almost falling off a step, which was in need of repair; and Helen was coming through the door, into the sunshine. She blinked in the light, hesitating; and then she smiled at me. I stood motionless; as she clicked by in her high heels, beautiful in that vast crowd, she let her hand touch mine for an instant.

I became electrified. Beauty does that to me. All my whole body burst into a cool glow, I could feel it. I practically forgot the Doc. I was turned on. How did the old Doc do it, create that beauty, while he himself is not much of an object to look at? How could he create when his business is the knife, and he is not the greatest artist in the world with that weapon, as I can testify; he did my circumcision.

But he tended to bring you through alive. Once in a while you had to apologize for the scars, but you came through just the same, both heart and lungs laboring inside a heaving chest. My heart and lungs were at it now, hammering and heaving.

Can you see Helen home?

Great knocking clappers of copper and steel, I burst out to myself, how can men be so blind?

Is the world round?

Are all men mortal?

A father, I said, should stand guard with a cannon. How can he be so trusting? Innocence, I practically shouted, is ignorance made holy. A father should buy up an old howitzer; he should train it on his daughter's bedroom. The enemy is everywhere, groping and prying. He should dig a moat and build a wall.

W H Y did I do it? Why? Not just that first night, the night of the stampede. That I could have chalked up to simple lust. I was horny. But I was with her again the second night—in the old Doc's garden. He was a great gardener. A real maniac. I was there the third night. When it got too dark for gardening and too late for politicking, Helen and I would be there. Night after night. Every day I gave talks all over the country, as many as seven in one day, every talk a remarkable success, and every night I drove like a maniac myself in my battered one-eyed hearse to get to Notikeewin and Helen and the garden. Three times we stayed together right until dawn. The heat was so great all day that the nights were just perfect, cool and not too cool; the sky was so empty of clouds that the nights were starlit, yet not too bright. Why? I asked myself. Why did I build a career all day and risk it all night? Me, a practical hardheaded man with soaring ambitions? Why did I do it?

I have never been so happy. That was one reason why.

When I was a kid I owned a little book on the Seven Wonders of the World, and I had a suspicion then that the Hanging Gardens of Babylon must have looked a lot like Murdoch's back yard. I won the book for writing a limerick about health, something about exercises or brushing your teeth, I can't remember. But in that garden I felt I was in another world. And to be there with Helen Murdoch—well, I guess I felt I had done it at last, I had outfoxed old Master Fate.

She was so wild and so gentle. It's no use pretending—we made love. Often. Remarkably often, Helen and I. Again and again, in that garden at night; we must have toppled a few old records. "What do you look like in the day?" I asked her. But she didn't answer; she touched me. With her beautiful hands, bold and shy, she touched me and daylight didn't matter that much. She was wild and gentle.

It should have made me age overnight, that folly; instead it made me young. Each night I was a virgin again. I really was. I've been quite a heller with women, sure. I've done well enough by anybody's standards. Especially when I worked on the boats, I remember one time, I begged for mercy; there were three women after me continually, one of them the chief engineer's wife, the chief a big Italian who would sooner stick a knife in you than smile.

But out there in the garden—I wanted to cry. Helen was all happiness, released and gentle and smiling, and me, I wanted to cry. Not that I wasn't happy too. I'd never been so happy before. I've never been so happy. But I wanted to cry. Maybe for all those times when it didn't make me happy; it's a great test of affection, you know. The way you feel the moment after. Sometimes you wonder how you got into such a fool mess. You want to kick your own ridiculous behind. Your naked arse. Or you want to pull your pants up off your knees and walk away and pretend it didn't happen. You know, the way you half-despise yourself and half-know the boredom has set in already, and how the hell do I bow out without hurting anybody's feelings? How the hell did I get here? You come, and then the arithmetic sets in. Add it up for yourself. How long is it really great: maybe eight seconds. If a man comes for the grand total of six days of his life he will go down in history as a heroic performer. One miserable week of joy, including a day of rest. And to do that you spend seventy years; three score and ten you spend, sniffing and pawing, crawling and begging and imploring, conniving, cheating, betraying your wife, inventing filthy lies, wasting your money, missing sleep, deceiving your best friends, risking the creation of further ridiculous life, wrecking your clothes. My God, a two-week vacation is longer.

But out there in that garden with Helen, I wanted to reach up and stop the old world from spinning. I simply wanted to stop time right there and say, "Helen, I regret to say the sun will not come up this morning."

But it always did.

Just in time for me to run home and shave and wash, etcetera, etcetera, and eat a bite and hit the road again. To my wife I said, caucus; we were caucusing all night, I explained. I hope she looked it up in the dictionary. Thus I earned her sympathy at last; she said I looked completely worn out.

Thus we had seven nights in a row in the garden, Helen and I. In Murdoch's garden. We did not get rained out once, and it would be nice if I could add, I regret to say. But I didn't regret it. All day I preached rain, and by five o'clock I was watching the sky for fear a cloud would blow up.

The smell of that garden at night; it wasn't a prairie smell, dry and stringent, parching the insides of your nose. It was an Eastern smell; it was lush, a green smell, heavy enough to be seen. I said to Helen one night, "He's done it, hasn't he? He's managed to create it right here in his own back yard—a little bit of the East."

"I know," she said. And she added, "You like it, don't you?"

As I say, it was cooler out there. "It beats a potato patch," I said, "with bugs stripping the leaves."

She laughed at me, for the way I said that, I guess. I got that impression. But she touched me too, bold and shy at the same time.

I've dabbled a little in gardening myself. The year I was in grade nine I produced two hundred squash. Heaps and mounds of giant squash. Then I couldn't find a single person who liked squash; I don't like it myself. My tomatoes, on the other hand, were touched by frost just before they were fit to eat; it made them rot very quickly. My cucumbers never came out of the ground. I put a lot of money into cabbage plants and the cutworms cut them off before I had time to put tin cans over them; tin cans with both ends cut out, it took me hours.

But the old Doc dreaded winter. He dreaded the first fall of snow. That forty-below weather raised holy hell with his shrubs and bushes and trees. So he wrapped them up in his botanic versions of winter underwear, and in spring they'd come back to life. Most of them. He had a knack, as you could easily tell.

All those rich scents were on the air, and after a while I could distinguish the smell of Helen's body. It was a sort of darker smell, musky and secret, and I guess she could find me in the night too, after I'd been out in the sun and heat and dust all day. Our eyes got used to the night.

The bad thing was—after that first time, I couldn't ever feel guilty. I tried. I felt obliged to try. I felt under obligation to feel guilty, but I only became confused; like at weddings or funerals. They're another thing I confuse. At my mother's funeral I couldn't shed a tear to save my soul. At my own wedding, a very splashy affair, I wept buckets. I cried a small deluge. Me, nearly six-four, a big man, thirty-three years of age and marrying into the plutocratic Burkhardt clan, I sobbed and wept. People were moved.

Out there in the garden—sometimes I had that same urge to cry. But not out of guilt.

I wanted to cry because there I was again, attracted to someone who did not begin to believe it would rain. I was attracted to Helen. And she could not for a moment believe a drop of rain would fall from the barren skies above.

Night after night we met, and night after night she teased me, well, it didn't rain, Johnnie. And I kept going back. Knowing how she would greet me I turned up nightly nevertheless, right on the dot. No cloudbursts today. As if I needed that punishment. As if I had somehow to be reminded that every word I'd spoken throughout the day was a rotten lie.

You've been listening to your own speeches again, I can tell, she could say with one breath. And with the next: Failure and you will have to get acquainted sooner or later, you wonderful big lout.

I had recaptured all that was gone and past. But how could I reply? The crops were drying up fast. It had to rain, and soon; it simply had to. The hay crop had failed. The wheat could make it if we got just one good soaker inside the next week. Other people's gardens were going brown, the peas weren't filling. The carrots couldn't split the ground enough to give themselves room to grow. But the old Doc, every after-noon he watered a part of his garden, with absolutely no apologies to the mayor of The Wild Rose City. And none were expected of an M.L.A. That garden was green and lush until you could hardly believe your own eyes when you stepped through the high hedge into his private domain. He was a slave to that garden, old Murdoch; he made roses bloom and cherries blossom; he made plums and apricots and crab apples hang so heavy on the branches they had to be propped up—and nobody else could keep a cactus alive. Patience and water, he'd say, patience and water; we've got the best soil in the world.

Helen and I would lie together under a plum tree, beside a little round sunken pool where goldfish drowsed amid the stars, and we were happy. She'd bring a quilt out of the house and we'd lie together, we'd make love.

I guess I was always a dreamer; right from the first, when I marched up those boyhood stairs to go to bed and stopped to look out the west window and saw all that distance out beyond; when I saw that horizon so far away. I was a dreamer, and in that garden I dreamed again; I dreamed and listened, an insect skating on the pool, a blossom yawning itself to sleep. Well, I exaggerate. But I heard my own breathing. I was breathing easy and slow; and every time I heard it it gave me a start.

"Tomorrow," Helen said.

"Tomorrow my arse," I said.

This was Wednesday midnight. That Wednesday night of the burial Mass; I understood her concern. The day of the election was twenty-four hours away. She was once again getting me ready for failure, as if by Jesus my life had been composed of anything else. She was nobly devoting her life to teaching a fish to swim.

"Tomorrow you should concede the election beforehand and try to make up with Dad. He could get you a job."

"Why?" I said. "Why the hell do that? On the following day the beer parlors close and someone will finally die of thirst. I'll be back in business."

She was looking up at the night; I was watching her mouth and eyes. "You joke about hating it," she said. "But really—I think you like what you do. I didn't know that for a long time. I didn't know."

"I hate what I'm doing." I moved my hand away from between her thighs; reluctantly, I might add. I was trying to make a joke. But I left one finger curled in that garden of her own.

"Why do you do it then?" she said.

"Christian duty," I said.

"Johnnie," she said. "Really. Why do you do what you do?" She moved my hand. "For a living," she added sarcastically.

Only a woman with a university education will ever persist in a question like that one. Why do you do what you do? It wasn't just hard times, I had to admit that to myself. Christ all fishhooks, I'm strong as a horse. I'm robust and vigorous. There are lots of things I could do in this world, there must be. "You see," I said. I was going to joke about making a fortune. But out it came: "I went all the way East to learn. Then—then just knowing that we die wasn't enough. I had to rub my nose in it. Maybe it's because I'm so goddamned big."

"Maybe I love you," she said. "What do you think, Johnnie?"

What in hell kind of question is that? She touched me. Without looking away from the stars, she raised her left hand. I was practically naked. I was trying to unscramble the sad confusion, trying to face the sad music of my soul. I was thinking very hard again, against my better judgment. The agony was almost unendurable.

"I've got more mortality than other people," I said. "That's the basis of the trouble. Christ have I got mortality. I've got mortality to burn."

It's a fact. To be so goddamned big and to be an undertaker. It's an injustice. All this dying to do.

She turned and bent and kissed my belly right where it's most ticklish. I was practically naked. I had kept on one sock in my earlier haste, a hole in its big toe.

"Look what's happening to your mortality," she said.

"Damnit," I said. "I'm being serious."

"But it isn't dead," she said, "after all."

"This is insane," I said. "This is madness. I'm only human. I've got to rest. I've simply got to get some rest." I was trying to be serious. Vicissitudes again. I wanted to talk about mortality; it haunts and afflicts me.

"You're so alive," she said.

"That's the whole trouble," I said. I was trying to remain sullen. "That's what makes it so bad."

"Don't raise your voice," she said.

"I have to," I said, "I can't help it."

"I know," she said. She waited. Her fingers tiptoed across my belly. "I've watched you, Johnnie. You talk. You hunger and thirst. You stride and thunder and roar. You're never still a moment. But in the end you smash."

I was lying perfectly still. I tried to frame a protest in my mind, hoping all the while that my stomach would not come up with a Jesusly big growl. Her ear was in a perfect position for hearing. But smash was the right word, nevertheless. She had said it without really intending to, I could see that. I've got these huge hands. Huge. Positively huge. And everything I touch I tend to smash it. I'm that way. And there I was with that beautiful girl; I had to face up to it; there I was compelled to put my big rough hands on happiness itself.

I had no idea that one girl could mean so much. I used to have a saying, stand them on their heads and they're all alike. Or sometimes I added—any port in a storm. But it wasn't working out. All day when I talked to all those meetings, I was talking to Helen. She wasn't there but I was talking to her. Rain, I said. Explaining and demanding.

Proclaiming even. Rain, I proclaimed. Rain, I exhorted. There were lots of poor people present. Always. You can always tell; the poor have a special way of combing their hair. Myself, I have this blondish hair which I keep neatly combed, and I sometimes push a slight wave into the front. I looked at those poor people, starving and hoping, their crops burning up, and I thought of Helen in her father's garden: marigolds and nasturtiums. Zinnias and phlox.

Believe, I said. Believe, I demanded, believe, Helen, believe it will rain.

"I smash," I said. I let my fingers touch her long dark hair, there in the darkness that my eyes had adjusted to, the starlight. "You're right," I said. "But I want to help. I want to help and I end up smashing. Something gets smashed. Once it was my Atwater-Kent. Once it was a fender, complete with headlight. Once it was Jonah Bledd's arm."

"Maybe I do love you," she said again; but she was putting the proposition to herself, not to me. I sensed that.

"Don't," I said. "Don't, H.P., you'll get smashed too. All busted up."

"Maybe just because you're so big," she said. She put her arm across me, resting her head on my chest while I touched her hair with my fingers. "There's so much of you to get hurt." And then she shook her head. "All day I fear you; and at night—"

"Helen," I said, "to face the music: what if it doesn't rain?"

"Make love to me," she said.

What kind of factual statement is that? "But what if it doesn't?" I said. "They believed and they'll get smashed."

"Now," she said. "Johnnie?"

I pushed her up, away from my chest. "What if it doesn't?" I said. My breath was quick in my chest again.

"Look," she said. She was pointing into the pool. "You can see the asphodels—reflected there in the water."

Eight inches of water, and in it you could see flowers, the moon, the wheeling stars. The moon was up; so bright it cast shadows on Helen's body; leaves and branches shadowed her silver body, except where nature had placed a shadow of its own.

I refused to budge, stretched out on my back as I was. "Christ, Helen, they're all banking on rain. When I shut up the women start in; new dresses, new curtains. For the first time in six years, they tell each other. They talk and jabber. And I can tell at a glance they don't have two nickels to rub together. Their hair tells me that. They're talking big because of me, because of what I promise. I start to feel guilty."

"Asphodels," she said, "growing upside down."

I stopped touching her hair. I touched her breasts, one, then the other, my huge hand confused; my hand wanting all, all.

"You're gentle," she said.

"No," I said. "I smash."

She held her hand over mine, holding my hand to her breast for a moment, holding my fingers still. "You're gentle," she said. Then she stood up. She picked a flower, a white bloom, one of her father's asphodels; she knelt and stuck it in my hair while I lay stretched out on the quilt and the grass.

I had rope burns from the quilt, one on the tip of my left elbow and one, somehow, one the inside of my right knee. My skin was abraded and very tender. Excoriated. But Helen touched my protesting hand with one finger; she raised my knuckles to her beautiful mouth.

She did that sometimes, she touched my scars. I would not stir off my back on this occasion, overcome as I was by a sudden stab of despair, but she kissed them. I have scars from baseball, from fights, from working on the boats, from love, from hate, from everything. I have plenty of scars and Helen could find every one. She kissed my elbow. Helen was like that. Never in my life had a woman kissed my elbow, least of all my wife Elaine; my elbow which had worn itself shiny on beer tables, on oilcloth, on stained linen, on bed sheets dirty and clean, on oak and pine and mahogany and maple, on iron and zinc, on the bare earth itself.

She kissed me, as I say.

That's another reason why I wanted to cry. Yes, in the midst of everything; I had the old impulse again.

How terrible. What a bastard I am. For my own mother, I could not shed a tear. I loved my mother. I went to her funeral resolved to cry. I strained and squeezed and groaned. I rocked and shook. But not a tear. And I am a deeply compassionate man. I reviewed the tribulation of my own life. I remembered my mother peeling onions, an onion raised to her peeling knife, her eyes red. But no tears came. I almost wept with embarrassment.

Out there in Doc Murdoch's garden, with nothing around me but happiness, I had to fight back the tears. I was filled with emotion. The thought of all my responsibility was too much. Helen touched my scars with her pale hands, her pale white hands and her beautiful mouth. She made me whole again. That's how it was, my feeling for Helen. Helen who kissed me. Who plucked a flower in my honor. For me who seven days earlier did not know an asphodel from a hawthorn. What blossoms did I know? Stinkweed and maybe the shooting star. Buffalo beans in the springtime. Wolf willow. Pin cherry. Foxtail. Does quack grass blossom? Does pigweed bloom?

"What if it doesn't rain?" I moaned.

In the Doc's house a telephone rang.

"Listen," she said. Helen kissed a scar of mine, visibly impressed by my cry of anguish. She was filled with admiration and pain and love. "Listen," she said. "What did I hear?"

A telephone was ringing in the silent house. You had to be deaf not to hear it. "Dad didn't get home," she said. "Should I run answer, Johnnie?"

Before I could open my mouth—before I could speak: somewhere in the high plum tree a bird sang, in answer to the phone.

A bird just burst out and sang; and in a sudden rage of ecstasy I leaped to my feet; I swept up my shirt and pants, my shoes and belt and the whole caboodle in my two long arms: I spun around and let go.

I stood naked before Helen. The branches of trees, the flower beds and the bushes blossomed anew in sweat-stiffened clothes, in clothes that were much the worse for wear. My shorts were nothing but holes. I stood naked and proud in that garden, one sock on my left foot, my feet tender, nevertheless, my hands raised up in stark humility to that hidden bird, the stars wheeling as they pleased. "Helen," I said, "it's all gone, and a good riddance of bad rubbish. I'm going to start over, from the ground up, from my birthday suit out."

And H.P. kneeling reached up to where I stood, a towering man, a looming man, nearly six-four; she touched again gently one of my scars.

Six long strides that sprang from my longing: into the middle of the Doc's sunken pool. In I marched, going full bore, stopping for nothing. The pebbles be damned, the goldfish be damned.

Helen did not answer the ringing phone. She followed. Helen followed, splashing me just a little, but her mouth was suddenly warm on mine; and together there in the water we fumbled in our silent haste. I have heard that certain acts are impossible under water, but that was not the case with us. Red hot blades are plunged hissing into water to temper the steel. A bird had sung in the darkness. The plum tree itself was a blue flame. And there in the darkness we coupled, damned near drowning, I might add; we coupled, me like a hippopotamus; we met and were joined, the stars wheeling, the night hushed into admiration; we coupled and we were one, Helen and I, my asphodel rudely afloat on the sloshing waves.

# THURSDAY

JUST AS THE SUN humped over the horizon I up
and hustled home. Or I dragged myself home; the
sock still damp in my left shoe. Thursday morning
had come as scheduled: the day before the election. High in that red morning sky a scattering of
fluff looked as if it would parch and corrode your
throat if ever you got a mouthful. The sky burst
flaming above the quiet streets, above the still
houses and the pulled blinds. Above the burnt
lawns and the caked flower beds. Above my
funeral home.

What a conundrum in naming that is.

Elaine was sound asleep when I got here. Or at least she didn't stir;
she slept a lot at the time. So I crawled in and dozed a few hours
myself; I had a hard day ahead of me.

Thursday was to be the climax of my electioneering. I was invited to
address a huge audience in Coulee Hill—in the very hall where old Doc
Murdoch had first skinned me alive. They were pretty excited, those
people down there. They all wanted to hear me now, those same

people who had laughed their heads off. They were very apologetic. They had recognized the error of their ways. I didn't have to rent the hall or anything; in fact, they agreed to buy my gas and give me a purse of five dollars to boot, guaranteed, no strings attached. I couldn't lose.

Or at least I don't feel I could, until the phone rang.

This was at ten forty-five. I was resting, so my wife took the call. Her splashing around in the sink had not entirely awakened me. I listened. I could tell, half-asleep and listening, that the call was for me. The bedroom was so warm I wasn't sleeping too soundly. It would have made more sense to sleep downstairs in the funeral parlor, but somehow I found myself making excuses not to do so.

"Who was it?" I yelled when she hung up.

"Doctor Murdoch."

My toes shot out at the bottom of the sheet, ten shiny toes suddenly greeted me, their nails clean but once again in need of trimming, reminding me again of the hundreds of little things I should have been doing instead of sleeping. No tent obscured my vision this morning, the spirit drooped. Reality, reality. Plus exhaustion. I was in the kitchen in two seconds, walking and pulling on my shorts at the same time, my chest bare. I have this hair on my chest which is naturally curly. The hair on my head is straightish, but thank God I am elsewhere a mass of curls.

"What the hell did he want?" I inquired.

I was gruff—because I sort of felt guilty about the old Doc. Maybe he'd got home and found all his goldfish washed up on dry land. The old Doc could put two and two together, he was human himself, as I often told Helen.

"What does he want?" Elaine said, repeating my question instead of providing an answer. "What does he think you are? His servant or something? His slave?"

That kind of indirection, that kind of righteousness coupled with deliberate evasion, is generally more frightening than a direct onslaught.

"What d'you mean?" I said.

"Ordering you around like that," she said.

I should have been suspicious; I really should have. "Explain, explain," I burst out. "And why do you have to have curlers in your hair at eleven in the morning?"

My wife has extremely straight hair. "Because," she said, "the church ladies are holding a raffle tonight, to raise money for the Bledd family."

That silenced me. I would have bet good money that the United Church women wouldn't do that for an R.C. She was pouring herself another cup of coffee, moving heavily because of her condition, carefully reminding me of what my rude lust and incontinence had occasioned. "What did he want?" I demanded.

"He wants you to come right away."

"Me?" I said. "To where? Who does he think I am? I have my rights. To his house?" My heart nearly knocked itself out of my bare chest. I wished I'd put on my shirt. But Elaine likes to see me bare-chested; when I expect trouble I sometimes leave off my shirt, it calms her. Also, she had not done the ironing. I lifted the flyswatter off a nail, thus uncovering a calendar; a picture of the Wise Men or the Three Shepherds or the Three Kings. I can never quite tell those Arabs apart. Also the date once again, alas. I swung wickedly at a fly on the oilcloth, just missing by inches. "I have this talk to give tonight," I said. "I'm very busy. At the Coulee Hill sports day. After all the ball games. They've canceled the dance just to hear me talk."

"I know." Elaine sipped some coffee out of her saucer. "I saw the notice in Wong's window. You never tell me anything, Johnnie. We never talk about what you're doing."

I was taken aback. Her tone confused me. But once on the defensive I could not quickly change posture. "I'm simply going to give a talk. Maybe on the joys of matrimony." I pretended to grin. "Or on the penal system," I added.

My wife did not crack a smile. She seemed to have on her thinking cap, thus her look of discomfort. Without abandoning her coffee cup she began to prepare dinner. "You should get to Coulee Hill early," she said. "Half the constituency will be there."

Such duplicity of intent unnerves me. I am basically a simple man, a trusting man. "Eight ball teams are competing," I agreed. "The winning pitcher will have to be a man of endurance and skill. One time in Coulee Hill I alone—"

"People from here are driving out there," she said.

That extravagance on the part of the local citizenry was quite astonishing to my better half, apparently. I had heard about the proposed excursion myself—something like thirty-five cars, a regular cavalcade. Murdoch's henchmen and sycophants, it turned out, were going out for the laughs. They wanted to hear what I had to say about rain on the sunlit drought-stricken evening before the election. Before the casting of the votes. I couldn't let myself think about it. In fact, I recognized the symptoms of nausea. I almost had a dizzy spell.

"Is it clouding up at all?" I said.

"He that has an eye," she said, "let him see."

She had not perused the Good Book without some success. "Has there been a forecast?" I pleaded.

"Turn on the radio and listen," she mocked.

Once again I had so innocently erred. "Where would I hear a forecast if there was one?" she continued. "Radios, or for that matter fenders, do not repair themselves."

My wife sounded wrought up. I said nothing. I had earlier and more than once tried to explain that her dear mother's radio fell over while I was making some minor adjustments; witness the gashes in my hand. Unfortunately the micky itself had come to light; the evidence gone, but the odor of evidence fresh and repellent.

"If only," she said, "you win that election—"

That's when I groaned. Her sarcasm cut deep. Sometimes a great groan comes out of my depths, distorting my face and filling the air. A soblike groan. I had less than twenty-four hours in which to lay on a cloudburst. And again the sky was nothing but clear, except for some fuzz that did not equal the pile under our bed. The heat was nearly unbearable. I was glad I hadn't put on my shirt. The air was still. When I'd agreed to talk, four days ago, I was confident it would rain in four days. I had just made a speech to that effect, to a curling rink full of breathless listeners. "I can't do it," I groaned. "I can't go out there and give a talk."

That's when Elaine just burst out suddenly: "It's on your way. You've got to. The baby isn't alive."

I was taken off guard. The old Doc never missed. For the first time I grasped the import of his call. "Then he didn't," I said, "bring this one into the world?"

Elaine gave no answer. She was dabbing at her eyes with a dish towel.

"Then he isn't at home?" I continued. "He's down at the Gunns."

"South of Coulee Hill, by the river," she said. She was pretending she had dishes to dry, though we hadn't yet eaten. "He said you know the way."

"Helen is driving down to get him," I said. Don't ask me why that came into my mind.

Elaine was shaking her head. "He said to tell you to come as soon as you're free."

"I'll put on my shirt," I said.

"Eat some dinner," she said. "I'm hurrying."

I shook my head and nodded. "This is fine. I can drop in at the sports day and cancel my talk."

"You can't," she said. A note I had never heard came into Elaine's voice. "Johnnie, you can't cancel it. Don't you see, Johnnie?"

I was literally dumbfounded. Unable to find my voice, I swung at a fly on an empty plate on the kitchen cabinet. On a plate decorated with various scenes of Niagara Falls, a memento of past carefree travels and forgotten joys. I brushed the fly off the plate onto the floor, hardly deigning to notice my success. Elaine could sweep up later. "I have predicted," I confessed, "to all potential voters, a certain degree of precipitation. Snow, hail, mist—or even rain."

"You can," she said, lifting the lid off a pot of boiling potatoes, sniffing the steam, replacing the lid, "beat them *without* rain."

A few flies were buzzing, the survivors. A cat yawned somewhere under the stove, somehow making a drowning sound. Having to drown kittens is, I suppose, one of the worst jobs on earth. I raised my bushy eyebrows. Elaine, standing motionless, raised a cup to her lips and studied the fly poison in the center of the kitchen table; the flies moved feebly over the damp brown pad, drinking greedily their own inevitable destruction. Elaine took down the cup from her lips; Elaine Burkhardt whose numerous relations did not exactly relish having an undertaker marry into the family fortunes. But why they should express their dissatisfaction in the privacy of polling booths was something I could not begin to fathom. I had a strong suspicion at that moment that even while Elaine was egging me on to risk my life and limbs for a few paltry votes, she had every intention of casting her own ballot for Murdoch.

She must have been reading my mind. "You can bet them *without* rain," she repeated.

I should confess—I do confess: the thought had never really seriously crossed my mind. The old Doc was invincible. The very thought of Elaine's suggestion rattled me; usually I'm very calm.

No rain. Win anyhow. I was staggered.

I laid the flyswatter gently on the table and put the tips of my little fingers in my ears and wiggled them. My fingertips. Unfortunately I have a natural impulse to disagree automatically with anything my wife says. "I could under no circumstances," I said, "beat Murdoch in an election. I may withdraw."

"If you give that talk tonight, you'll win."

"If I go out there tonight," I said, "I'll be tarred and feathered. I'll be suffocated in a rain barrel full of gumbo dust."

"Johnnie," she said, "tell them it didn't rain."

"They'll be able to guess that," I ventured.

"Tell them," she said.

Women, I recognized once again, will never succeed in politics. "Sure," I said.

"Just tell them the truth," she insisted. "Be honest with them. Tell them it didn't rain. Those Murdoch idiots have put up posters all over town—of you holding an umbrella."

Miracles will never cease. My wife, cloistered and devoted as her life may seem, was of my political persuasion. My own wife, descended of the Burkhardt clan, implement dealers par excellence. Minions and agents themselves of the Fifty Big Shots. Retrievers of defaulted hayrakes. My dearest wife applauded, in her heart if not verbally, my withering attacks on the high-muckie-mucks. She had heard about me, no doubt, in church. It was quite a jolt to my religious convictions. I was moved.

"I have to go see the Doc," I persisted. "He sent for me. I have to cancel my talk."

"You cannot cancel your talk," she said.

"The doctor sent for me," I said. "He sent for me. I have a duty."

"Duty duty duty," she said. She was checking the potatoes again. "Duty, shit."

That word should give you some idea of the magnitude of my wife's concern. I had no idea she knew the word even by hearsay. I expected, duty, horseradish. I wouldn't have been more surprised if she had walked over to the kitchen cabinet, opened the left door, lifted down the teapot off the top shelf, and taken out one of her tailor-made expensive cork-tipped Sweet Caporals. Why didn't she roll her own like other women?

"I have a duty," I repeated. "I have never ignored a call from Murdoch, regardless of how I may judge the man."

"Let the other undertaker go," she said.

"That deaf atheist," I said.

"Johnnie," she said, "don't you see?" She touched her own prominent breasts. "I'm a little bit scared, Johnnie."

"The Doc will usually pull them through," I assured her. "A couple of slaps and away they run, take me for example."

"It isn't that easy," she said.

"I have a duty," I said. "Elaine," I said, "Jesus, even if old Gunn is penniless, I have a duty to perform."

"You have a wife and child to support," she said.

That was a slight exaggeration. She was bending over the stove again. My wife was fond of saying not only that she was eating for two, which excused her gluttony in a time of hardship, but also that she was sleeping for two, praying for two, passing water for two. By God, some days I couldn't buy my way into the bathroom. "That's why I'm going to where Murdoch is waiting," I said, irrationally. "I need the business."

"No," she said. "Johnnie, listen. We haven't got the money to see a doctor. Do you realize that? I missed my appointment this month, to save money."

I felt pretty bad. I was taking an honest look at myself. I was a poor provider, I could see that. Here I was, raising my voice, bragging and swaggering all over the constituency, and my own wife and child were being deprived. I felt terrible. "Elaine," I said. "I've been a poor husband."

I expected her to say, I know. Elaine can make a whole conversation out of those two words.

"No, you haven't," she said.

Of all the things she could have said, that was the worst. Why didn't she nag in her usual fashion? Sometimes we'd sooner have wrath than forgiveness. I felt terrible. Wrath can be a great consolation. But she had to go on: "We're well off, compared to the Bledd family. We have our health. Or the farmers who can't meet payments on machinery and land. Or the business people. Three more places on Main Street are closing this fall, if there's no crop. I heard that in church last night. A third of the street is empty or boarded up now, Johnnie. The women always say to me—'Your Johnnie is such a go-getter, Elaine.'"

I nodded my head. Also, I wiped the sweat off my brow; the heat was asphyxiating. I took down plates from the kitchen cabinet, I looked for knives and forks; in a flash I was setting the table. Elaine was pregnant, as I say. I'd never noticed how much until now. She had a hard time moving; you could tell, she wanted to sit down. Her feet were swollen, for one thing. I did that, I said to myself; the price for being a heller with the opposite sex. Twins, probably.

"You worry too much about everybody," she said. "You should think about yourself too. You're so generous."

Elaine, at this time, was serving up food out of pots into bowls. I was overwrought. In silence I left the flyswatter where it was, smack on the table instead of on a nail where it belonged; sometimes I move it with great deliberation as a little moral lesson.

"Sit down, Johnnie," she said.

My chair at the dinner table is strategically placed so that if I stand up or sit down without bowing deeply I glue the back of my head to a sticky brown fly hanger and clothespin which I must inevitably share with a lot of struggling flies. For dinner we had warmed-over coffee, boiled potatoes, boiled wieners and sauerkraut. My wife was supposed to go easy on fried foods. I have never especially liked sauerkraut, as my wife would be the first person to know.

"I'm sorry there's no butter for the potatoes," she said.

I ate my sauerkraut. I stuffed it all down, and just to show how good a husband I was I asked for a second helping. I don't just dislike sauerkraut. My wife gave herself kind of a swing and hoist and stood up. She gave me a generous helping. I detest the stuff passionately; that's the way I tend to live.

Anyway, right after that I felt a little gas on my stomach. Sauerkraut always does that to me, which is one reason why I am not fond of it. It bloats me.

"You should drop in on my cousin, there in Coulee Hill," Elaine said.

"Which of your cousins is that, dear?" I said.

"She's been engaged for three years. They can't afford to get married." Elaine put three spoonfuls of sugar into a new cup of coffee. "Those poor people, what a pity."

"Terrible," I said. "Terrible. What a shame."

"You'd think," Elaine said, "that a pretty girl like that Murdoch girl would be looking for a husband."

"Yes," I said.

"She came to church one evening, bringing flowers. A very pleasant person. More potatoes?"

My wife's compassion had rendered discussion impossible. I accepted the additional potatoes and ate hurriedly.

I went to the bedroom and put on the one clean shirt I had left, a black one, in which I look very good because of my coloring. I selected from my wife's dowry a yellow tie, one that her father liked, and silently I put it on and knotted it. I went back to the kitchen and silently bent over where Elaine sat, her feet out of her shoes now, the flyswatter in her right hand, the left on the handle of a cup, and I kissed the top of her head, her hair.

"Take care, dear," I said.

"You can win, Johnnie," she said.

I went to the car shed. I examined both fenders. With some difficulty but not without success I resisted the urge to pick up a maul which lay exposed on an empty antifreeze container. I very gently chased five cats out of my hearse and gently got in and slammed the door. Only to have to get out again and find a coffin; and to once again evict the cats. As gently as possible, I started the engine.

To tell you the truth, I had no idea where I was headed; I simply kept stepping on the clutch and changing gears. And as it happened, pretty soon I was pushing down on the gas pedal, vaguely aware of the telephone poles in the corner of my eye.

B∪T the road always cheers me up. It always has that effect; I like to feel I'm going somewhere. Pretty soon I was spinning along, the sun dancing on the chrome radiator of my hearse, on the chrome thermometer on the radiator cap. On the fenders. The wind was singing in at the open windows, of its own accord wiping the sweat from my brow; my spirits simply rose. Sure, my ass was sticking to the seat, whose doesn't on a day like that? But I really feel free on the road. I feel all the pressures let up and I'm rolling along, going somewhere and doing something; my mind starts to travel and whirr.

My wife had given me an idea. By God, I could win that election without rain. Tell them it didn't rain, she said. Sometimes that woman is a genius. Tell them, she said.

Be honest with them.

Yes sir, I saw it. It came to me in a flash. I was buzzing along that road, the gravel flying, the dust in a cloud behind me—an honest man. One honest man, I saw; One Honest Man could save the day. Sometimes that woman is a positive genius. I saw her point immediately. She had figured out the very thing that had me buffaloed. Of course, tell them straight out. Why beat around the bush? I was no performer of miracles. Me, I was just another mortal, like anybody else; I suffer too. I feel hunger. Pain is my lot in life; anguish my heritage. The heat and the cold afflict me too. My throat gets dry. Desire and temptation are the scourge of my existence. Also cats.

Also repentance. Also humiliation.

Who was hurt worse than I was by the failure of rain to fall? Who was going to look foolish, be mocked at, scoffed and kicked? I should get a nut-protector from some hockey player and wear it at all times. My wife was all right. She had a good head on her shoulders, a Burkhardt head, I could see that.

I was rolling down that highway, heading straight east, glancing to left and right. Some of the farms were deserted for keeps, you could tell without trying. The curtains were gone from the windows of the houses. It was a hard thing to look at, like looking into the torn empty sockets of vanished eyes. Windows were broken in half the barns. It was funny; windows were the first thing to change; the whole business of people wanting to see out when they're in, wanting to see in when they're out. I was that way myself. But the yards changed too; weeds began to grow without feet to wear them down: the worn old boots of men and the bare feet of kids and the hoofs of horses and cows and the toes of chickens.

One man could redeem the whole country; not twenty, not ten, but one. One Honest Man could sire a new age. I'd just march right up there onto that stage with the flags hanging limp in the still air, the crepe paper wilting in the heat. Damn all the bankers lined up at the back of the hall, waiting to split their sides; I'd lay it on the line. Straight from the shoulder. No holds barred.

My dear friends, it has not rained and I'm sorry and I'd like to go up to the Parliament buildings this fall and make amends. I'm in this with you. This poverty is our poverty. This drought, my dear friends, is our drought. We need new blood. We need action; enough of words and promises and filthy lies. And the Lord said, If I find in Sodom fifty righteous within the city, I will spare all the place for their sakes. Or for twenty. Or for ten. Or—yes, my dear friends, yes— One Honest Man can do what a gang of cutthroat schemers, agents of the Fifty Big Shots, has never done. Has never been able to do. Never will do. One Honest Man, my dear friends—

I began to feel much better. My wife was all right. There she was, about to have a baby, alone all day while I was electioneering all over the place. What went on in her mind? Concern for me, I'll bet. Worry. About me on the road alone, with a broken-down worn-out car, facing strangers, trying to argue with bullheaded farmers and sharp-dealing businessmen. Trying to be good to people who hardly deserve it and getting no thanks for my efforts. Nothing but rebuffs and insults. There she was alone, Elaine who is scared in the dark, especially living in a funeral home. Who could blame her? I asked myself. And all day she had to worry about the child's future; boy or girl, it depended on me. I who had not turned out to be such a hot provider.

The green was almost gone from the countryside. The poplar groves looked dry and withered, the leaves hardly quaking. The birds themselves, commissioned to sing, had given up hope. They were silent. The wind in my ears, the gravel, the motor under the hood— and no other noises. On a good day you'd be startled by a meadowlark, singing yellow-breasted on a telephone pole. But hope was faltering. The willows in the ditches were dying too early, some kind of worms making little yellow pods on the spotted leaves. The stinkweed was shriveled and small, clinging to life low on the shoulder of the road; even the thistles, Canada and sow, looked stunted. Stunted and mean. The wheat fields themselves seemed to be praying for water, stirring as they did dumbly before a small wind. Only the crows looked happy; far away across the fields they flapped in the sky, complete masters.

Confusion is nothing new to me. Again it began to disturb my calm. I was on Highway 313, driving hard for the old chaos. I could whip into Coulee Hill, where a sports day was in progress; where three ball diamonds were swarming with carefree people. I could take the cutoff and go straight down to the river where the Gunn family was trying to scratch a living out of the gumbo flats among river hills: to where old Murdoch was half-expecting—well, expecting my arrival.

I was undecided. I get very excited at ball games; on one occasion I was very nearly arrested for swinging at an umpire and putting my fist through his mask. More scars. But at that moment the thought of jail was an immense consolation. The simple life of the hoosegow.

I whizzed along.

Five towns between Notikeewin and Coulee Hill, a beer parlor in every town; and I had already passed the first two without blinking. You'll find it hard to believe. There on my left was the turnoff into Burkhardt, the third town, the dirt road bouncing over the tracks, past the whitewashed cattle pens. There across the tracks and up past a couple of grain elevators stood the Commercial Hotel, its beer parlor open, two cars parked in front already. Company inside. Men willing to talk about the important things. Willing to give advice, consideration. And what did I do? I wheeled on by. I chose to drive on toward the next town.

I thought of Helen. We were to meet at midnight, in the garden again. We'd made that arrangement. I thought of her, and pretty soon my clothes were all ropes and knots binding me to my infinite miseries. How could I endure? My hidden nakedness cried out. I wanted everything, everything in life was hardly enough, and now I was faced with total confusion. My wife had a good head on her shoulders. Helen had actually pleaded with me in the opposite direction: fail, she said. But Helen had qualities of her own. My God, she could have converted me to Buddhism. I understood Jonah at last. A funny thing.

I thought of Helen, her patch of darkness when she lay in the moonlight. Her legs newly shaved, not bristling. My clothes had me all knotted up and tied, sticking to the seat. The undersides of my knees were itchy. My foot ached on the gas pedal, straining so hard against the floorboards. There is no real zip in a hearse. I glanced up at the sky.

Helen would understand about its not raining. My wife, for all her good intentions, would be unable to resist a little sarcasm. But Helen would understand. She had a compassion for failure. What should I say to her, after I had boasted so freely? For your father, I wanted to lose. But she wouldn't believe it; what should I say? That's me every time, Helen, you might as well know. I fail. I set out with millions of grandiose ambitions, and I fail. That's what happens. Always. Touch me, Helen. Touch me; and help me forget. I promise, I plan, I scheme, I devise, I manipulate, I contrive. And I fail. *Toujours, toujours.*

I worked with this guy from Montreal when I was on the boats, the only close friend I had. He always said *toujours. Toujours;* something like that. Do you love me? the girls said. *Toujours,* he said. Did you get that goddamn grain unloaded? the skipper said. *Toujours,* he said. The skipper hated foreign languages. Why *toujours*? I said to my friend one day. My closest friend. Why *toujours*? *Toujours* is no answer. It's the only answer, he said. Think about it.

The sun was beaming down, reflecting bright and shimmery off the fields of dying wheat. I thought of the garden. Why did I never sneeze from all those flowers in Murdoch's garden? The flowers at a funeral make me sneeze without fail. What mystery was concealed right there?

But Elaine had the right idea. I could do it without rain. Honesty is the best policy. That's the whole trick in life, doing without. Get used to that right now, I said. Johnnie Backstrom, buck up. Stick out your hefty chest. Flex the muscles in that pitching arm. Prepare your declaration.

Elaine was absolutely right. Elaine who had suffered and learned. My God, what that woman put up with. Consider the husband she had to endure.

Driving along, tearing down that road at a high speed, I thought of my wedding dance. Eighteen minutes before it was to commence I was pronounced incommunicado. The greatest moment of any woman's life had arrived; Elaine was to trot a new husband onto the floor for the first dance and the first sweet round of general applause. Elaine who at thirty-four must have despaired of any applause whatsoever. And what was to mar her happiness?

Consider. I who had so often consumed gallons and carried on. On this one major occasion I consumed only what could be acquired by stealth, and yet I was rendered unable to navigate. The reception was held in the United Church basement. I passed out on the stage in front of one hundred and fifty-four guests, all of them professed teetotalers. My wife counted. I was stretched out in my new black suit, a purchase I had made with a dual function in mind, my head in a cardboard box which had contained a wedding gift, a baby's tub, a gift which had come none too soon, my arms akimbo. I mistook the box for a pillow. My wife kept it; she keeps it in her attic. I was very drunk. I lay down and found I could not arise, so I chose to slumber. Eighteen minutes, as I say, before the orchestra was scheduled to strike up, "Here Comes the Bride." My wife timed me. I have often heard the statistic quoted since. One hour and four minutes later it was decided, by whom I do not know, that the dance must proceed without me. The orchestra, as is the custom, struck up "Here Comes the Bride." It took six men to carry me home to my marriage bed.

Beginnings and endings.

Jonah Bledd, who seldom cracked jokes, remarked after Elaine's rather sudden engagement that he was unable to tell if the shower was for a wife or a child.

And so I was to be father. Riding along, eating up the miles and not knowing where they led, I remembered touching my wife's belly with my giant clumsy hands, touching with one finger, then with two, then with all five. Feeling the baby move. Little kicks and pokes and jabs going on inside. Somersaults and handsprings. Rehearsal. For the foolishness that is life. Let me out. Let me at them. A new J.B., powerful and eager: I tried to think of possible names. But I thought of my parents instead. Was it my mother or was it my father?

They were both insane in their own ways. My mother, a teetotaler and a very devout person, throve on rhubarb wine and a sudden passion for a Church of the Nazarene preacher. Which was a shame, because I think the old Doc loved her. I think he once proposed; she hinted as much. The wine was diuretic, she claimed. Also, after a few drinks she would claim to be chronically constipated. Congenitally constipated is what she said, but I believe she was confused by words.

My father was a gentle man. He reserved all his dissatisfaction and sense of outrage for the institution called warfare, and he died in battle, blown to smithereens by an exploding shell, thus rendering a funeral unnecessary. He wanted to come back from the war and start a sawmill—out on the prairies. A kind man; he had a great belief in self-sufficiency.

I myself combine my mother's vitality and my father's political idealism. Thus I became an undertaker.

I don't understand. *Toujours* be damned.

Never.

A shadow came over the road. At first I thought it must be an airplane or a dirigible about to crash into my hearse. I hadn't thought there was a big enough cloud in the world to cast a shadow. But it went away in a moment; then the sun was hotter than ever. I saw two horses in a yard, a gelding, its tail putting up a vague resigned resistance to all the swarms of flies, and a stallion: a big stallion, pale blue, ignoring the flies, pawing at the post to which it was chained.

Horses, wheat, crows, drought: but no people. For mile after mile the farmhouses looked empty and deserted. I assured myself: a lot of people are gone to Coulee Hill. Everybody is gone to Coulee Hill for the sporting events.

I wasn't thinking, you understand; or I was thinking about other things. The dust was up and blowing before I saw it rise. The horizon was blurring already when I became aware. A field of summerfallow seemed to lift up and hang suspended; only now I saw it was drifting like smoke across the road ahead of me. A storm was on the way.

And then I thought to myself, this caps it. I'll get up to talk tonight with the dust sifting in around the windows, dust hanging on people's hair, in their clothes. People coughing dust out of their throats and scratching it out of their ears and blowing their noses and looking at the dust in their handkerchiefs. I'll get up to talk and people will be wishing they'd saved their rotten eggs.

And instead of mentioning rain I'll point to Murdoch's cronies lined up and aching to laugh in the back row. Look what blew in, I'll say. The land and the seed and good times blew away. Your fields and buildings are blowing away. But the bankers and lawyers hang on. So things can't be so bad that they can't get worse. There's a little milk in the old cow yet. There's a little loot yet for the robber gangs. A little plundering left to do. And then I'll suggest— Maybe, I'll say, Maybe if One Honest Man just speaks his mind—

I had to swing the steering wheel like a maniac. A pedestrian, in all that blowing dust, was marching down the center of the road. I had to wheel for the ditch, slamming on the brakes; I stopped and he came up beside me, a little man, still marching to unheard music, still in the center of Highway 313.

He completely ignored me, as if he might be deaf and blind. I had somehow got into the left ditch, almost hitting a culvert. The brake on my right front wheel was shot. I had stopped dead and he went right by me, that walker, so I called out, half-trying to be courteous, half-bellowing out my mixed emotions:

"Going to the sports day?" I called.

I was a little surprised to find I was going there myself.

But I pried a hand off the steering wheel; accidents frighten me. I shifted gears and pulled up a few feet, driving carefully and stopping carefully again, the way you do when passing a whole herd of cattle. That pedestrian didn't stop; he just suddenly snapped to attention.

He looked up, turned eyes left, and when I recognized him it was too late to drive away. It wouldn't have been polite. And he was just as unwashed as ever. I should have broke his neck the first time I saw him.

My short-peckered friend, the prophet. He climbed into that hearse as if he owned it. As if he'd been expecting me for two hours and was just a little miffed. I might have been his lackey and driver. He didn't let on that he recognized John Backstrom, candidate for public office, whose face was known to all. He didn't seem to know who I was. He sat up straight and pulled his overcoat around him before he slammed the door, damn near taking it off its hinges. I expected him to start brushing the snow out of his beard. He looked as if he was shivering.

"A bitch for heat," I said.

"A sure sign," he said. He brushed at his beard. He arranged it as if one solitary hair had got out of place and he must put it back before he could continue. He arranged and patted. He might have been fixing a bowl of flowers. I almost drove into the ditch, starting up again, but I had to watch. I could barely take my eyes off him. He stroked that filthy beard once more, and then out of all its tangle came, "It's going to come down."

I should have wheeled for the ditch and smashed into a telephone pole. I should have broke his neck the day I laid eyes on him, me with my unlimited strength. I should have. I'm a big man, the law would have been on my side.

But it's no use arguing. I might as well confess. I didn't have time to call him a raving fool and a jumped-up little turd before a drop of water hit the dust on the hood of my old hearse.

I thought maybe the radiator was boiling over; it was a terribly hot day; I'd been driving the old hearse hard. I thought maybe it was a bird, a crow flying overhead that had let go at the opportune moment—God knows I've been shit on all my life.

"It's going to come pouring down," the prophet said.

He was deigning once again to speak, that little pedestrian. I glued my eyes to the road; I didn't watch the dust on the hood at all. I hadn't had occasion to wash the old bus in recent days, another error in judgment. "It's going to rain cats and dogs," the prophet said. He was arranging his beard as if he expected to be laid out in a coffin; he seemed disturbed at the way I drove.

To expect gratitude from any human being is to expect too much. I was very busy, trying not to notice anything. But that feat was impossible. I do not use a deodorant myself, I confess; why should I plug up all my pores? But that man stank.

He had the gall to imply by a glance that my driving very nearly upset him. This little prophet. "It's going to rain pitchforks," he said.

I looked around finally, I had to, I'm built that way; that story of Lot and his wife has always touched me deeply. I looked back just once and the sky in the west was positively black. As if a great fist had closed the sun's eye. As if a range of mountains had broke loose and was galloping straight at me. The whole west was one great galloping cloud of smothering dust. I reached to turn on the lights.

And then the shiver turned to elation. Because I saw the windshield again. A drop of rain had hit the windshield. A drop of genuine water. Even while I was watching, right before my eyes, a second drop hit.

My bowels melted. That's when I first realized: I had forgotten what a rain cloud looks like. In a flash I remembered. That hint of purple behind all the blackness. You understand—earlier I had *believed* it would rain. While all the time I suspected that every cloud is made of dust. Now I *knew* it would rain. There's a terrible difference.

All of a sudden I wasn't just driving down that gravel washboard out toward Coulee Hill; I was floating. There'd be a harvest after all, thanks to good old Johnnie Backstrom. There'd be fat golden kernels under those barley beards. Stooks in the fields. There'd be wheat in the granaries and feed in the feedbox and a new washing machine on the back porch and beer in the cellar and water in the wells and the jingle of coins throughout the land: and tomorrow the voters could show their appreciation.

I'd done it, I knew.

Those old poplars would be stiff and straight, busting with life again. The ditches would be full of muskrats and bulrushes, mallards and pintails and thousands of croaking frogs. Little kids would have new clothes for school in the fall. Taxes would be paid. They'd be selling gas again, in the filling stations. Fill her up please, and three cheers for Johnnie Backstrom. I just knew it. Let's take the kids to a movie, ma, and a tiger for Johnnie Backstrom. I had to express my joy to someone.

"Great burning testicles of Peter and Paul," I burst out to the prophet. He was sitting there like a stick. I thought I'd rub his nose in some of his own foolishness. "She didn't end after all, did she? The old world?"

"She will," he said.

That jumped-up little turd. Why did I speak to him at all? My short-peckered friend, why did I pick him up in the first place? But

I'm just as bullheaded as the next guy when it comes to hard facts. More so. "Sure it will," I said. "In two billion years or so. That worries me to death."

"No," he said. "Tomorrow."

I should have laughed him right out of my hearse. But I didn't. I didn't want him to catch a death of a cold in that coming rainstorm. For some fool reason I went right on trying to argue. "It was supposed to end a week ago. And instead it just got off to a good start."

He didn't bat an eye. That beard was moving again; it positively cast off dust into the air; dust swirled in my old hearse. I was tempted to sneeze. I pressed a finger to my upper lip, listening nevertheless.

"Tomorrow is Friday?" the prophet inquired.

"Correct," I said. "Friday. At last, by Judas. Precisely. Tomorrow is the big day."

"Tomorrow she will end," he said.

Past failures didn't seem to faze him at all. "Tomorrow is election day," I said. The individual drops on the windshield were blurring into one lovely smear; we were really clipping along. "Just watch my dust tomorrow," I said.

"Put aside your vanity," the prophet said.

"Vanity be damned," I said. "I ate a pile of dust. I'm going to kick up a slightly larger pile."

"Vanity," the prophet repeated. "Put aside your earthly pleasures."

"I'll put aside about one-and-a-half kegs of them," I said, "as hair of the dog for the day that follows."

"Vanity and vanity," the prophet said.

Nothing irks me like pointless repetition. I was sitting there in my hearse beside that man with all his swollen self-confidence, and that's when I began to lose my temper. I got mad. Ordinarily I am the picture of good nature. But I got mad; and I took it out on that unwashed little wonder sitting there beside me, ramrod stiff, so damned self-satisfied and pleased that the world would end tomorrow. His clothes were rags, they were hardly decent, they hardly covered his nakedness. Sure he wore an overcoat, to hide himself; a military coat. God knows what war it was from. Rags and ribbons. Rusty nails for buttons. In another week he'd be stark naked; no wonder he wanted the world to end.

"How could the world possibly end tomorrow?" I said. "Go see a doctor, young fellow. I'll pay for it myself. But you're joking."

"Tomorrow morning," he said. "The end will begin tomorrow morning. By tomorrow night—darkness."

"I guess so," I said. "I guess there'll be darkness tomorrow night. There was last night, I noticed."

"Darkness," he said. "A new darkness. Not the old darkness."

He was a creepy little bastard. I've seen people get that way from the Bible before. That man my mother married, the second one, was close enough to that sort of thing himself. One time he tried to heal a girl that had scarlet fever; he caught it himself and damn near died. The old Doc pulled him through; the same Doc who must have been tempted to let him kick off, wanting to marry my mother the way he did.

"Tomorrow," I said, "the world will begin to turn green for a change. The cows will get an honest-to-Jesus bath, which they badly need. The slough holes will fill up and run over. The river will rise. The grass will come alive. The crocuses will be so confused they'll think it's spring and they'll bloom all over again, likewise the buffalo beans, likewise the sleepy-heads."

I felt a strong impulse to lay it on a little.

"And the wicked shall be punished," the prophet said. Sitting there ramrod stiff. "Get rid of your earthly vanities."

I should have kept my mouth shut. There are two things a man should never open: his fly, his mouth. I've read the Bible myself. I have a firsthand acquaintance with many a chapter and verse. People have been spouting all kinds of crap for years. "Tomorrow won't be the same," I said.

"Precisely," the prophet said. "That's right."

You see what I mean? Everything I said, he twisted it around. That's one thing I can't stand. I drove faster and faster. The road was getting quite greasy. Honestly. From the rain. I had to turn on the windshield wiper. I'd forgotten to. It stuck for a second, and then away it went, making its own special noise, suck, suck, the mud washing thin, then just a thin film of something like oil, then clarity itself; the clear drops smacking the clear glass. I was delighted that the prophet on his side couldn't begin to see.

But damn that nature of the world. Why is happiness constituted the way it is? Why? Pretty soon I wasn't enjoying myself at all. Hardly at all. The evidence was in my favor: the windshield wiper positively drowning in rain; the mounting din of rain on the leaky roof of my hearse.

Against all the great weight of evidence and keen logic, I began to feel depressed.

Self-confidence is very depressing to me. I was sitting beside that idiot prophet, straight as a poker in his self-confidence. Maybe my driving scared him. There he sat, malodorous and reeking; and he was tickled to death at the prospect of a final end. I had to drive fast. Pointing out to him the facts of life was a sheer waste of time. Blindness is hard to reason with. I tried, reasonably, to explain: the sun will not overnight snuff itself out. The earth turns on its axis. Galaxies explode, but very slowly. The flowers come and go, do what we will.

And pretty soon a terrible doubt had hold of me. I confess. A suspicion. The more I confronted the facts, the more I was overwhelmed by a terrible realization.

I had nothing to do with the rain.

I had not a thing to do with the coming of the rain. That realization came to me in the form of an emotion. I don't trust emotions. I have a goddamned good reason for not trusting them, they tend to run riot over my mind and body night and day. The rain had just happened. By sheer accident. And here I was, about to cash in on an accident.

I am basically an honest man, I hate to masquerade under false colors. Here I was, the sky full of rain, the clouds about to burst at last, and my anguish was still running full throttle. My throat was still parched.

I couldn't do it. I couldn't get elected on such fraudulent grounds. Merit should be what earns rewards. Thousands of voters were about to assume I had brought this rain, whereas in fact I had had nothing to do with it whatsoever. The sky overhead was now a roaring mass, a sharp line dividing the black roll of clouds from the emptiness of sky. The dust was settling, I can tell you. But I felt that one hundred yards up ahead of that cloud that chased me, I'd be back in my drought. I sped like a man insane, like an innocent elk in front of a prairie fire. I argued, hardly able to keep from raising my voice, the vehemence straining within me.

"No man," I said, "has the slightest damned idea of what's going to happen in this world."

"Tomorrow it will end," the prophet said.

What could I say? What clincher of an argument would open his eyes? "It didn't end last week," I said. I was practically embarrassed to say something so self-evident.

"Tomorrow it will end," the prophet repeated.

I hate to deceive people. This rain would drive the crowds in off the ball diamonds. I had hoped to get to Coulee Hill early, in case they needed a good umpire for the final game. I am an excellent umpire, always fair to both sides, quick-sighted and sure of judgment. Now it was going to pour rain, obviously, for some time. In Coulee Hill in a rainstorm the obvious place to go to keep dry is the community hall. That hall would very shortly be full of hundreds of people. Someone would set up a stand selling hot dogs and coffee. In a few minutes I could be in Coulee Hill, I realized. Up ahead about two miles I could either stay on the main road and zip the four miles into town. Or I could cut south, avoiding the town altogether, and plough mud directly toward the river hills and old Doc Murdoch.

I am, let me repeat, an honest man basically; I didn't want people to be deceived about the rain. But also, every man has a little streak of pride. I didn't like to think the rain came *without* me. That was the most unbearable thought of all. It turned my knuckles white. Maybe that's why I had to insult that little prophet.

If I couldn't lick him fighting fair, I'd fight foul. I hate to admit it, but there it is: I like to win. I hate to lose. And I was losing, so I swung with the intention of hitting below the belt.

"You must miss your old Model-A," I said.

I swear that at that moment he decided to pull a bluff. I swear he did. He turned around to me with those squinted innocent bright blue eyes of his, the only part of the man that was clean, and his dirty beard waggled again. "Model-A?" he said.

I was taken in for a second. "Model-A," I explained. "Your automobile. A car."

"A car?" he said.

"That old car you got rid of at the auction sale. That goddamned wreck of a Model-A you tried to palm off on me, that's a car. Don't pretend to me, you old faker."

"What car?" he said. He was peering intently into my face as if I might be loony. As I say, he had these clean blue eyes. He brushed at his beard with his dirty fingernails.

"That heap of scrap iron you left parked in the middle of somebody's yard. That pile of nuts and bolts and haywire that wasn't worth a wooden nickel." I was becoming upset. "Don't give me that innocent look. You're a two-bit little chiseler. You pedestrian fraud." I have that trouble with my vocabulary; it gets out of hand. "You jumped-up little overgrown turd," I said. "That *car*," I shouted. I had to get through to him. He had these innocent clean blue eyes; he could have caused an accident. I bawled at the top of my lungs, *"That goddamned Model-A."*

"Ah," he said. Very softly. "Yes. Of course. That was mine." He gave me that unbearable fake innocent look of his, that why-are-you-shouting look that my wife is master of.

One of my great sighs came out of me, a huge helpless sigh. "Correct," I said. " That's right. Absolutely—"

"My Model-A," he said.

"Right," I said. "Right."

"I won it," he said.

" The hell you won it, you lost it," I said.

He looked at me as if I was claiming to be Napoleon. "I won it on a wager," he said. His staring made it hard for me to watch the road. "I never lose. I've never lost a wager in my life. God provides."

"I'll bet you haven't," I said. " You've never lost?"

"Correct," he said. "Indeed. Would you care to make a small wager yourself?"

"I don't gamble," I said. "Name it," I added.

" Your choice."

"Anything," I said. " You name it. I'll take either side and win."

I was in that kind of a bullheaded mood.

"Fine," he said. "I say that tomorrow—"

I had no choice. Absolutely none. Sometimes one act of violence is necessary to preclude other acts of violence. Thus the right hook. The rabbit punch. Thus hanging, electrocution, the rack. Thus war. I slammed on the brakes. It really was raining pretty hard; I stopped so fast I believe I actually felt the wheels skid. "Get out," I commanded. Maybe I simply couldn't endure the stench. "Before I split your skull with a left uppercut. I once pitched three men through a third-storey window. I was fairly sober."

"I wish to get out," the prophet said.

You'd think he'd never been in a car before, the way he looked at me.

" Well, do it," I said. "*Do* it." I was losing my temper. "Get to hell out," I shouted.

"I wish to," the prophet said. "I want to. Please stop the car."

The car was rolling; we were on a slight incline.

He got out very politely.

As if I were a wild beast, he didn't want to excite me. He stood with the door open, letting the rain hit the expensive cushion. A hearse is not an economical means of transportation. He thanked me very politely for the ride. " Thank you, son," he said. "God bless you, son."

"Slam the door," I said. "It doesn't work too well since the accident."

" The accident?" the prophet said.

He began to look very much alarmed. Maybe he was afraid the rain would wash off some of his dirt. If there is such a thing as virgin dust, there it was on his neck and ears. Streaks formed on his face; as if he was about to dissolve. I almost burst out laughing. It was very odd, to see that self-satisfied little prophet look alarmed. I almost relented. Even behind all his whiskers and dirt, you could see he was human.

Maybe that's why I asked a question. "Look," I said. "I can see you've been around a lot. You've seen the sights. I had a little accident—"

He slammed the door. I thought he was gone: but the nails that served him as buttons appeared in the open window. The tip of his beard was there like a wet root, so I went on: "If a body is in a bottomless hole?" I asked him.

It was hard to hear, the rain on the roof of the hearse, the engine idling. Maybe he answered and I didn't hear him. "If you see what I mean," I said, "a man has a duty. If your job is preserving the dead—" Suddenly I interrupted myself: " What could be more useless?" I cried.

A voice that seemed to have no head burst into a maniacal laugh.

Up until that moment I was on the verge of asking the prophet to get back in; having learned his lesson, he might have been good company. But at that moment I drove away. I kept my eyes on the road, not looking in the mirror to see where that prophet went or what he did. I kept my eyes on the road. A man my size is a large target for the brute knuckles of existence. I was being pummeled.

IT'S a funny thing: I had to go see the Doc. All my life I'd gone running to bend his ear; when my bowels churned I ran to Doc, and that's the way it was again. It's nothing physical; I can eat anything. But I only had time to dodge a few chuckholes, and there I was in the river hills. We had a pretty rough time of it. Not a word was spoken except, Lend me a hand here, Get that corner, will you? Give us a lift. I mean, the trouble was the pouring rain. It was coming down in buckets. We couldn't keep anything dry. It didn't let up. My pain and misery were taking the form of rain. That, after all my big talk, was almost more than I could bear.

It came down by the barrelful. The air we breathed was suffo-
cating, it was so full of water. You needed gills. You could drown
standing up on a raft. And to make matters worse, night was falling.
By the time we were ready to leave the Gunns the mud was ankle-
deep in the middle of the yard. That damned old hearse could no
more budge than fly. We got stuck in Gunn's lane before we ever got
out to the dirt road. It was no use. We had to wait for Gunn to harness
and hook up a team and lend us a wagon; he brought us out a gaunt-
looking pair of crowbaits, a team of blacks.

We put the little white coffin in the wagon and covered it over and
Doc and I climbed up on the springboard seat. Amos couldn't leave
his wife. What about the team? We asked him; but he just stood
where the hearse was stuck in mud up to its axles in the middle of his
lane and he shook his head. There were holes in everything he had
on; when he tried to take a step we heard the water in his shoes. "Just
tie them up somewhere," he said. "To a fence post or something.
Anywhere you like."

The Doc and I, neither of us could be described as a skilled driver;
each of us was waiting for the other to grab the reins.

"You drive, Johnnie," he said. The Doc.

Gentle baldheaded Christ, he almost broke my heart right there.
You've got to understand. Saving that child meant the world to him.
He took it as a personal defeat. He worked at it for nearly thirty hours,
without ten minutes of sleep. That old farmer out there, he never
expected to have a child and then his wife got pregnant. He was crazy
with joy until the trouble began. It would have been a son. Old Amos
would have been the happiest man in creation, the Doc could see
that. Rain or no rain, that old man would have been nothing but
tickled. He would have forgot his troubles and his poverty. Look at
the mattress his wife was on. There was no money hidden in that
mattress. A dollar bill would have made a lump.

We drove through the rain and darkness, Doc and I, both of us
together under a binder canvas sitting up there on that springboard
seat. I hesitated to speak. I wanted to explain a lot of things.
Sometimes you just want to blurt out everything, about the way
you've cheated and lied and everything; other people's goodness can
make you want to do that. We kept fairly dry except for our knees. My
knees which were raw and scraped to begin with.

In that wagon it was a two-hour drive back to the gravel road. We
were bound to have lots of time to talk, so I didn't push the Doc to get

started. I listened to the rain; it was nearly pitch dark, with the rain falling not in sheets now but steady. The three-day kind of rain. It might go on for a full week, you can always guess. It was coming almost straight down, heavy and steady, soaking the earth. Everything was mud or water. Everything. The whole world was mud or water.

"She's a soaker," the Doc said.

"A real souser," I said.

"Just what we needed," the Doc said.

How could he say that? If I'd been in his boots I'd have been cursing and raging, shaking my fists and stamping in the mud, demanding justice. His garden no more needed rain than my knees needed it.

"There won't be much of a crop," he said. "But at least they'll get their seed back. And feed for the winter, and little to sell, enough to pay the bills until spring."

He was right. I'd been promising a bumper crop. But this was all we could hope for. I didn't think an Easterner could know that much about farming.

"Just enough to hope on," he said. "That's the main thing."

What a dismal view of existence; I changed the subject. He hadn't mentioned my connection with the rain. "You should have stayed with the farmer and slept," I said. "I saw a spare cot in his living room."

"Helen," he said, "should be waiting for us when we get to the gravel road. She phoned from Coulee Hill. She'll be waiting at the turnoff and we can put everything in the car and head straight back to Notikeewin."

It was unlike the Doc to forget to mention a call. I could see how tired he was. "We could be back at Gunn's place in no time," I said.

"No." He lifted his head with a little jerk, moving it briskly against the canvas that dripped above our noses. "Good Lord, Johnnie, I rode a plowhorse fifteen miles when you were born. And I'd never seen a prairie trail up until then. I never mentioned this to a soul—but I very nearly got lost out there. That would have left you in quite a fix."

I could see the old Doc wanted to talk. "I'm in quite a fix most of the time," I said. "You know that better than I do, I guess."

"I guess I do," he said. He started to say something. "But when I should condemn you, I end up sympathizing. I've been in a few fixes myself."

That was hard to believe. The Doc had been on top of the heap since I could remember. I asked him about it. I said, "Doc, you've been a budding tycoon since I was big enough to hope you'd give me a dime and tell me to blow it in immediately."

The old Doc had to laugh. "I was your age before I finished medical school. I had to work for years, saving money. There wasn't much extra cash in those little Ontario towns back when I was a boy."

It had never dawned on me that the old Doc had struggled like the rest of us. I felt uneasy about some of the things I'd said while electioneering. I had sort of let on that the Doc hadn't done an honest day's work in his life. Immediately I wanted to make amends. I wanted a chance to square the records. But that wasn't going to be too easy; sometimes it's the expected that catches us off guard. The way that light did.

You see, I guess when Helen phoned out to the Gunns' place, I guess a lot of people rubbered. Amos Gunn was on a party line. Each family had its own ring—the Gunns' was three shorts and a long. Here it was, dark out, and after a while as we drove on our way, the Doc half-dozing, me watching the road and the horses' backs, having to stare hard into the darkness, I noticed a light up ahead.

It was a pleasant change from the clop and suck of hoofs on the road, the jolting of the iron-rimmed wheels; from the jingle of tugs and the creaking of the doubletree. Those things can lull you to sleep. Just a pinpoint of light made the difference.

It turned out to be a lantern. There it was, almost pitch black out, and when we came to drive past a farm, a man and wife were out at the end of their lane, waiting. You could see they'd been there quite a while. The woman's scarf, over her head, was soaked through. The man's big woolen jacket was hanging heavy with rain. They were there, the two of them, a couple, the man holding the lantern, the woman holding something else under a towel. The man raised the lantern when I pulled up on the reins. He was half-shy to begin talking.

"We came home to do the chores," the husband said. He didn't want us to think they couldn't afford to attend a sports day.

But his wife broke in on him: "We heard you were going by."

On the phone, she said; she said they thought it might be serious so they rubbered. They'd heard we were out on a night like this. They listened, farmers take that liberty during an emergency, and they were waiting for us with a pot of hot coffee and sandwiches. I was absolutely famished. Gunn gave us porcupine for supper, his intentions were the best. At least he claimed it was porcupine. Gophers would make me throw up on the spot. He said it was a delicacy, cooked it himself, killed it himself, too, he assured us. The Doc ate as if he relished it. I need a beer or two when consuming such delicacies.

But I never tasted a better cup of coffee, never in my whole life. I wanted to say so to those two people standing there by the wagon wheel. I wolfed down a couple or three sandwiches, intending to express my thanks.

But an embarrassing thing happened. I thought they'd come out because of the old doctor. Everybody knew him.

But when I handed down the empty cups and the wet plate from the wagon, that woman—she reached up and touched my hand. She wanted to touch my hand. I could hardly believe it. My hands which have done so many wicked things. Even at that moment they must have smelled of horses, I'd helped old Amos hook up. I was born on a farm. Leather that has often been exposed to excrement has the damnedest smell when it gets wet.

"We want to thank you," she said. "We'll be in there tomorrow, somehow. If we have to swim."

It was a good ten miles from there into town. Eight miles at least. I was very embarrassed. The old Doc was sitting right next to me. He couldn't help but hear; the coffee had revived him a little. The rain was starting to soak through the binder canvas, we could feel it on our backs. Cold on our necks. The canvas would be ruined, they shrink. I didn't know what to say. I let the woman touch my huge hand, dirty or clean, and then, speechless, I took hold of the reins and I just clucked my tongue and that team started out again, by no means eager, slogging through the mud.

I didn't know what to say. The old Doc must have been pretty tired, he was half-leaning on me. I'm quite big anyhow. We started again and the smell of sweating horses came up to us, with the various smells of canvas and mud and rain and leather.

"You just try to get a little sleep, Doc," I said. "I can handle this."

But the old Doc wouldn't give in. He tried to make conversation, just to show he was still game. As if he had politely not listened. As if we were casually at ease in a nice warm beer parlor. "Your wife didn't show up for her last appointment," he said.

"I'm surprised," I said.

"She isn't peeved or anything?"

"Not a chance in the world," I said. I felt very uneasy. "She never has hard feelings."

"I wonder why she didn't show up?"

"Busy, probably," I said.

"What could she be doing?"

That one stumped me. I had nothing to say.

"You hope it's a daughter?" he said.

"We tend to have mostly sons in my family," I said. "I come from a long line of sons."

"I'd like to deliver that baby," Doc said. "I was afraid maybe Elaine was peeved."

"You will, Doc," I said. "I'm sure you will."

"No," he said. "I'm not so sure." Then, before I could dispute him, he said, "Good luck, Johnnie. The very best."

I didn't know how to reply. We still had miles to go. Words always fail me at the wrong time; I should have argued with him. But he seemed so sleepy. I wanted him to rest. Or I should have brought up the topic that was on my mind; about this rain, Doc, I should have said. I should have blurted out: it was a sheer coincidence, Doc. Nobody knows it the way I do.

But after a while there was another light ahead of us. Up ahead in the rain, another lantern. I knew this time what was coming. I had to prepare myself. I had to exercise iron control.

"That daughter of mine," the Doc said. "She is all I have left. At least remember that much, Johnnie."

I nodded. I suppose he couldn't see me in the darkness; maybe he felt the canvas move. I couldn't speak; I was so busy trying to control my various emotions.

A family met us with a warm drink, hot cocoa, teetotalers again, a couple with two little kids who just wanted to see me. Little pale kids who looked thin and sickly shivering down there beside the wagon wheel, their big eyes staring. See me of all people, Johnnie Backstrom, a mere undertaker, sitting up there on that springboard seat beside an M.D. The lantern just barely managed to light up the streaking rain. If I'd been alone I think I would have cried. The father picked up the little kids one at a time and raised them closer. But having the old Doc with me that way, I was embarrassed.

I was a fraud, that's why. I knew it and I wanted to make amends. I had to reach out and touch those little kids, one at time, the boy, then the girl, me smiling a big smile. It was expected of me. But deep in my heart I cursed that rain; it could have come one day later with little further harm to crops or men. It could have simply waited; without rain my pain was at least a simple pain. Pure drought had its virtues, I could see that. I had to turn my face away from those little kids watching me, staring silently. Say thank you, the mother said to the little girl. To Mr. Backstrom, she added. I could hardly finish my cocoa.

The scum from the cocoa stuck to the roof of my mouth. I nodded. I slapped the reins on the horses' backs, the horses nodding, me nodding; and when the wagon jerked I had to steady the Doc with one arm and drive with the other. I drove, I escaped, and still in my head there could be no peace, only the tumble and din of my thinking. The roar.

"Helen," the Doc said. We had gone past a couple of deserted farms. Or maybe the people were in town. Or hadn't rubbered. He seemed to be half-delirious. "Helen, you should have—" He started to fall and I caught him. I cradled him in my right arm; pretty soon he was actually snoring.

It was an endless drive, but thank God Helen was waiting when we got to the gravel road. She was sitting there in the big Chevy, the lights on dim, pulled off the gravel as far she dared. The old Doc was sound asleep. How a man could sleep on that seat was a miracle itself; we need better roads. But he did it.

Helen came out of the car and up beside the wagon when I pulled on the reins. It didn't take much encouragement to stop that team. Helen, even before she spoke, before she finished buttoning her yellow slicker, reached up and guided my ankle where I was reaching over the side, my size thirteen foot dangling in space, trying to find the wheel to step on. My shoes were ruined. I found the rim of the wheel, all mud itself; I got down from the wagon.

"You must be dead," Helen said.

My joints were creaking. "It was a tough trip," I said. "Your father is taking it hard."

He was slouched double on the springboard seat. I stepped up on the wheel again and got hold of his shoulders and pulled him out from under the canvas; we managed to get him into the car, Helen helping me, both of us sliding and slipping, our feet picking up the gravel.

Then we were standing at the back end of the wagon. We had an awkward moment there, Helen and I, together. For one thing, it was raining. It was raining cats and dogs again. Raining pitchforks. The little white coffin was one I'd had in stock a long time. Some salesman loaded me up with coffins when I was opening shop. I was green. I thought I was in a sure-fire business. Now that same coffin was covered over with a torn quilt and a horse blanket, both of which simply soaked up the rain.

"I came from Coulee Hill," Helen said.

We couldn't approach one another. We were standing two feet apart, yet the darkness might just as well have been made of cast iron. "Well—" I said. And then I went on: "I hope the roads are passable."

Helen had to clear her throat; something women very seldom do. "That crowd that expects to hear you talk—"

You understand, we had not announced the topic of our conversation. "That was three hours ago," I said. "At the exact moment when I was supposed to appear, I was feasting on stewed porcupine. I made a mental note."

"They're still there," she said. "Everybody is still there."

She didn't have to say anything; remember that. I didn't ask.

"They're just getting out of the rain," I insisted. I tried to laugh. "Some of us don't know enough—"

"No, Johnnie," she said.

"But it must be nearly eleven," I said. Then I quickly added: "You never know till it's over. It's like a ball game in that respect."

I believed that Helen shook her head. "I was only just there; everything in town is empty except the hall. Even the beer parlor. They're waiting."

Naturally, I should have been pleased. Helen was standing tall in the darkness, beyond where the Chevy's dimmed lights showed up the streaking fall of rain. We had made an appointment to meet at midnight. I was standing right there myself, and God forgive me, for a terrible moment I wanted to seize her in my arms. But for once in my life I spoke up instead. My heart was wrung. "The rain had nothing to do with me. Nothing in the world." My cowardice overcome, I felt improved. "It was a natural phenomenon," I said.

And the next thing I knew, Helen had her head against my chest; I couldn't tell if she was crying or what. I was bracing her up, rather than holding her. I wondered if I should put my arms around her. But consolation and lust, in me, even they became confused. So I simply blurted out: "Helen, don't worry."

Then, of all things, she kissed me. That was the warmest, loveliest kiss I have ever run into; and it took me completely by surprise. My head was bent against the rain. My whole body was one long shivering chilly ache, and all of a sudden two warm lips, the tip of a tongue, infused me with new life. I was tempted, just for a fraction of a second, to repeat the event of the previous night, as it had occurred in the Doc's garden. Her head found my shoulder, the memory of her warm mouth, her cool cheeks, fresh in my mind.

"H.P.," I said. "Don't cry, H.P."

She gave a little convulsion, a sob escaping her throat; and I had to take hold of her. I put my arms around her; I groped in the darkness, finding the slicker smooth and wet, and then softer where her breasts yielded to my groping. I am forever condemned to grope.

She was crying. And kissing me at the same time. Crying and standing on her tiptoes to kiss my neck. I had this terrible revelation: Helen was forgiving me. That must have been it. She could not really regret the rain; she was kissing me out of sheer love. My wife had been full of advice; here was love. I thought of my wife. Back in Notikeewin, The Wild Rose City; in the funeral parlor. Up over it, I should say; what isn't she up over? She was scared to death in that place when it rained. But Helen was moved. She was proud of me; she clung to me there in the darkness, in the rain, proud of what I had done.

And then once again I remembered that I had done nothing. Nothing, nothing. "It was a natural phenomenon," I said. "He loves you," I added. "In the wagon, when he was half-asleep—"

"He knows," Helen said.

Let me say right out: what astonished me most was my own calmness. Really. It was as if I had all along been expecting this remark and had the answer ready. It was as if my silence itself was rehearsed and simply waiting for its cue.

She stepped away from me. "When I phoned him from town— He said, 'I called last night. Was something wrong? Where were you?' And instead of lying I simply said, 'I was with Johnnie out in your garden—'"

"How could you do it?" What was it that triggered me? I don't know. But suddenly I struck out my arms as if I must somewhere switch on a light so I could see her face. "To him," I said. "To *him*. How could you do it to *him*?"

I struck the darkness itself. I had to cry out. I put a hand to my own throat, one of my own huge hands. I staggered away from Helen. A bolt of lightning might just as well have pierced my head. A great tree of lightning, blossoming up from my ears. From my split skull. The horses should have started and fled.

I turned to look and they were standing silent; black and wet and bowed in the pale glow from the Chevy's headlights. Exhausted.

"It had begun to rain," Helen said. "It was the rain."

She was standing there, not a yard away. Little H.P. She was the garden, the forest of my soul; a forest tangled and scented. A forest wild. She was the turf and torment of my raucous love. My own wife, that bundle of consistencies, is all straight hair at one end, a twist or two at the other. H.P. was the paradox of my dreams.

But instead of bringing relief, her remark is what plunged me into despair. Don't you see? You've got to understand. That's why I yielded to despair. For a moment I really did, I gave up completely. Because of her remark—it was a prophecy of all to come. It was the alibi the world would use to cudgel me. If I took victory now, the world would mock me with: who couldn't win? You've got to see, I was utterly defeated—by her quietly saying, it was the rain. Because I could have gone straight into Coulee Hill barehanded and bare-knuckled and I could have whipped old Murdoch fair and square: *I could have done it without the rain.*

And that's why I hesitated. I wavered for a moment as I experienced despair; I had to hesitate. Helen saw that. Or felt it.

"What is it?" she said.

Selfishness is man's greatest enemy: I saw my duty.

"It was a natural phenomenon," I said.

"Johnnie, stop it," she said.

I was sizing up the little coffin. "It's an odd size," I said. "That car won't be an inch too big."

Helen was behind me, waiting, silent. She could feel things about me—she always could, right from the beginning.

"What did he say?" I said.

"'He's an attractive man, Helen,' is all he said."

I'll tell you something. I could have got that coffin into the car. I've wrestled my share of coffins. But instead of doing it I simply said, "It won't go. I'll have to drive this outfit into town. I can get help in town, I'll borrow a pickup truck."

I don't know why I said that. I didn't want to go into Coulee Hill at all. I didn't. I swear I didn't. All that rain, I was risking my health for one thing. I was stiff and sore. But what could I do? I had to explain.

I had to make amends. It was all clear as day. I'd explain to that hall full of people waiting to hear from me. That would be best. I'm here to apologize, I'd explain. Please vote for Murdoch. I'd beg them. Command them. He knows the ropes. I want to be the first person to vote in the morning. My dear friends, I'm casting my ballot for Duncan L. Murdoch, who is the better qualified man. That would bring the place down. Vote for Duncan L. Murdoch, M.D. My integrity would swing everyone to old Doc. He'd win by a landslide.

I climbed up on the wagon, stepping on the hub and then the rim and then hooking a leg over the box. I should say tank rather than a box; it was a tank wagon, for hauling grain. The seat had got wet. Man's innocent ass, I thought; I lifted the canvas over my shoulders. I unwound the reins from the peg on the front of the tank. It would take me an hour to drive into town.

But I was a man of determination. "Tell him not to worry," I said aloud. I didn't dare look back leaving Helen. If I'd looked back once, I'd have lost my determination. Beauty does that to me. "I'm going right now to explain," I said. Aloud. To Helen; to the rain and the darkness. "I have to."

I reasoned with myself for a long time—I had to make amends, and I'm not ashamed to admit it, suicide itself was among the possibilities. I thought of my wife actually shedding tears, the neighbor women heaping the kitchen table with cookies and salads and pies, scrubbing the floors. The men in various beer parlors: well, I guess old Backstrom finally did it, as I knew he would, just parked his hearse on the railway tracks. Was it his nagging wife that drove him to it? Odd bird, he couldn't handle his liquor. Car troubles, somebody said; plus fear of getting no votes. I recognized: that damned rag of a Notikeewin newspaper would have a field day: BACKSTROM SHOOTS SELF: HOLE IN SOCK FINALLY OF USE.

But I also knew what my luck is like. Big Backstrom, the belt buckle gave while he was hanging himself, he broke both legs on the edge of a chair.

Or even if I did succeed: that pudgy deaf atheist of a hardware dealer would get the customer, unwilling to charge a decent price.

I had one hour to think.

People would hear the wagon. Especially on that gravel road, they'd hear the horses, the wheels. One hour to mediate on the nature of raw ambition and man's ultimate end. I had no choice but to drive slowly, that team was totally exhausted. One hour in which to prepare a speech. They'd probably come out to meet me; out into the rain, hundreds of people, running and waving and cheering in the rain. Over and over I tried different approaches. "My dear friends," I said, speaking directly to the horses, that coffin joggled along behind, "my dear friends, I met tonight with Duncan Murdoch, the man who delivered..." Beginnings and endings. I had to make amends. By God, the world is a wicked place. A man could get piles, sitting so long on a cold wet board. "My dear friends, the time is at hand. We've had enough suffering. Enough crying. We've had enough pain. Enough dried codfish—" No, damnit, no. Explain, explain. "We must forgive, my dear friends. We must forgive the selfish, the proud of heart, the whoremongers; we must forgive the plutocrats on easy street, the teetotalers, the pious—" No no no no. A man has to make amends. I owed it to the old Doc. I'd fight my way tight-lipped into that hall. I'd be up on that stage before I opened my mouth. We must make amends in this world. "Rain," I would have to begin, the flags stilled about me; the crowd tense and waiting. I'd be soaked to the skin. I let the binder canvas fall to the floor of the wagon; hunched I sat, stubborn against the rain, soggy and alone as a creature of the deep. It was blistering cold in the wet night, I have never been so alone. But I had a duty and I couldn't stop; somehow I would have to begin, "My dear friends, rain..."